ᴬHIGH
PRESSURE
SYSTEM

Tor/Forge books by Ken Gross

A Fine Line
Hell Bent
A High Pressure System
Rough Justice

A HIGH PRESSURE SYSTEM

KEN GROSS

A TOM DOHERTY ASSOCIATES BOOK
NEW YORK

A HIGH PRESSURE SYSTEM

This book is printed on acid-free paper.

A Forge Book
Published by Tom Doherty Associates, Inc.
175 Fifth Avenue
New York, N.Y. 10010

Forge ® is a registered trademark of Tom Doherty Associates, Inc.

Library of Congress Cataloging-in-Publication Data

Gross, Ken, 1939-
    A high pressure system / Ken Gross.
        p.   cm.
    "A Tom Doherty Associates book."
    ISBN 0-312-85444-7
    1. Women journalists—New York (N.Y.)—Fiction.
    2. Mayors—New York (N.Y.)—Election—Fiction.
    3. Politicians—New York (N.Y.)—Fiction.   I. Title.
    PS3557.R583H54   1994
    813'.54—dc20   93-43987
                                                                CIP

First edition: February 1994

Printed in the United States of America

0 9 8 7 6 5 4 3 2 1

For Andrea

^AHIGH
PRESSURE
SYSTEM

1

JANUARY

THERE WAS SOMETHING deeply unsettling about the crusty old driver of the stretch limousine. "I'm Sol," he declared, standing smug beside the rear door with his arms akimbo. Bonnie Hudson smelled coffee and mint and trouble in the puff of steam that came out of his mouth. "Watch," he cautioned a second too late, after she banged her head against the roof. As she sank into the plush leather seat, Bonnie turned to show him her fangs, or at least a scowl, but as she looked up she was restrained by the sight of stiff spikes of white hair poking out of the fringes of the driver's ancient cap. A wave of cold air off the Hudson River shook the fingers of Sol's white hair in her face.

After he mounted a high cushion in the pilot's seat of the silver Cadillac, wiggling to make himself comfortable, Sol let Bonnie know who was boss. "Make yourself at home, don't be shy," he said, twisting for better position on his perch. "You got a telephone, something to drink in that little cabinet. Peanuts. Magazines. Anything you want, you name it." She realized that it was a declaration of equality, not generosity. She was a prisoner of an old limo driver who, in the name of high egalitarian principle, wouldn't hesitate to unleash a barrage of opinions and rules and comments on an upstart passenger.

They were outside Bonnie's apartment building on Fifteenth Street in Lower Manhattan and Sol was running through his preflight checklist. He had his clipboard, he had his change for the tolls, he had his paper towels, he had his trip voucher, which she would get around to signing, and he had his map. Everything neat, tidy, and within reach.

Bonnie leaned forward on the soft leather seat and spoke: "My name is . . ."

He cut her off. "I know who you are. I can read." He held up the voucher with her name printed in block letters. Then he turned around to face her. He waited a few seconds before speaking. "Take a guess how old I am."

Bonnie felt the push of his personality. She had run across this type of geriatric bully before, mostly in her family; people who believed that age had given them a license to abuse anyone on the sunny side of youth. "I'm very bad at guessing," she replied mildly.

"Don't give me that," said Sol in his oppressively spunky manner. "Go on. Take a chance. Live a little. I happen to know you take a few guesses about the weather. I see you on the television—cold front here, warming trend there, and don't forget the humidity or the windchill . . ."

"Fifty-three," she said just to shut him up.

He laughed, shook his head. "Not even close."

"Ninety-five," she snapped.

He looked shocked that even for an instant someone could mistake him for being so old. He turned away. Then he mumbled his standard punch line, even though she had flattened his pride. "I will be seventy-four on my next birthday."

"You think a man your age should be behind the wheel?" Two could play his off-balance game.

He looked at her in the rearview mirror, trying to see if she was a mental case. "Never mind," he said finally. "I been driving cars before you were born."

"That's what worries me."

* * *

Bonnie Hudson hadn't intended to take a bite out of the old man, but he'd asked for it, and besides, she was the paying customer. She was in no mood to be manhandled by Henny Youngman. She was too distracted, too frazzled, too far out on a very shaky limb to be a good audience. Tossing away a career and a good man were enough blows for one day. She had hired a limousine for privacy at a moment of high drama in her life. Sol was not in the plan.

It took him a minute to regain his composure. Then he said, "I hope you don't mind me saying, but you're a lot better looking in person." This was worse than dealing with an out-and-out curmudgeon. Now he was faking nice. Not that she was fooled. This was standard golden-age cunning, she decided. It was transparent, but potent. If she had to be honest, she was aware in some dim, modest crevice of her own self-knowledge that it was true—in person she was attractive. At the age of thirty-two, she could still pass for a brooding college senior. She was compact and lush and there was an unmistakable and exotic intelligence in her brown flashing eyes. Nothing gaudy, nothing that would show up on a blunt instrument like television. Still, she knew that the old fox in the front seat was just trying to win back his audience.

"You know, Sol, now that you mention it, I do look better in person. In fact, so do you. Much better in person. Frankly, I'm impressed, a man your age, looking the way you do. You must watch what you eat."

He was taken aback. He didn't know what to make of her or how to talk to this one. She was so quick, so prickly. There was something actually volatile and vaguely ominous about the way she came back at him. Usually, he had them eating out of his hand—which is exactly the way he described his effect on passengers to his wife, Bertha, who was always impressed by Sol's polished gift of gab: "I got them eating out of my hand," he told her night after night when he came back from the road. Bertha

believed that he was a sage and a smoothie, and that was the way
she described her husband's professional style to her friends:
"Before he even starts an engine, he's got them eating out of his
hand."

Even Sol believed it, but he couldn't gauge the impact with
this one. Was she joking? What gives?

Tamely, he tested the water. "Yeah, it's the truth, television
doesn't do you justice," he added, pulling out of the parking spot
and almost killing a kid on a bicycle. "Rat bastard!" he screamed
out of the window. "They shouldn't let them in the traffic," he
said turning to her. "Am I right?"

"That's right, Sol. They've got no business in the middle of
the street with those dangerous bikes. Let 'em stay on the sidewalk where they belong, I say."

He was bewildered, and his reply, which under different
circumstances he had always offered as a reasonable alternative
to uncontrolled bicyclists, sounded feeble. "They had lanes.
What happened to the bicycle lanes?"

"Gone. Lanes went the way of trolleys. Damn shame." Bonnie tried to head off further trouble by turning away, looking out
of the window. She saw a woman bent with age inch painfully
down Broadway. Lately, she had made a habit of violating the
unwritten urban code of avoiding eye contact with the homeless
and downtrodden—a tactical rule born out of shame and fear.
But noticing, looking, had become a personal issue for Bonnie
because of something that happened just before Christmas. She
had been walking along Fourteenth Street when, out of the
corner of her eye, on a far fringe of defensive awareness, she
sensed one of the ubiquitous urban nomads. In the Reagan
Eighties they had become a liquid presence in America. The
woman was standing against a wall holding an outstretched
paper cup, the universal appeal for a donation. The woman did
not appear particularly dirty or drab or diseased, but it was no
longer possible to tell with certainty who was an economic casu-

alty, what with charity shelters giving donated designer clothes to the needy.

So, considering the season and her mood, Bonnie dropped a quarter in the woman's cup. Both of them watched in shock as the coin sank into a cup almost filled with fresh coffee. The woman looked up, Bonnie grinned, took the container, and handed her a dollar bill for a new cup of coffee. The woman—an ordinary upper-middle-class pedestrian—had been waiting for a friend and sipping coffee. It was then that Bonnie realized how easy it was to make a mistake, how easy it was to slip through the safety net of perception. She resolved to pay more attention.

And so, as she rode down Broadway in a hired limousine four weeks later, she stared at the woman bent with woe. When the car came abreast of the woman and paused for a light, Bonnie saw that she was not old after all, just crushed by circumstance. She was a bag woman, pulling a shopping cart filled with plastic sacks. Her hands were raw from the cold, and her face was wet with mucous. The woman turned and saw Bonnie looking at her and the expression on her face turned suddenly fierce. She began to shriek and look for something to hurl at the car and Bonnie was grateful when the light changed and the limousine pulled away.

"Listen, you mind if I stop for gas?"

"I'd mind if you didn't." She couldn't seem to control the edge in her voice. It was disappointment more than anger. She had looked forward to a luxurious ride in utter solitude and peace. To dwell on Jack. To measure the loss and stack that up against the gain. The freedom. The loneliness. Poor Sol had to endure her pointy elbows and sharp jabs and smart-aleck insults.

The gas station was on Seventh Avenue and the limousine was so long that it took up two pumps. As they waited for the tank to be filled, another limousine pulled alongside with three passengers in the back looking like members of a wedding party. The driver leaned out of the window and asked Sol how to get to LaGuardia Place. He had a thick Hispanic accent and had to repeat the question twice. Finally, Sol shook his head. "Never heard of it," he said. When the second limousine pulled away, Sol spoke to the rearview mirror. "Can you believe that? The man doesn't even know where he's going."

"Well, LaGuardia Place, it's a small street—I heard of it—but I'm not even sure where it is."

"Off Houston Street," said the old man, casually reeling off the correct answer. "Near West Broadway."

She opened and closed her mouth, absorbing the implication of what he just said. "You mean you know where it is?"

"Of course. I didn't start driving yesterday."

"Why didn't you tell that man?"

He looked disgusted, shook his head. "Why should I tell him? That's his responsibility. He should have checked it before he went out on the job. How can you go to work without knowing where you're going? When I leave the garage, I always check the route, I make sure the roads are open, and I bring along a map. They don't do that. They don't check, they don't prepare. You know who they got driving today? People who can't speak English. They can't read a road sign. They bribe someone to get a license."

He expected applause for his conscientious approach to the job. Instead, he got a smoldering silent rebuke. That's when Bonnie made up her mind—she and Sol were not going to make it through the day together. The incident turned her back to thoughts of Jack. He would have been mostly amused by Sol. Playfully tolerant of the old man's bitter nature. It was his forgiving spirit. She felt, at that wavering instant, the absence of Jack like a stone.

They were past the Lincoln Tunnel and onto the turnpike heading south for Atlantic City when she reached for the paper bag inside her coat pocket. The bulk of the contents of the bag was both comforting and a little scary. Money was a dangerous thing. A paper bag full of hundred dollar bills had potency. It was like carrying a loaded gun on a hair trigger.

The open road loosened Sol up again. "You know, I had some boys in the car two, three weeks ago. New Year's Eve. Musicians." He shook his head. "What a life! They had regular jobs, but they made extra money on the side with a band. One was a mailman. Another was, what? A collection agent. And they play in a band. Murder."

A band, she thought. Well, why not? We romantics all chase some wisp of drama or glory, even in dreary pubs and tinny VFW halls. Her own pursuit had begun in a dusty city room, where she had first come fresh out of college, besotted with the sentiment of journalism. At the time, she didn't notice the filth, only the word "PHILTHY" written in the greasy dirt on the wall by some iconoclastic finger that had long since moved on. She was a yellow-dog newspaper fiend and she chased fires and murders and calamity out of raw instinct, and in the grim recitation of the facts, she found a comforting profession. She was good at the job because she could see the stories in the gaps. She wrote well enough and could usually identify the villains. Her heroes were defeated newspaper wretches who kept trying to sneak hard truths between the shifting lines drawn by timid editors.

In time, Bonnie became a dazzling reporter with a style of her own. She was the New York City correspondent for a Long Island newspaper, but the paper's audience grew squeamish about so much gloom, and one day the editor called her in and suggested—demanded—that she lay off depressing stories about the plight of the homeless and the downtrodden. The editor said that the reader surveys had shown that subscribers wanted up-beat stories with a happy ending. And if that's what the readers wanted, that's what she should want. After all, they were in daily competition for readers with the "style" sections of the bigger papers. By then—the Reagan-Bush Eighties—Bonnie had grown brittle with rage and she quit. Despite all of her obvious talent and the small cult she had attracted, the newspaper's modern new editor/manager/viper, Toby Warner, accepted with barely disguised glee. Bonnie's insubordinate ways didn't serve Toby's ambition, which was, like all ambition, without limit. It was an ugly moment when they faced each other in that final showdown. Bonnie couldn't back out of her threat to quit and knew that she was doing just what Toby wanted her to do, but she was Bonnie and she couldn't stop herself. Finally, she stood up, seeing the way things were going, and leaned across the desk, causing Toby to flinch in fear, and said between clenched teeth, "Go fuck yourself!"

Bonnie was not without admirers. Harvey Levy, a talented editor forced out of his job at the paper after defending Bonnie, had become managing editor of a local television news show. After a long campaign, he convinced Bonnie to try television. He suspected that her personality would shine on the air. After eight months without a job, Bonnie was willing to try. To her amazement, she turned out to be a natural. The camera lingered on her, as if waiting for one more witty wisecrack, and she returned the compliment by delivering. Harvey made her the weather reporter and she stunned a slumbering audience with her no-nonsense approach to the subject. "It's raining, take an umbrella," she said. When great heat waves struck the city during the summer, she looked into the camera and declared, "What did you expect? It's August!"

And when the anchorman blamed her for a drought, using her as his foil—as all anchorpeople use all weather reporters—she didn't let him get away with it. "Do I blame you for the Middle East?" she said. On the air. It was unheard of. His face, as the camera returned to him, went through a sunset of colors.

She was described with shameless praise by critics as a breath of fresh air.

But it was her nightly sign-off—"Hey, it's only weather!"—that endeared her to an audience hungry for some sign of intelligent life in that media universe. It had a Vonnegut-like irony, an

Ellerbee-like smirk, a Swiftian wink that launched her into local superstardom. Not that she didn't have qualms. When she begged her friend Harvey Levy to get her a press card and send her out on stories of consequence, he sympathized but pointed to the robust ratings. Since she had insulted the sportscaster (suggesting that sports was for men what fashion was for women—essentially trivial—rendering him speechless, unable to read the scores from the TelePrompter, simmering about the blasphemy) the station had become number one in their market. Every outcast in the tristate area tuned in to see who was next on her hit list.

As time passed, Bonnie saw that she would never be allowed out of the studio hothouse to report stories of significance. She was trapped inside a cushy bubble with lowbrow egomaniacs and high-paid fools. But she bristled. She refused to become a media hag; she refused to settle for minor celebrity on a third-rate station. She refused to grow ambitious, which was the only alternative. There was a book in this, she believed. She wanted to write about slick anchorpeople who had never read Russian novels, studied philosophy, or been enchanted by foreign cinema. And soon after the first of the year, soon after her encounter on the street when she suspected she might be becoming callous, she decided enough was enough.

The first step was the hardest. She wrote a cowardly note and handed it without comment to Jack. It said all the known things: they were not cut out for each other. The unwritten subtext was that he was an ex-cop with little education and secret moods and she was a disappointed intellectual with wild, unformed ambitions and snobbish reservations about a commitment to a blue-collar gladiator. He didn't even argue, just packed and left. In that same destructive and reckless moment, she phoned in her notice.

She quit to the sportscaster, who shouted "Hooray!" It didn't feel like much of a departure, not without hearing Harvey Levy beg her to stay. But this time he had beat her to the punch. He had gone to a new station. She wouldn't go with him when he asked. She had other plans.

She would write. It would be a blistering account of the way things really work in "the media." Only books take time and she did not have a lot of money in the bank. So she had withdrawn what she had, stuffed it into the paper bag, and found herself on this last-ditch journey down the New Jersey Turnpike in a stretch limo, rented for a languid, lingering moment of privacy. And maybe she did it like blowing on cold dice, for luck.

She turned away and looked out of the side window at the monotony of the turnpike. The center strip and the shoulders were planted thick with shrubs and trees and grass, burnt brown from the sulfuric car fumes. And empty beer cans were sprinkled along the byway like contempt. A fast-food wrapper floated in the wind, trapped by the toxic currents.

"You know, when the dispatcher told me it was you, I says, I know this girl. I watch her on the news. She gives me the weather. What's that thing you say, 'Hey, it's just the weather!' I say that all the time. You know, when I get frustrated. When someone acts like an animal back there." He tossed his thumb over his shoulder at where Bonnie was sitting. She flinched. "You'd be surprised."

" 'Hey, it's only weather!' " she corrected.

"What?"

"The sign-off. It's 'Hey, it's only weather!' "

"Yeah, that's what I said."

She didn't argue. She told him to stop at a service area. "I'll be a few minutes," she said, clutching the paper bag. She walked across the cement strips that broke the parking lot into fascist geometric sections. Her head was down against the wind. She stopped and looked up and was struck by the gray, flat, aching gloom of the industrial gash in the earth that was northern New Jersey. In the shimmering distance were the blisters—gas storage tanks—and the spidery threads of overhead power lines and the dense plumes of smoke from the factory chimneys. The air was blurred by soot and ash and the moist, suffocating blanket of chemical smog. Her nose burned from some active fire—a portion of the New Jersey meadow was always on fire—and from the sour, rank stench of nearby landfills. A soup of carbon and methane and garbage. The cars whipped by on the eight-lane highway at crushing speed, and the faces of the people in the cars had no expression, except the numbness of long-suffering souls who expect no relief. Even the hopeful pilgrims heading for the gambling casinos in Atlantic City walked across the parking lot softly, as if they accepted as fact that flesh was outranked by steel and stone. Bonnie was dizzy and felt as if she might be on the moon.

"Take your time," yelled Sol sarcastically.

She turned, startled, as if the voice had no business out here on the great breathless plains of the service station. Sol was smiling and waving an arm out of the window, as if he were seeing her off at a train station. He was making the sarcastic point that he would wait like a martyr in the car while she did whatever she had to do in the service center. She stood there for a moment, feeling the force of the wind blowing hot and cold in her face. She smiled and waved back.

There was a woman ahead of her walking slowly toward the restaurant. The woman was shaped like a bottle and she walked like a sailor rolling on a pitching deck. As Bonnie caught up to her, she saw that the woman was breathing hard, devoting all her energy and attention to the task of locomotion. She was one of the passengers from the bus parked in the reserved area, headed for a day-outing in Atlantic City. The woman wore a cloth coat buttoned to the neck and had her purse clutched tightly with both hands. She looked like one of life's brave fullbacks waiting to be tackled from the blindside. Bonnie held open the door to the restaurant and the woman smiled gratefully. They sat at adjoining tables. Bonnie watched her set out her snack of banana and prunes on a paper plate. She added a can of juice and made a place setting with a napkin and plastic utensils. It looked like a ritual.

Bonnie had a hamburger, french fries, and a Coke. "Could I use your ketchup?" she asked the woman, who smiled again—a warm, welcoming smile—and handed it over, then looked with a raised eyebrow at Bonnie's meal. "I know," said Bonnie, "but I can't keep track of all the food groups. Besides, I like red meat."

"You must be very young," said the woman.

It was a nice, warm voice. Bonnie laughed. "Do you mind if I join you?"

"No, certainly not. Just don't try to make me take a bite."

Bonnie was curious; she wanted to know how it worked—the plain facts about the cost of the bus and the details of arranging travel to Atlantic City. And the motive. Why did the bottle-shaped woman endure hours of bouncing along the turnpike to feed the casinos? What was the lure? It wasn't the money. Not the expectation of a big payoff.

The woman had no hesitation; she wanted to talk, as if she had been thinking about all these questions, formulating reasons and explanations. She said her name was Roberta and she was a regular on the Yonkers-to-Atlantic City run. She was sixty-eight years old and she was a widow and came twice a week, gambling the twenty dollar bonus money that the casinos gave away as bait to lure in little old ladies so they could steal their social security and pension checks.

"I just play the slots," Roberta said. "Some of the other girls play blackjack and roulette, but they can't beat those games. I stick to the slots and I play real slow. So's I don't run out of quarters. You play fast and lose, you get itchy palms if you have to stick around and watch. You get bored. You have to throw in some of your own money. So I have my lunch—you know they give you a free lunch—and then I take my time. Unless I hit one of the jackpots. Then I speed it up a little. As long as it's their money. I don't play with my cash, not me, honey. I couldn't afford that. No, they don't get anything out of me. But it's a nice outing, you know? The ride and the company and the excitement. All it costs is the $7.50 bus ticket. I once hit a $500 jackpot. I played for months on that." She paused, allowing Bonnie to think of the intricacy and thought that went into her recreational strategy. Then she said, "This is like my nursing home, only the food's better and I'm an outpatient."

Roberta laughed and it was a happy, uncomplicated sound. Bonnie laughed along with her.

Bonnie sipped her Coke and, using her tactic of allowing lonely people to talk, discovered that Roberta came on the same bus with the same driver every time. His name was Carlos, Roberta said, pointing to a thin man in his thirties who was eating a donut.

"Listen, I lost my ride," said Bonnie. "You think Carlos will let me buy a ticket?"

"Sure," said Roberta, who went over and arranged the deal. The driver took ten dollars extra for his trouble and added Bonnie to his passenger list. Bonnie walked to the bus with the bottle-shaped Roberta between herself and Sol's limousine. As she sank into the window seat next to her new friend, she saw Sol get out of the limousine, circle impatiently, glance at his watch, and talk to himself. She felt a nice glow of sinful satisfaction, wondering just how long he would wait until he went in search of his passenger.

It was a cheerful group on the bus that rolled out of the service center and headed down the turnpike. One of the men—a former store owner from Queens with sharp eyes—recognized Bonnie. "You're the weathergirl," he said, leaning across Roberta.

She threw up her hands. "You found me out," she said.

For the rest of the trip, she was the celebrity guest and the other passengers all made a visit to her seat, giving her tips on which games to play, how much to bet, what to eat for lunch, where to walk in safety—and joking about the rotten weather she provided all year. She didn't mind it from them. They

planted health food cookies wrapped in napkins in her lap and
Bonnie felt protected and safe among them.

Atlantic City was a Potemkin village, with glittering rococo ho-
tels and casinos and make-believe castles rising at the shoreline
of the great ocean. Behind them, blotted out by the false mina-
rets and costumed staff and half-naked showgirls, were the real
slums and shacks where the wretched year-round residents lived
like Russian serfs.

At the Taj Mahal, where the indoor lights made it seem like
a domed stadium, Bonnie headed straight for the pit boss and
told him her intention. She had to speak up, above the clatter of
chips and wheels and gears and excited players. Roberta headed
for the assembly line of slots, rattling her quarters in a deep cup.
The pit boss looked at Bonnie, then said he would have to check
with the floor manager. She began to feel a welling of excitement
as the noise and lights and full realization of what she was about
to do came upon her.

The floor manager's office was next to the cashier—a large,
tasteful room intended to subdue troublesome losers who
wanted more credit than the casino was willing to give. The men
were all doused with cologne, wearing freshly pressed suits,
flashing glittering watches, staring at her with intimidating ferocity. At first she thought that the floor manager was a young
man—he had that youthful corporate look of blow-dried hair
and tolerant smile. He nodded when she told him what she
wanted to do, asked if she had any identification, and she showed
him her company ID and a few credit cards and her driver's
license. He rubbed his fingers expertly across the surfaces. The
pit boss whispered something in the floor manager's ear.

"You're the weathergirl!" said the floor manager, who was
not really so young, when she looked closely. Could have been
crowding fifty, but carefully clipped and tended, like a garden.
"The one with the, oh, what's that expression?"

"Hey, it's only weather!"

He nodded, laughed without making a sound. He must have swallowed all natural noise to rise to floor boss in this temple of gambling.

"How about it?" she asked. There was a certain amount of bravado in her offhand manner. She might have been grateful if they turned her down, sent her home with her money intact. But now that it was public, she was committed.

"You have the cash?"

She took out the paper bag from her deep pocket and handed it to him. Her hands trembled and if he noticed, he was professionally trained to ignore such signs of nerves. He looked inside, took out one of the bills, held it up to the light, then pushed a button on his telephone console. "Get me Manny," he said.

They were all silent while they waited. There was an awkward clearing of throats. Then the floor manager pushed the button again. "Some coffee," he said. "Hold it." He looked up at Bonnie questioningly.

"Coffee's fine," she said. She did not know whether she could swallow. But her mouth was dry, and it would give her another thing to do.

Manny was different. He wore thick glasses and an ill-fitting suit whose sleeves didn't reach his bony wrists. He had the sallow look of someone kept in a back room. He blinked in the artificial sunlight of the casino. His movements were awkward, except when he touched the money. He handled cash like a magician, turning it around in his hands, testing the texture, examining it under a jeweler's glass. He plucked three bills from different sections of the stack and he took his time. By now they were drinking coffee and sitting on the sofa, giving Manny time and privacy to perform his work.

"I've never seen you here before," said the floor boss, whose name was Larry.

"I don't gamble," Bonnie said.

They all laughed, except Manny, who never laughed.

Larry leaned over and said, "You don't gamble?"

"Sounds funny," she agreed.

"You are about to bet $37,000 on a single roll of the dice—
you don't consider that gambling."

She hadn't when she dreamed up the plan, and when she
asked the casino officials to lift the house limits so she could place
her life savings on a roll of the dice, she didn't consider it
gambling. Not in the technical sense of the word. She wanted
one roll so she could get it over with quickly. See the results.
Have an immediate answer to the question of whether or not she
could afford to stay home and finish writing her book. Thirty-
seven thousand wasn't enough—she knew that. She needed at
least seventy to pay her rent and keep up a semblance of her
lifestyle. She was not willing to move into a roach-infested East
Village tenement.

Manny had tested fifty bills at random and was willing to
render his opinion.

"Looks good," he said.

Larry nodded, rose, and asked Bonnie to wait in his office.
He had to check with the house manager. "You gonna call
Donald Trump after this?" she asked.

He turned and looked at her, revealing a somber, fiduciary
side of his personality. "This is a lot of money," he said. Now he
looked fifty.

The house manager was a silver-haired CEO, who appar-
ently seldom descended from his penthouse to the casino floor.
A path opened through the crowd that had started to collect
outside of the floor manager's office. "Jeff Fields," said the house
manager, smiling, holding out his manicured hand, looking over
at the stack of bills. He was tall, not bad looking, and probably
had a reputation as someone solid. He looked solid, like someone
you'd trust with your money, which is what she was doing.

"I've heard of you," she lied.

He raised his eyebrows. House managers were like under-
secretaries of state. No one ever heard of them, apart from the

inside baseball staffs. He chased everyone else out of the room, poured some fresh coffee in her cup, then straightened the crease on his slacks. "Are you certain that you want to do this?" he asked without looking at her.

"I've thought about it," she said. Her voice was husky.

"I hope this isn't your last dime," he said, facing her.

"Call it a whim," she said finding her television voice, the one that came to her when the camera turned her way.

"That's a big whim."

"If I win it'll be a whimfall."

He sighed. "I know who you are. I have had your references checked. By the way, did you know that you were reported as a missing person on the New Jersey Turnpike? A limousine driver said you vanished, possible kidnapping. There are a lot of people looking for you."

She laughed softly. "He was a very annoying driver."

He nodded, as if all things were comprehensible to him.

"Well, then," he said, standing up, his decision made. "We are here to accommodate our customers and you are a customer."

"So I can bet the $37,000 on one roll of the dice?"

He paused and gave her a very grave look. After a few seconds, he said, "We will stand by our bargain. No limit. One roll of the dice. I must warn you, however, if you lose, this is for keeps. You won't get your money back."

"I understand," she nodded.

"But there's another danger."

"What's that?"

He poured himself half a cup of coffee and sat down again. "You may win," he said.

She laughed.

He smiled. "It is a very real possibility."

"I certainly hope so."

"That may not be the end of it."

"Just one roll of the dice. Win or lose, I'm history."

He looked at Larry's teak desk and the rich curtains and he spoke facing away. "We won't stop you, either way."

"What's that mean?"

He got up again, searched for the words. "People get caught up," he explained. "They get excited. You may want to double the bet. What I'm telling you is, we will not stop you."

She shook her head. "One bet, win or lose."

"The house seldom loses."

"Unless you give me loaded dice, I'm ready," she said, rising with him. She stopped because the motion made the room spin. She asked if she could use the bathroom. Of course, he said, and it struck her that the casino men had the steady tenderness of intensive care nurses.

Larry's office had its own plush bathroom, which had casino lights and wallpaper with a motif of cards and dice. The towels were linen and crisp. Bonnie looked at her face. She was sweating. "Do you really want to do this?" she asked herself in the bright mirror.

She nodded back. Then she choked and turned and heaved her hamburger, french fries, Coke, and some cookies they had fed her on the bus into the toilet. She flushed, cleaned the bowl, then flushed again. She washed her face, put on some fresh makeup, and emerged smiling.

The house manager examined her. "Still time to change your mind," he said.

She shook her head. "Ready," she said, heading out into the hushed casino.

A table had been set aside especially for Bonnie. The crowd parted, clearing a path through the eerie silence. She could feel the secret watchers in the ceiling, sense the hidden cameras on the pillars. In the crowd she saw Roberta, who was smiling and shaking her cup of quarters.

It went by in a swarm of images, none of which remained steady. She felt as if she was about to fall, but she held onto the table. She stood at the head of the table and the pit boss offered her a choice of dice. She picked the first two. At every move, a murmur shivered across the casino floor. "The lady is about to roll," said the pit boss mechanically.

Someone wanted to bet with her, and the floor manager shook his head. "This is a private game," he said. "No other bettors." The floor manager placed thirty-seven $1000 chips on the table. Bonnie took a breath and rolled the dice. The first one hit the back wall and stopped. It was a one. The next was a three. Her point was four. Little Joe. The hardest point to hit. A sympathetic groan passed behind her. She gulped, counting herself a loser. She forgot the odds, but it was something long and not in her favor. If she rolled a seven before she rolled another four, she lost.

In the background she could hear side bets being laid. She picked up the dice and rolled them again, her spirits flat and resigned to defeat. Her heart thumped and she had a grimace of a smile pasted on her face.

"The point is four," said the pit boss and then the dice came to rest and the noise and respiration in the room stopped. The first die was five and the second was three. "Eight," announced the pit boss, and she would have to roll again. She didn't even bother to look. The tension was too high. The big gamblers had taken seats in a balcony, watching with lizard eyes. She flung the dice against the side of the table, and when they stopped a scream went up from the spectators. "Two and two," cried the pit boss. "The lady makes her point." He used the long stick to move thirty-seven more $1000 chips to her pile.

She watched and was unable to take it in. She had won! She had never believed it was possible. Even in her hope, there had been some guilty feeling about earning money this way. She had doubled her money! She could not believe it. All the overtime and scrimping, and in two minutes at a dice table, she had $74,000. She picked up the long, rectangular chips and stuffed them in the paper bag.

"Congratulations," said the house manager, Jeff Fields, smiling, holding out his hand. She saw the look in his eyes and she laughed.

"No," she said, "I'm through."

"Fine, fine," he said. "We'll go back to Larry's office and I'll write you a check."

The people in the crowd were clapping her on the back, clucking about her victory, making chirpy, optimistic sounds, as if they had beaten the house. She could feel the lightness of the mood. Then she thought, Jack would quit. He would take the winnings and walk away and consider the game over. Maybe that's why she hesitated. In the midst of the celebration, after someone handed her a glass of champagne, she stopped. It wasn't over. Damn! It should be over. They had been right, the professionals. The civilians bet on dice, the professionals bet on human weakness. The pit boss looked over at Jeff Fields.

The house manager nodded, then said to Bonnie, "I warned you."

"I know," she said grimly. She looked up, and the lizard pros had not budged after the first roll. They had been waiting for the next roll of the dice. "Let it ride," she said with a sickly smile. "Hey, it's only money!"

$$\boxed{2}$$

A T 8:30 IN the morning, John Fasio bolted out of his official car and charged into the borough hall of the county of Queens. The citizens scattered when the intense borough president blitzed his way into his domain with his hair flying, his necktie floating behind like a wind sock, his suit jacket flapping like the fins of a happy seal and his breath sending smoke signals ahead of his dramatic approach. Fasio simply had no patience for the wheezing front door or the glacial pace of pedestrian traffic or the clunky elevator that rose like a hacking cough through the 1930's Works Department building. He pushed, he plunged, he forged ahead.

Not that there was anything urgent to drive his engine. Fasio was simply the sort of man who stirred a whirlwind in his wake. It was his inexhaustible energy and raw force, not his physical measurements, that gave him size. On the cusp of forty, he took the stairs in athletic leaps, as if he were being chased. Not by a person, but by some inkling of failure. His fans boasted that he was the youngest borough president of the largest outpost of New York City, as if that combination of youth and vitality implied vast dormant possibilities. And, in fact, when he had come to public office four years earlier, it had been in an uproar of youth; now the people who chronicled and forecast such things skipped over intermediate, minor ambitions and spoke of the Senate or Governor's mansion. They deliberately left open the rest of his future, with a deep and knowing silence. And so he ran the way he did, in part, to keep up with the expectations of his supporters.

He ignited the air with his crackling commands, his crisp instructions to his staff and his sarcastic wisecracks about pompous big shots. The sound of his heavy tread thumping down the unventilated corridors of local power set in motion a retreating tide, as nervous officials ducked behind closed doors until they heard his footsteps ebb.

"Hey! Hey! Hey!"

The one-legged Vietnam veteran who operated the newsstand and cigar counter under the winding staircase yelled hello, and Fasio yelled something back. "Do me a favor, sarge, don't give me any more hot tips, okay?" cried Fasio. "The last four horses ran out of the money. I'm gonna have you busted!"

"Hey! Hey! Hey! I only tout 'em—I don't run 'em. I can't run." He thunked the wooden leg with an iron weight that ordinarily held down a pile of newspapers.

It was a friendly, familiar battlefield salute between two soldiers. Then Fasio remembered something, stopped halfway up the stairs, twisted with surprising grace, almost like a dancer, and called over his shoulder in a clear voice: "Cigars!" His trailing chief assistant, who was also his driver, bodyguard, and companion, Murray Gerber, scooped up a handful of the Garcia y Vegas at the newsstand and nodded, thus completing the transaction. Almost. The wounded veteran would add their cost, and then extra cigars as a veteran's bonus, on Fasio's tab.

"John, I gotta talk to you," said one of the city councilmen who had been floating in the second-floor hallway, waiting in ambush for the gust of Fasio's morning passage. Sam Morris was one of the old-timers—a halfhearted liberal. He had come to public office thirty-odd years ago, in his forties, a public-spirited defense lawyer with left-wing sentiments who had, in time, turned into mush. He found the city council to be a body largely ceremonial that ratified local ordinances. The real power lay with the mayor and the five borough officials who controlled the day-to-day operation of the city.

Now Sam Morris was elected to the city council out of pity. His constituency cast their votes as if they were dropping a handful of spare change into Sam Morris's political beggar's cup. Besides, it didn't really make any difference. Not in a calcified, pragmatic civic body ground down to bare survivalism. Everyone knew that the members of the city council rubber-stamped whatever the political bosses told them to approve. And for their votes they collected a small paycheck and those meager perks that made living in New York possible—a free parking space, a miniature badge that gave them immunity from speeding tickets, little gifts and free vacations from corporations that counted on tame and toothless municipal watchdogs.

Fasio smiled and nodded; it was enough to pull Sam along past the guards outside of his office who enjoyed giving everyone a hard time. Fasio paused to look at the messages that always piled up like leaves on his secretary's desk. He started to read them, then stuffed them into his pocket when they blurred, and marched into his own office, howling "Coffee and bagels for everyone!"

Sam Morris, who was seventy-five years old, stood while Fasio fell into his soft leather chair and began thumbing through his daily calendar. Fasio kept his fingers and his mind in constant motion, mostly because he was restless and frightened of being bored.

"Sit, Sam, sit!" said Fasio.

Sam Morris sat perched on the edge of his chair and remembered sitting before Fasio's father with the same anxious knot in his belly. It was Sam's brief service in the army airforce during World War II that settled his rank forever. He would always be an enlisted man.

"So, what's going on, Sam? The wife okay?"

Sam nodded. "Fine."

Fasio knew that she wasn't fine. Her true condition was written in thick black lines under Sam's suffering eyes. Gerry Morris, a retired schoolteacher, was dying. At the age of seventy-eight she had slipped and cracked a bone in her hip, and it had proved to be one of those irreparable geriatric injuries from which people never recover. She had been in bed for a year already.

"John, it's about the incinerator," said Sam.

Fasio was relighting his cigar and for a second was confused. Jane, the secretary, had deposited a tray of coffee and bagels with a schmear of cream cheese on Fasio's cluttered desk, and without even looking, Fasio had grabbed a bagel, had swallowed half in one bite. Now he looked at the match and he looked at the cigar; then he remembered Sam's incinerator and smiled. The incinerator. No one wanted one. The city was sinking under mounting alps of garbage and still the "homeowners" fought against the only sensible, albeit imperfect, solution. Someplace else, was their battle cry. Anyone with a brain could see that one day an incinerator would have to go into business in Queens.

But Sam lived in Bayside, an unblemished section of the borough astride the great bay in Long Island Sound. Once, it had been the site of mansions for rich industrialists—a safe commuting distance from gritty urban woes. Now the great homes were broken into condos and Bayside was a bus and subway ride from midtown, and the golf course was open to high-priced plumbers and iron workers, not to mention middle managers. As if that wasn't enough, the city wanted to build a new incinerator in Sam Morris's backyard, along an empty stretch of shoreline. It was a logical site, even a fair choice, given the spread of incinerators from Brooklyn to Harlem. But Bayside hired potent lawyers and fancy lobbyists and made it one of those make-or-break litmus tests for local office. Sam Morris, who wanted his wife to die at home in peace, was opposed to the site.

"It's gonna kill the goose," said Councilman Morris. He meant the bountiful campaign donations, the fat fundraisers, the abundant tactical support provided by Bayside residents and private interests for public undertakings. There were year-round dinners and fetes and appeals that never went unanswered. They all kept the financial pot bubbling.

"I understand, Sam," Fasio said, puffing the unlit cigar to life, wiping away the cloud between them. "I personally hate smoky incinerators. But, you know, Sam, there's an important truth you people have failed to grasp."

"What's that, John?"

"Well, every morning I have half a grapefruit. It's a nasty habit, I know, but it makes Irma think I eat healthy." He shrugged. "Guess what? I do not eat the outside. I put it in a bag and I put the bag in the garbage pail and I put the garbage pail outside of my door. I have no idea what happens after that, but every night when I come home—a miracle!—the pail is empty. What do you make of that, Sam? You think maybe there's a grapefruit fairy?"

Sam nodded. "Okay. I get your point."

Fasio became artfully solemn. "I'm not sure you do. You know, the landfills are full. They're farting methane. And that stuff is lethal. We gotta do something. Methane or carbon. Take your pick. I pick carbon. I have every intention of picking something less toxic when it comes along. But for now, we gotta put my grapefruit rind someplace." He smiled and held out his hands, palms up, a supplicating gesture. Then, his voice taking on a touch of irony, he said, "C'mon, Sam. What's your story? You think only people in ghettos should have incinerators?"

Sam ignored the provocation. This was business. "I think something could be done—a compromise. A place where it doesn't hurt industry, cost jobs, ruin property values. You know the problem is political. It really is. The trouble is, we need a

man in Gracie Mansion who understands—truly understands—
the balance between business and the ecology. Somebody smart,
maybe, a man like you . . ."

"Are you crazy? You think I could stop the incinerators?"
He shook his head. "No one can. Listen, I'm not crazy about it,
I know the downside. I know the true benefits of our wonderful
industrial age. We poison everyone equally with toxic emissions.
I also appreciate the fact that people are lazy and recycling is a
pain in the ass. I just want to make sure that your average citizen
appreciates the fact that he doesn't hafta quit smoking. It won't
make any difference. The incinerator next door is a good two
packs a day. I know all this shit. But tell me a way out?"

"We really should have more studies . . ."

"Bullshit! We've had more studies . . . than cockroaches." He
waved at his desk, piled with well-prepared documents. "Environmental impact studies. Technology forecasts. Site selection
studies. So many studies that I had to get my environmental guy
to do a study on the studies. I'm still waiting for his summary,
which will wrap it all up and I'll present it to the mayor, along
with my recommendation. The mayor is counting on my report.
And I gotta tell ya, right now, I'm really leaning towards an
incinerator."

"Listen, John, there are two million people in Queens.
These are good people, John. Voters."

Fasio shook his head. "Don't start on that crap."

"You'd be a good mayor. A great mayor. Never mind the
incinerator. Forget the garbage. I'm talking about City Hall.
Gracie Mansion. This city is falling apart. Literally. The bridges
have holes in them, the subways are sinking, the water pipes
can't hold water. And, there's no leadership. None. No rudder.
We need someone strong to take over . . ."

"Cut it out, Sam. I don't want to be mayor. I don't even
want to be borough president."

The old man smiled. He didn't believe Fasio. According to
the sacred political code upon which he operated—ancient

bureaucratic shrewdness handed down like the wisdom of Confucius to all those who fed at the public trough—everyone wanted to be mayor. Everyone wanted to be borough president. Everyone wanted the limos, the young volunteers dazzled by the stench of power, the fawning maitre d's at the first-class restaurants, the instant seating at hit shows, the public recognition— the movie-star celebrity perks, the endless, endless adulation. Everyone wanted some of that. Or so Sam Morris believed.

The light on John Fasio's phone console blinked. "Your mother," said the secretary.

"Sorry," Fasio said to Sam, who had taken the cue and was gathering his things to leave, "I gotta take this."

Fasio watched Sam vanish into the adjoining office of his assistant, Murray Gerber, then punched the telephone console button where his mother's light flickered on hold. "Ma! How's it going?"

Celia Fasio was seventy-five years old and living in the Golden Years Nursing Home in Westchester County. At another time, she would have been living in a room in her son's home. Her mild eccentricities and lapses in memory would have been shrugged off lightly as the usual cargo of family responsibility. It was a constant source of guilt to John, her eldest son, that his mother and his wife, Irma, could not survive under the same roof. *We had to put my mother in a home.* He said it out loud whenever he was alone in his office and the words had the impact of a hammer on an anvil.

"Johnny, Johnny, Johnny!"

She was sobbing. The tears were spilling out some twenty miles away into Fasio's earpiece and he could almost taste the bitterness. He knew that his mother had managed to sneak into one of the offices to get to a phone. Whatever she was crying about, she had that unanswered grievance of having been placed in a home by her son.

"Ma, Ma, I'm gonna be there Sunday. You remember, Ma? We're gonna have a party."

It was her birthday. An event. He would bring her a gift. It wouldn't make her smile—in fact, it would make her weep and he wouldn't know whether it was for joy or sorrow. But he would bring the gift and the cake and the strained, synthetic joy.

"Johnny, I'm hungry. Johnny. Did you hear me? I haven't eaten all day!"

He stopped. Was she serious? He couldn't tell. She could slip back and forth between adult coherence and childlike raving. He spoke delicately, uncertain whether he was speaking to the indignant parent or the muddled child. Maybe it was him, his own eroded compassion. The men on the street who spoke of their hunger, begging for spare change to buy something to eat—he didn't believe them, either. Food was such an easy thing to find.

"Listen, have you had breakfast, Ma?"

"They take the food and they sell it. Did you know that? They sell the food from our mouths. I have to beg to get a crust of bread."

"Did you have breakfast today? Just tell me what you ate today."

There was a long silence on the phone. Then he heard a dignified voice. "A bowl of cereal."

"See, Ma, you had something for breakfast."

"With sour milk!" she howled. Then, when that sank in, she added, "When I told them it was sour, when I complained, they took away the cereal."

"I'll call, Ma. I'll call right away. You'll get something to eat, I promise. And I'll see you on Sunday."

He hung up before she could start again. He didn't want to believe in her hunger. But it sounded plausible. He told the secretary, Jane, to call the nursing home and make certain that his mother had something to eat.

"Don't make a thing out of it," he said. "Just make it, like, a question. I don't want them to know that she called to complain."

Jane was standing in the doorway, her hand on her hip.

"Gimme a suggestion," she said. "What makes me ask this question about your mother?"

He shrugged. "I don't know. You're calling because I was thinking of my mother and wondering what she had for breakfast."

Jane's face curdled.

"Okay, just say I'm worried if she's eating. Her appetite. I worry if she eats. She's had a problem with her appetite. Humor me. Tell them to humor me."

Jane turned to make the call, but her expression showed that she considered it a pretty thin excuse to make a fool out of herself.

Murray Gerber, who generally trailed his boss like a sulfuric cloud, sat behind his cluttered desk, peering up at Sam Morris like someone looking up from a foxhole, showing as small a target as possible. Gerber was fifty years old—an ex-cop who had spent his whole adult life in a bad mood. It was Gerber who defended Fasio against the steady onslaught of annoying pests who gravitated like metal filings to the office of the borough president. The office of borough president belonged to Fasio, but it was Gerber who said yes or no to almost every entreaty, and there was seldom any appeal from his rulings.

"Is he gonna go, or what?" asked Sam.

Gerber lifted his shoulders. He didn't speak unless he had to—operating on the theory that anyone might be wired.

"It's getting close," persisted Sam. "We got less than a year 'till the next election."

Gerber nodded.

"You want him to be mayor, don't you?"

Gerber nodded.

Sam knew that somewhere under Gerber's ex-cop's haberdashery was a gun. A licensed gun, but a gun, and under the gun beat a heart that was perfectly capable of using it. He knew this, and it made a difference in how he spoke to Murray Gerber.

"So, what we want is to get Carmine Tanana to do an environmental impact study," said Sam Morris, cutting the chitchat and getting down to business. "He's an expert. Former sanitation commissioner. Credentials. A name. You want someone who knows the territory."

Gerber nodded.

Sam Morris continued, "In order to get Tanana, we gotta make the summary inconclusive. You're gonna see it, control it, put it under his nose. Just raise some doubts about things like, you know, the habitat. What's an incinerator gonna do to the wildlife? The birds at the airports? What you hafta do is make sure that he knows it's gonna take one more final, comprehensive study. And I would think that a comprehensive study will take at least another six months. And maybe then there could be some controversy about the results, which would also take some study. You know, there are some tidal pools around Bayside, which could have very adverse ecological effects if they are damaged. And an incinerator could do an awful lot of damage. We have to do this, Murray."

Gerber looked away. He had lost interest in the incinerator. He was like a bored husband, keeping the guise of wedlock alive while conserving his passion for an undisclosed tryst.

Sam realized that he was not going to get a satisfactory conversation started and handed over a thick envelope. They were alone in a windowless room, but Gerber looked around just the same. He took the stack of hundred dollar bills out and counted them with the speed of a teller. When he was satisfied that he had 150 bills, he placed them back in the envelope, nodded, and slipped the envelope in his top drawer under one of his old service revolvers. Just then they heard the door.

"You still here?"

Fasio poked his head into Gerber's office. He didn't see the envelope or the exchange, but he did see Sam Morris's face turn bright red. He guessed at the reason for the blush—some conspiratorial maneuvering by Sam with his corrupt chief assistant.

By now, it only tickled the old compunctions he felt about his assistant's plastic scruples. Don't let me catch you, he had told Gerber when he had seen a case of liquor in the corner of the adjoining office. Little sins, he told himself. Small favors, small gifts. If there were envelopes bulging with hundred dollar bills, he refused to see them. There was a simple reason he tolerated the corruption: Murray Gerber was a petty thief who would remain in his debt forever. He could be relied on in a tight spot because Fasio had spared him from disgrace by ignoring the trivial blemish.

"Just leaving," said Sam quickly.

When he was gone, Fasio stared at Gerber for a moment. His assistant looked a little uncomfortable, shifted some papers on his desk. Fasio wondered what he had interrupted. It had the stench of something ugly. But he didn't chase it. They had a bargain. Still . . . he felt uneasy.

"Remember Sunday," he said.

"Right," replied Gerber.

"You ordered the cake?"

"You know you can trust me," said Gerber smiling. Then he turned away from Fasio's scrutiny to catch a pencil before it rolled off the desk.

3

B ONNIE HUDSON WAS not famous for her cooking. She would have starved without restaurants, diners, and friends moved by pity over her culinary bungling. If it came down to it, she could put together a sandwich, but nothing too complicated. Nothing that would require applying live heat to, say, a raw piece of meat. She was safe with store-bought ham and cheese or lettuce and tomato, but even here she fussed uncertainly with condiments and was never convinced that mustard wouldn't make a more interesting dressing than mayonnaise. Usually, she forgot which she preferred, got it wrong, and wound up eating half a sandwich.

In the end, most of her meals were prepared by strangers and consumed at isolated tables in modest restaurants under the canopy of scowling waiters who didn't approve of single women eating alone. The march of feminism notwithstanding, tradition-bound restaurant staffs believed that a single woman suggested a range of sad possibilities, from the whiff of disgrace to the shadow of madness. Women were supposed to be sunny, social creatures, cheerfully balancing pots and plates and providing the glue for family life around the hearth. And if that wasn't enough to justify their unfriendly attitude, there was a bottom-line slander—single women were bad tippers. In spite of the fact that Bonnie wildly overtipped, she found that it made no difference whatsoever in the low caliber of the service.

It was not laziness that accounted for her inability to cook. Bonnie's retreat from the kitchen was a matter of self-preservation. She couldn't be trusted near an open flame because she was too easily distracted. She usually forgot what she was doing. Her attention wandered to an interesting passage from a book, or something she saw on the street, or the possibilities contained within an old remark. And as she turned these thoughts and events and worries over in her mind, she would be jarred by the piercing shriek of the smoke alarm. Neighbors always knew when she was cooking.

It was just too much trouble for such a quick payoff and all that cleanup.

And so on the Saturday after her excursion to Atlantic City, she was playing it safe. She was waiting to take her old boss, Harvey Levy, out to dinner. She sat dressed and perfumed, glaring at the pile of bills on her desk—bills that would have to wait, now that she had so quickly and carelessly tossed away two years of solvency on a single roll of dice. Even now, in the dim evening light of her living room, she could see the snake eyes of the dice looking back at her from the green felt of the casino table. She could hear the sucking sound of sympathy from the spectators as they watched the chips gathered in by the pit boss; and she could hear the trill of satisfaction from the gamblers who once again had had their faith in human weakness restored.

There was also the memory of a tinsel-thin sound—her own voice, rising operatically to an off-key pitch of near panic as she tried to shrug off the damage: "Hey! It's only money."

As a result of that sudden surge of avarice, she now had to grovel and present a reasonably sane and plausible front to Harvey Levy to land a miserable job she didn't want in the first place. I should have paid a couple of months' rent in advance, she thought, then cursed again the dice that had forced her into this humiliating predicament.

She tried to buck up her spirits: Good old Harvey, she thought. One of the guys! Never management. A boss, true enough, but a prole at heart. He has a powerful union sentiment left over from his youth as a street reporter. Good old Harvey!

Of course, he has an edge and that's good. You need an edge, especially when dealing with people like me. But not a corporate edge. Not a clock-watcher or a piecework overseer edge. A good-guy edge. Not that he'd let me screw the company. I mean, the company has to live, breathe, sign the checks . . . But, you know, he can be a son of a bitch. Especially when he doesn't get his way. And his way is not always my way . . . No, no, no. A really nice guy. But maybe I played too rough when I told him where to shove the stupid job and his tempting gold. People are funny about specific anatomical insults; they take it personally. Maybe he already has another weather reporter. Someone who cheerfully uses the idiot maps with the moving clouds and cartoon letters and military arrows; someone who doesn't let her rage show up on her segment like some exclusive accu-weather satellite shot of her own emotional storm clouds.

Somebody who can cook!

Okay, okay, she told herself with that calming inner voice that made her think she was a slight loon, let's not fuck it up. She would not eat much, just touch at the food and remind him of her wit with clever conversation. If only she could remember not to rant against everything from wooden-headed Elvis schmucks to that annoying phony humble act by Mother Theresa. She would be immensely rational, she decided. Harvey would see in the afterglow of dinner that she was wasted on the weather, with her newfound mildness and sagacious approach to life and the world.

The sound of the doorbell broke into her strategic planning. She looked at the clock above the refrigerator and it read 8:05. When she went to the door, there was Harvey smiling back at her. She didn't budge. Finally, he asked, "Did I come on the wrong night?"

She laughed, and it was a nice, shining laugh, spraying friendly familiarity like an air freshener. "What's a right night?" she said, stepping aside, ushering him into her apartment.

In one hand he held a bouquet of flowers and in the other a bottle of wine. He expects me to cook, she thought. He expects me to serve him a dinner right here in the apartment!

She took the flowers and the wine and then reverted to her old newspaper ways: "How'd you get into the building?"

"I gave the doorman your name and he said, 'Good luck,' and let me in."

"He's not supposed to do that," she muttered, annoyed, while she fussed with the violets. He followed her into the kitchen where she pulled the bouquet out of the paper and forced it down into an old wine carafe. "He's supposed to buzz," she said of the doorman, turning accusingly to Harvey Levy. "God, I hate that!"

Levy smiled. "I guess he thought that anyone who said that he was coming to see you wouldn't be making it up."

She absorbed that, and swallowed the retort which was on the tip of her tongue: Maybe it's because you look so fucking harmless!

Instead she smiled winningly and said, "Help yourself to a drink," then vanished into her bedroom to put on her coat.

He had taken his first sip of whiskey when she emerged from the bedroom. He looked her over and she detected an unmistakable and unwelcome longing. She always assumed that they were pals, maybe even friends. Adversaries, of course, but adversaries of the closest kind. The sort who could spit out insults like bullets and still be friends. Now there was this shivery undertone of courtship. He was wearing an Armani jacket, a Nicole Miller tie, a Calvin Klein shirt. His shoes were polished, his voice had a husky rasp, his eyes were a little moist, and, most alarming of all, he had a schoolboy awkwardness. The predominant impression was that of warmed-over, desperate, middle-aged charm.

Of course, now that she was face-to-face with the look, she should have expected it. She should not have ruled out Harvey as a potential suitor. She was definitely within his range of interest. After all, he was unattached, a widower, only forty-nine years old, which put him in the ballpark. It was simply that she had never thought of him as a romantic possibility. The man was . . . well, Harvey. He was someone to argue with about headlines, deadlines, and leads. Career things. Theories. Ethics. There was almost twenty years' difference in their ages—but then Jack was in his low forties. Of course, Jack was young, no matter what age, while Harvey was . . . Harvey. Solid. Authoritarian. Difficult. Smart.

"I heard about you and Jack," he said.

She ran a hand threw her lush hair, then shrugged. "It's okay," she said. "We're both lost souls. Searching for ourselves. He's looking in Queens and I'm looking in Manhattan. Which happens to be the last place I was seen in public."

"Too bad. I like Jack."

"Get out, Harvey."

He looked stunned. She pointed to the door.

"Let's go to dinner."

Thirty years earlier, The Lion's Head on Sheridan Square, in the heart of the bohemian section of Manhattan's Greenwich Village, was a scurvy newspaper bar filled with dipsomaniac reporters who lived on the edge of poverty and the thin gruel of local fame. They had bylines or columns, but it didn't count for much. One story was pretty much like another in a time of calculated sentiment and cookie-cutter opinion. Other reporters knew of their outlaw touches and important scoops—knew it from the lips of the culprits, themselves. They were men, for the most part, who stank up the room with smoke and beery outbursts against gutless publishers, heartless editors, and the worst, the very worst: the well-groomed, blow-dried, soulless, empty-headed television news things who called themselves reporters. Heirs of a warrior tribe of fierce journalists, these television things—according to the howls growing louder in the night as the liquor and beer turned up the heat—were the brain-dead children of their age who would mouth only the most convenient and popular banalities. They didn't cover stories—they covered their ass. So said the remnants, as if that explained their decline.

There was no hope and no charity, in that unforgiving den four steps down from the street, for the fools and serpents who ran the world according to their insatiable materialist creed. The stories that couldn't get printed were roared aloud by the impotent lions of the press. They were a pathetic lot, even when they pushed each other into the jukebox or staged some wavy, toothless fight in which punches seldom landed.

In those rowdy, clammy days the food at The Lion's Head was bad. The customers who had stumbled into the back room for dinner after soaking themselves in liquor couldn't taste the difference. But then The Head had fallen on good times. A chef had been employed in the kitchen and the inch-thick hamburgers and oil-drenched french fries vanished, replaced by nightly dinner specials of fish and pasta. The print reporters had grown old and timid, and there were nights when the long curling bar was inhabited by the disabled, exhausted relics of their profession who stared into the bottom of glasses that contained soft drinks. Even the cloud of smoke was gone as the smokers died out or were driven east to the junkie part of the Village. The great sentimental and heroic sagas came from the mouths of investment bankers and public relations experts. Treason was only a memory in The Head.

Still, out of habit, Bonnie came to the Head. She was fond of the old bones she found around the bar, and the back room, with its old books and working fireplace, was congenial for Harvey, too. They sat under movie posters for *Morgan* and *Doctor Strangelove* and ate bread and ordered drinks and gradually recovered from the shock of having stumbled into a purely social encounter.

"I would have cooked," she said smiling. "But then I would have had to watch you try to eat the food." She shook her head. "I am living proof that women do not belong in the kitchen."

"I'm sure you could do it, if you tried," he said with conviction. "Christ, you can do almost anything."

She shook her head again. "I can't clean. Sometimes I spend a whole day just cleaning the bathroom. Nine, ten hours. In the bathroom!"

"Really? I missed it. Sorry I didn't get a chance to see it."

"Well, actually, it doesn't really get that clean."

"It doesn't?"

She shook her head. "I usually bring in a book—I don't like to go anyplace without something to read. Most of the time I'm on the floor, holding the book in one hand and a rag in the other, polishing the brass. There's one stretch of pipe—right where the light is best—that really shines."

He nodded. He understood. It was Bonnie. And he kept looking past her, over her shoulder, as if he couldn't trust himself in a head-on blaze of her eyes.

"So," she said, "how's the new station? How's it working out there?"

His head wavered, like a dog sniffing the air. "Oh, it's not so bad." He didn't sound convincing.

He smiled and Bonnie felt the distant chill. When they both worked on the Long Island newspaper, the one thing that they had always agreed upon was that bosses were bad and jobs were terrible.

It had been two years, and Harvey had created a new career as a television editor for a local station, but now he had been lured away to work for a new station—the one recently purchased by a British media mogul, Basil "Thatch" Conway, who wanted to launch himself into American society since he was considered too lowly to be a British blue blood. He set out to

become an American aristocrat with typical shrewdness.
Through the media. Television station owners had instant access
to power. Conway even became a citizen to satisfy the Federal
Communications Commission's guidelines. Having gone that
far, he surrounded himself with a king's court. At a dinner at the
Museum of Modern Art, Thatch had been seated next to Harvey Levy, who had dazzled him with his inside bitchy gossip
about everyone, his smart chatter about style and fashion and
power.

By the end of the evening Thatch had offered Levy a management job at Channel 9. Levy wanted to bring Bonnie with
him, but she had turned him down.

"You know," he said, cutting into a chunk of burnt fish, "I
like opera."

"I didn't know that." She didn't want to know that. There
were some revelations from the heart that only spelled trouble.

"Do you like opera?"

He was staring into her face now, a soulful look that made
her want to shake him and say, Let's go back to the old Bonnie
and Harvey. "No, I hate it." That sounded hard—too hard. But
that didn't stop her. "I can't understand a word. Not even when
I've got the libretto right in front of me."

Harvey felt the blast of her rejection.

"Is everything all right?" The waiter's name was Sydney. He
wrote it on the checks. Spelled it out in block letters so that he
wouldn't be mistaken for "Sidney." He stood over them, his
hands clasped together, smiling his Sydney smile.

"How do you get the damn charcoal off the fish," snarled
Harvey.

Sydney gave a brief lecture on scraping with the seam of the
fish, then withdrew rapidly. "I've been thinking about your
offer," began Bonnie.

Harvey looked up. His face showed shock. "The opera?"

"No," she said, annoyed. "I hate opera. I mean the other
one. The job. You know."

He twisted in his seat, adjusting himself, finding the right spot. Bonnie was uninterested in the opera, or Harvey Levy for that matter. He had gotten it all wrong. She was after a job.

"I thought you hated doing the weather."

That was the voice—a scratchy slice of sarcasm. That was the Harvey Levy she knew and wanted to work for. He was chewing the blackened fish—charcoal, bones, skin and all.

"Well, I guess you don't have anything in street reporting . . ."

He munched on the bones. She could hear them break. "There was a story in the newsroom," he said. "A rumor. According to our media guy, you quit Channel 11 . . ."

She shrugged. "Yeah, well, that was no rumor."

". . . and were seen in Atlantic City on a gambling binge. The rumor, or story, had it that you were dysfunctional, if that's the word, crazed with gambling fever, and that you blew the bankroll, the whole thing, on one roll of the dice, and that they had to cart you off to the Betty Ford gamblers' clinic."

She shook her head. "God, I can see why people hate reporters."

"You need a job?"

She nodded. He had recovered from his embarrassment. No scabs showing—just teeth.

"I can put you on a payroll," he said, holding up his hand for Sydney. He wanted coffee. Bonnie wanted a scotch.

"What do I have to do?"

He smiled, leaned over the table, and whispered gleefully, "The weather."

She ran her hand through her hair, looked around, realized that she had no choice. "Will I get a shot at doing some other stories?"

He bent closer. "Hey, the job offer is simple. It's only weather!"

4

S UNDAY MORNING BROKE cold and gray. At 6:50 the light was
just starting to crack open the sky. A crust of ice had formed
over the flesh of Queens. Murray Gerber thought that his hand
might stick to the metal when he pulled open the car door as he
started out to meet John Fasio. It was a few miles from Murray's
lonely monk's cell in Fresh Meadows to Fasio's restored Victorian home on Bell Boulevard in the stylish region of Bayside. But
it was a pleasant drive down city streets that almost looked like
country lanes; Gerber lit a fresh cigarette off the stub of his old
one and shuddered, shaking off the morning chill.

He passed the usual dawn patrol of newspaper delivery
trucks and bakery vans and slow, drowsy police cars moving in
and out of dim streets like stalking cats. The ice in potholes and
puddles crunched under the wheels of the sector cars inching
through the streets, ready to pounce on an early burglar. In this
upper-middle-class section of Queens—not far from the home of
Councilman Sam Morris—the streets were almost deserted on
the last Sunday of January. The neighborhood was buried under
a winter hush, with an added blanket of the Sabbath.

Near Twenty-ninth Avenue, as the boulevard fell toward the
bay, where the yacht club windows were tucked under canvas

ready for heavy weather, Murray pulled the official city car to a stop, half on the sidewalk and half in the street. He let it idle as he waited for the boss. A police cruiser passed by and the patrolman in the front passenger seat nodded solemnly, letting Murray know that the local sentries were on guard and had checked him out.

It was warm inside the car, and Murray loosened the scarf around his neck. He glanced over and saw that the house was still dark, but he knew that Fasio was inside, pumping away on the exercycle.

A ride to nowhere, he thought. Got to get him going somewhere. Time was running out; soon it would be too late to enter the next mayoral election. But Gerber had a serious problem getting his man to jump into the race: John Fasio was happy as borough president. He didn't want to be mayor. But when Murray thought about it—without even having to utter the title, Mayor, aloud—he felt a tingle of tempting possibilities. The piddling little shakedowns and payoffs for delayed municipal incinerators or contract favoritism were nothing. A few thousand here, a few thousand there, it didn't add up to real financial safety. And that's what Murray needed.

Murray Gerber had seven secret accounts in seven different names in seven different banks, and still it was not enough to make him feel secure. Maybe it would never be enough. Even when he was a cop in uniform shaking down storeowners on Queens Boulevard, he'd always wanted more. His partners and superiors had been astonished at his brazen demands for money. What they didn't realize was that Murray was always waiting to get caught. He never thought it would last. One arrest and he would be broken from the force without his pension. He had to get it all while he could. The other cops thought that he had no fear, but he quivered with fear.

He wasn't afraid of going up against a psychotic killer; he had enough awards and medals to attest to his courage. But he expected backup. He expected to be protected, rewarded, and not just given some marks on his career jacket. He wanted the flak vest of retirement accounts. He wanted financial security. Murray believed he had earned the payoffs. Wearing the blue gave him permission. And so when he took his own bonuses, he was well within his own ethical guidelines. After all, if he put his life on the line to protect the citizens, why shouldn't they pay him directly, without the middleman of taxes?

Gerber had an uncanny sixth sense about just how far he could go in his entrepreneurial avarice. When he felt the unfriendly breath of an internal investigation, he quit the police department. He became John Fasio's full-time bodyguard and driver and assistant. Fasio took him on because he felt an obligation. It was an old debt. Murray Gerber had been a volunteer in the seventies, working for Fasio's father, Big Jim Fasio, who was a big shot in the Queens Democratic Party, until the disgrace. Big Jim was the party's fund-raiser in Queens during a crucial congressional race in 1972. In spite of the fact that he managed the backbreaking chore of running a car agency, Big Jim was a splendid fund-raiser. During that momentous campaign, however, everything seemed out of control. The structure of the party was in disarray, the campaign manager was incompetent, the candidate—who should have been a shoo-in—found himself without a coherent strategy. Big Jim stepped in and put some shape into the organization, all the while juggling the financing and the car agency. Gerber was a dervish, delivering the candidate to his appointments, performing menial and important chores without complaint. Even when a discrepancy was found in the financial accounts under Fasio's control—they were short fifty thousand dollars—Gerber remained a sobering and calming influence.

Under the threat of a big investigation, Big Jim accepted the blame for the missing money, but he always insisted to John that he hadn't taken the money. John never knew if his father's claim of innocence was merely technical.

The quick admission of guilt was a great relief to the high

Democratic leaders. The Democratic bosses didn't think that the party would survive a full-scale inquiry, never mind win the disputed congressional seat. Big Jim went to prison for a year, and when he came out, he was a broken husk of a man. A felon, he couldn't go back into private business, and he was a pariah in politics. He grew more and more silent and withdrawn.

There was a small, stubborn body of opinion—held for the most part by lowly storefront workers—who insisted that Big Jim Fasio had never stolen the missing fifty thousand. They speculated that the only thing Big Jim took was the blame, for the sake of the party. The opinion never amounted to anything more than windy sympathy. But John preferred to believe that unauthorized version of his father's ruin. And John never forgot that Murray Gerber was one of the rare supporters who had offered Big Jim something more concrete than a speculative alibi.

That counted high with John.

Murray Gerber had remained an open friend after the prison term, spending a lot of time with John's father. They went out together on long drives and lonely walks. They were almost inseparable. Until the morning when Big Jim Fasio walked into the park alone and put a pistol in his mouth and blew the top of his head off.

Later, when John Fasio found that he had a gift for politics, and Gerber offered him his services, he didn't hesitate. There were some—advisers, gossips—who said that it was a mistake. And there was the undeniable link with the old scandal. The connection might taint young Fasio's career, he was warned.

The smart money pointed out that there were persistent whispers about Murray's questionable moral standing, rumors about corruption. They insisted, without proof, that Gerber had taken too many free cups of coffee. All the admonitions had the opposite effect on Fasio. It was whispers and rumors that demolished his father. Out of staunch loyalty to his dead father and gratitude to Gerber, he gave him the job. The old slander didn't matter. Besides, Fasio argued, there was always a whiff of smoke that clung to a brave cop. He closed his eyes to the small moral lapses.

In the four years since, Murray had discreetly enriched himself with payoffs for smoothing access to his boss, or subtly controlling one project or another. But he'd suppressed his more flagrant impulses of greed and had kept the hounds at bay. He had his reasons. For one thing, he didn't want to damage Fasio. He was too valuable. The little kickbacks and payoffs were costume jewelry. He sensed diamonds in the distance.

Now he felt it. He saw his big opportunity in the lingering and frustrating gridlock over wiring the borough for cable television. One great conquest and he could retire. If he could just get this guy interested in the mayoralty!

At 7:30, Gerber saw the light go on in Fasio's bathroom. He knew what was taking place inside the house. Irma would be awake and stirring while Fasio got into his shower. They would both be aggressively silent and grim, the night's sleep leaving both exhausted. There was no rest for those two.

Murray lit another cigarette.

Inside the Victorian house, John Fasio lingered under the steaming water of the shower. Then, when the muscles felt soothed, he shut off the taps and shook himself like a dog. He stepped out of the shower onto the plush carpet and dried himself with the thick towel. He took his time dressing, preparing himself to visit his mother. When he came downstairs his hair was still damp, and his necktie hung loose like the rails of a train track, and he could feel a flutter of disapproval cross his wife's countenance.

Irma had laid out a place for him in the breakfast nook, which featured a clear view of the bay. Silently, he drank the juice, ate the four prunes, swallowed the dry toast, and managed to get the decaffeinated coffee into his belly. Obediently, he took the vitamin capsule. It was the price. Now that their son was dead of a brain tumor, his was the life that hung by the thread of Irma's intense and relentless ministrations. A small, dark woman, she seemed to shrink in the terrible aftermath of her son's death. Only her eyes—two great teardrops in the center of her face—grew.

Fasio had no doubt that Jimmy's death had unhinged Irma. The boy was just ten when he died. The onset and the outcome of the tumor seemed to have occurred instantly, overnight. In fact, the ordeal had dragged on for six months. At first, they thought that it was a simple thing. Jimmy banged his head—no big deal, an active kid gets bumps. But the bump wouldn't subside and the headaches persisted and the neurologists repeated the CAT scan, and then, instead of reassurances and relief, they proposed more consultants; second, third, and fourth opinions and cloudy, windy obfuscations. They said that they had to be certain. When they summoned oncologists, John and Irma Fasio knew everything.

The doctors were all uniformly conscientious, flawlessly sympathetic and unanimously unyielding in their opinion—they held out no hope at all. Except a miracle, which drove Irma even deeper into a spiritual trance.

Sometimes, the doctors said in their soft somewhat detached professional tones—distant airy academic lectures that drifted past their heads in the austere hospital offices—sometimes, they said, it happens like this. A blow, even a mild blow, will set the cells dividing wildly. Sometimes, they said with an embarrassed and tactful professional shrug, such things happen. As if cataclysms on such a scale were simply part of life's quirky bends and turns. As if John and Irma should be good sports and accept the death of their beloved only child without running into the street naked and screaming like animals; as if people sometimes, because these things happen, did not tear out their eyeballs and scald their own flesh. In their insufferably calm voices, the doctors sensibly argued that food must be swallowed, work must be performed, life must go on. These things happen.

Just before Christmas last year, Jimmy died. He passed away without a complaint. He simply closed his eyes one crisp afternoon when all the medications and radiations had run their predicted course. Afterward, Fasio watched Irma change. The emphasis of her life shifted suddenly and she became convinced that whatever happened to Jimmy, she was, in some part, to blame. To compensate, she took complete charge of her husband's routine. She monitored his meals. She counted his calories. She brought the exercise bicycle into their bedroom—not that there was much else going on there.

But John Fasio was not prepared to surrender to her grief. Not wholeheartedly. He had dealt with calamity before, when faced with his father's disgrace and suicide. The scar tissue left behind was indelible, but he would not allow it to cripple him. He had a defiant pride about his father, and he had a grim determination not to let Jimmy down by dying along with him.

"When do I get my eggs again?" he asked quietly. He could hear the car idling outside.

She was fussing with the decaffeinated coffee and he saw her back arch. "Okay," he said softly, "I tried to go along with the dry toast and the juice and the hot water instead of coffee. I really tried. But, listen, Irma, honey, I gotta eat. I'm hungry!"

"I'm trying to see that you eat right."

She turned and her eyes were brimming with tears.

"It's been more than a year," he said gently.

She turned away, looking out of the window, as if she would find a place to hide, at least a place where her gaze could rest. A clock ticked in the dining room. For a moment, it was the only sound in the house. A dead child left behind an arid house sucked dry of air and sound.

"I gotta go," he said finally, and she turned. He could see the relief in her face.

Murray Gerber watched the progress of the lights as Fasio advanced from the kitchen to the foyer. He punched up the heater as he saw the front door fly open. Fasio ran out of the house with his topcoat draped across his arm, his necktie still dangling undone. He stumbled down the small incline and fell against the car, pulling open the door and collapsing in the passenger seat.

"Coffee," he said, as Murray put the car in gear and inched off the sidewalk and into the traffic lane. Fasio slid the necktie high enough to hide the unbuttoned collar. "No butter on the bagel," he said as the car pulled up outside of a deli on Thirty-fifth Avenue.

"Plain?"

"A schmear," replied Fasio. "Two sugars," he yelled after his driver, who knew by heart how many sugars the boss took in his coffee. Fasio watched from the passenger window. He saw the bag with food and coffee pass over the counter and his assistant run back to the car. He didn't see any money change hands. He could have jumped out of the car and gone for the bagel and coffee himself, made certain that the transaction was unblemished. But he didn't.

Fasio finished his bagel before they hit Northern Boulevard. It took him four large bites. Then he emptied the coffee, packed the papers in the cup, and told Murray to stop at a Dunkin' Donuts. Fasio jumped out, dropped the bag in a wastebasket, then went into the franchise and came out with two plain crullers. It occurred to him as he fell back into his front seat that he had not paid. Hell, he told himself, it didn't matter; he would make it up next time.

Birthdays were always painful for John Fasio. They began with great suds of celebration—balloons, champagne, cakes, sweets, presents, the holiday flicker of candles, golden wishes—but there was always a subtext of sorrow.

His mother's forty-fifth birthday had fallen on a Sunday in February 1962. He was ten. He had planned and prepared for the occasion. He wanted to surprise her with something weighty, something of substance to mark the event. For five months he had saved every cent that he could lay his hands on—money from running errands, returning deposit soda bottles, skimming his own snack money. Whenever his father gave him a dime for a treat, he put it away. Together with all the other change he had saved in his campaign, he had managed to accumulate $19.75.

His father, Big Jim, joked about the milestone, told Celia that forty-five was not old, but even at ten, John could see that it made his mother wince. She was not even looking forward to the usual family celebration at the usual favorite restaurant on Main Street in Flushing.

John's gift would save the occasion, he thought. When he went into Benny Stern's jewelry store on the Friday before the birthday—his money rattling inside a glass jar—he pointed to a bracelet in the window. He'd had his eye on it since the day in November he and his mother had passed the store and she'd remarked casually that it was pretty. Mr. Stern was very nice and took John into the office, where they emptied out the jar on the desk. They separated the quarters and the dimes and the nickels and pennies.

The look on Mr. Stern's face told the story. The bracelet cost $65, and that was without taxes. Crushed, John was ready to settle for something less, but Mr. Stern offered to work something out. He would take the $19.75 and John would work in the store after school cleaning up.

"I'll do this, John. However, you should not get into the habit of debt," said Mr. Stern solemnly. Thrift and discipline were high on Mr. Stern's list of desirable attributes, and John admired the jeweler's high principles, even if it meant ruined weekends and long hours of sweeping and cleaning in the store.

In the end, it was worth it. Celia Fasio wept when she opened her son's gift at the Chinese restaurant on Main Street with the dragon breathing fire over her shoulder. She wore the bracelet on every important occasion, in spite of the fact that it was only paste and it really didn't suit her style.

When John showed up the first time for work after school, Mr. Stern told him to forget it. The only payment he asked, he said, was to be mentioned to his father. And his father, John learned much later, who had moved into a manager's position in the campaign by then, hired one of Mr. Stern's nephews to work as a Democratic canvasser in the local precinct.

It was, in a peculiar way, unsettling that the debt was unpaid in the conventional manner, that the business was concluded behind a curtain of unspoken agreements and understandings. John Fasio sensed that there was something wrong with it, but he could not raise all the questions that the irregular process awakened. He marked it down to his own ignorance of the way of the world. One thing he would not do was to question his father's integrity.

The uneasiness about money cropped up again on his twentieth birthday. He was a senior in college, and he thought that he might have to drop out because the family finances were shaky. Big Jim was now heavily committed to running a congressional election in a hotly contested district. He had no time or energy left for the car agency.

John was worried, but it was a birthday—an event—and the family went to the same Chinese restaurant, where the dragon still breathed fire on his neck, and when they were stuffed and laughing and breaking open fortune cookies, his father handed him an envelope. Inside was his real fortune—a receipt for his full college tuition. John didn't know where his father had gotten the money. He suspected a loan. He fought off the same troubling sensation of wrongdoing he had had when he was ten.

He finished college and later—much later—when his father was convicted of misappropriating campaign funds in that congressional election, John thought of the night in the Chinese restaurant. He believed his father's version that the campaign money was stolen by a third party, and he was taking the blame to avoid a bloodbath, but the memories of birthdays and celebrations were blemished, and he never again ate in the restaurant with the dragon breathing fire down his neck.

* * *

"Too hot?" asked Murray Gerber, and Fasio shook his head. He enjoyed the blast of warm air on a cold day. She should be in her own home, he thought. Seventy-five wasn't old, not nowadays. He saw them every day, lots of women, walking, shopping, leading their own independent lives. She was too young to be fed with a plastic spoon like a baby by an underpaid and indifferent "caregiver" and staring at a blank wall.

It was true that she had moments when she went blank, or worse, began raving over imagined insults, long-settled grievances. She tuned to channels that didn't exist and read the guides and ordered films and couldn't be convinced that cable had not yet come to Queens. She was not always able to hold her water. But that wasn't so bad. They had things to handle weak kidneys. And if she saw strange plots and spat at strangers, well, worse things happened under his office window every day. That was no reason to put her in an institution. Not in John Fasio's eyes.

The doctors said that she would vanish into the Alzheimer's, that there was nothing they could do to reverse it. Fasio acquiesced and fed her into the home and felt like a criminal. There were moments when the clouds disappeared and the old Celia came forth, the one with the clever wit who didn't miss a trick. But they were rare. Maybe she just didn't want to show herself anymore. He could understand that.

"You get the cake?"

Murray nodded at the backseat, where the two shopping bags were wedged in snugly to keep them from spilling. Fasio craned his neck to look. The cake, the party plates, the soft drinks, the candles, the pretty box with the new sweater—all there. Fasio touched the small bag in his coat pocket. Inside was the bracelet he had bought her thirty years ago. She had left it behind when she went into the nursing home. Intentionally, he thought. A clear demonstration of an intelligence still capable of being vindictive. Irma insisted that it was an oversight. Nothing more. John had it cleaned and the stones reset and wrapped it in "Happy Birthday" paper.

"Oh! Did you get the shelter dinner arranged?"

Fasio had been trying to stage a fund-raising dinner for the homeless. But times were rough and there were other urgent calls upon the public's charity—AIDS research, MS, abused women . . .

"It's slow," said Gerber. "I got the Hyatt and they'll give us a price, but it's a heavy night. People are busy. It's not like you're the mayor."

"Don't start with that crap!"

"Okay, okay. I'm just saying. I ask about food kitchens and clothing drives and job training and I get this dead fish on the other end of the line."

"You think if I had big-time clout you'd have big-time clout?"

Murray shrugged. "Not an entirely unreasonable assumption."

"Just try to get the fucking dinner moving. You got six weeks."

Of course he knew that Murray was right. He had some leverage as a minor public official, but he couldn't move the earth. He couldn't pick up a phone and get the *New York Times* to pitch his charity. It was good being borough president—a lot less pressure, a lot more free time—but a lot less power.

At the Golden Years Nursing Home, there was the sour smell of old age. The lobby was crowded with tentative, middle-aged children—men and women afflicted with guilt, who averted their gazes, who fussed with packages of unwanted gifts. They didn't know what to expect when they saw their parents. A further stage of deterioration. More withdrawn, more childlike, less alive. A slow, painful snuffing of the candle. Guilt, not merely at their own default, but guilt at their own heightened enjoyment of life with their burden gone.

And the staff at the home, with their forced geniality, their false sprightly mood, chirping on about how this one finished all of his lunch and that naughty one wouldn't touch her Jell-O, stirred a mute rage in John Fasio. He thought that there must be some residents who were mentally intact. There must be some who found the insult of being treated like children unbearable.

A tear rolled down his mother's face when she saw the gifts. She remembered the bracelet. Not all the tapes had been erased. She looked at her son and smiled and pulled him close and kissed him and he could taste the tears.

It was a plain room, institutional, with dusty Rembrandt prints and plastic chairs and a steel bed that looked like an open coffin. The linen was old and rough and a pitcher of stale water stood on the cluttered nightstand. The window, blocked by discreet bars, overlooked a lot strewn with abandoned cars and old tires and broken bottles. In the distance there was a parkway. It was more of a cell than a room.

After Celia blew out the candles, they cut the cake and the male practical nurse, Marty, handed out the paper plates and the soft drink. Then something happened—his mother's face grew wistful and she clung to Marty.

"We're going to be married," she said, looking up at the acne-pocked face of the practical nurse.

For a second, Fasio was stunned. Then he looked at his mother and the nurse. Celia was radiant, but her joy seemed qualified. Marty was half smiling and half cringing. Fasio tried to reassure the youth with a look of understanding. It was a joke. He was a big youngster—big in the shoulders and in the gut. Maybe not so young, now that he looked carefully. Somewhere between sullen adolescence and wasted middle age. Late thirties, maybe even forty. Premature sagging jowls. The face of a drinker and fighter. One day, Fasio thought, that face would be crisscrossed and dented from all the cheap liquor and hard fists that it came up against.

Marty was shoveling in the cake, pushing back a stray wisp

of hair with a hand covered with icing. Fasio's mother was stroking the nurse's leg like a cat. It made Fasio's skin crawl.

"So, Ma, do you like the sweater?" he said sitting on the edge of the bed, holding it up for her inspection.

"We're going to be a married couple." Her voice had flown away, up into that high atmospheric range beyond reason.

Marty was clearly unhappy. He dumped the rest of his cake into a plastic garbage bag at the side of the bed. Fasio could see, between the flashes of his smile and his blush, that he had a mean temper.

Celia never took her eyes off the nurse, gazing at him as if her disposition depended upon his approval.

"What's wrong, Ma?" asked John.

She shook her head, perhaps because she didn't want Marty to notice that she was so bound to his feelings. Fasio was irked, but still unclear about why she was the way she was. "Look," he said mildly, "I brought some candy." He revealed the chocolate–peanut butter cups, and her eyes flashed for an instant at the thought of the sweets, then resumed their sentry duty over her nurse.

"Marty," she said, pleading. The male nurse rolled his eyes impatiently. "When we're married, you'll have to protect me, won't you?"

Marty was now watching Fasio closely. "They get very dependent," he said.

Then Fasio saw the bruises on his mother's arms and legs. They didn't look like accidental bumps, more symmetrical, up and down in a line, as if she was systematically beaten.

"I'd like to talk to my mother alone," he said to Marty.

"I'd better stay," replied the nurse, standing up straight. It was a border-guard reaction and it made Fasio bristle.

"If you don't mind," he said.

Marty pushed out his chest, displaying himself, and he was thick and strong.

Murray had been watching, waiting to see how this developed. He didn't want it to go too far, not with Celia in the room. He counted to three in the face-off, then tossed his cake in the garbage and took Marty under the arm. His fingers dug into a pressure point and he could have broken him then and there with a little more force, but he was a professional and he used his strength with a measured amount of power, just enough to exert his will. The nurse's face turned pale and he was breathless with pain.

"The boss wants to talk to his mother alone for a minute," he said mildly, ushering Marty out of the door.

"You shouldn't have done that," said Celia when she was alone with her son. Her voice had dropped, but she still looked worried.

"What's wrong, Ma?"

She began to weep. "Look at me," she said, and he saw that she was wearing a dress badly in need of cleaning, her sweater was buttoned wrong, her hair was unkempt. "I haven't had my nails done in . . . I don't even know how long."

5

J ACK MANN COULD hear the sound of hunger rolling around
like loose cargo under his belt. He thought, as he listened to
the low thunder of his stomach—along with the drift and moan
of the eighteen-wheel traffic on the nearby expressway—that it
was a mistake to skip breakfast. And a particularly bad idea to
go on a job interview with a noisy belly.

He stood in front of a half-dead building on the service road
of the Long Island Expressway, in an industrial section called
Maspeth. The building looked bare at ground level. The signs in
the window said FOR RENT and CLOSED, and the sheetrock had
begun to peel. But there was life above the street. Over the
abandoned beauty parlor and empty insurance office was the
headquarters of THOMAS J. HOLMAN & ASSOC.—INVESTIGATIONS.
Jack laughed. Tommy-the-Clown was an "associates"!

How ironic. Tommy Holman was a cowboy cop, or at least
he had been when Jack rode shotgun with him in the squad car
in downtown Flushing a decade ago. This was a man whose tin
shield went straight to his head—happens like that with some
cops. Like the first hit of crack cocaine. The minute they had the
gun and the shield, they were lost with power, out of control.
"Tough Tommy"—a name Jack planted on his wayward part-

ner in a spirit of gentle irony (but which Holman embraced in weightless ignorance)—had to be restrained or reprimanded after every run for busting innocent heads or smacking hand-cuffed suspects. Invariably, Tommy picked on the wrong person. Once he tried to muscle a highly respected mob guy, and it took every diplomatic effort to save him. In the end, Tommy had to go crawling and begging for his life to an intermediary in Little Italy. That was when Jack dubbed him "Tough Tommy."

Surprisingly, Holman lasted four years on the force, then opened his own private agency using broken down ex-cops as his infantry. For some reason, the business thrived. Holman had an "in," and nobody knew what it was, although, given his temperament and history, he could be doing backgrounders for Hitler. But someone or something kept him alive in the recession.

As Jack gathered his courage, nursing his broken pride, he decided that he would not go into this interview with a stomach pleading for a handout.

There had to be a diner—after all, this was Queens. Circling the block, he spotted a closed meat market and a Korean deli with a winter sentinel out front. Further along, there was an empty lot where oversized cars crowded every inch. Even the ones with NO RADIO signs had been stripped and looted. All the windows had gray masking tape to keep out the weather.

If I work for him, he thought, this is where I will park my car—among all the other broken-down wrecks and derelicts.

There were very few homes in the neighborhood. It was the expressway noise, no doubt, which must have been like an earlier version of an airport nuisance. The few houses that remained were lopsided wooden shacks out of another era. The walkway surfaces were cracked, steps were missing from the front porches, windows were broken and gave them a haglike, toothless look. No one fixed up a home in this section of Queens. If you had that kind of money, you moved.

On the final lap of the block he found the diner. It was half hidden by a blur of stop signs and highway directions. It had been there for a long time, long before the sheetrock boom of the fifties or the real estate bubble of the eighties. It remained in business because of the local car mechanics and factory workers and truck drivers and food handlers—blue-collar men with cannonball muscles. They worked in the tin factories and body shops and wholesale markets spread across the cheap landscape that shook under the passing traffic of the expressway.

The name of the diner was visible beneath decades of grease and soot: THE EXPRESSWAY. Below the name was a silhouette of an old propeller-driven airplane, a tribute to nearby LaGuardia Airport, which, at the time the diner went up, was a local marvel. The windows of The Expressway were papered with blunt, artless specials. The Four Deuces: two eggs, two strips of bacon, two slices of toast, two pancakes, for $3.95. The luncheon special was a meat loaf platter, with potatoes, a vegetable and bread, $4.65.

Through the seams in the blaze of specials, Jack saw the gaunt slouch of defeated customers accumulated along the counter. There was no pleasure, no talk—just the grim spadework of getting the food into mouths. If he got the job, this would be where he would have his morning coffee and juice. He would become one more hump in the long ridge of broken backs. If he was lucky.

He wondered, as he looked through the window, if Holman would give him an advance. He had let things go too far and now the rent was overdue and he didn't know whether he could cover the checks to the utility company and the phone company. He had stopped keeping track of his checks somewhere along the line, and writing them had become a little like closing his eyes and walking out on a ledge.

It was because of the breakup. He was behaving more than a little recklessly since he and Bonnie had separated. It was too abrupt. There was no reason. But that was silly. When he thought about it—which he tried unsuccessfully not to do—there was every reason. They were doomed from the start. She was a dazzling television star, and he was an emotionally shattered cop slipsliding through life.

They had met six years earlier when he was still on the force and she was a celebrity weathergirl longing to be an honest reporter. They were chasing the same villain at the time. Somehow, he hadn't resented her persistent, annoying interference in the case. He'd welcomed it. She pursued witnesses, pestered investigators, alerted suspects—almost getting herself killed—and it didn't matter. None of it. Not to Jack Mann. She was a comforting presence. When she spoke or delivered an opinion, he felt the same overpowering sense of security he felt when his wife wrapped herself around a topic. A deep intelligence was at work. A reliable and steadfast colleague was in his corner. They followed the case through to the end, captured a spoiled, killer cop, and then—for the first but not the last time—broke apart.

It was, he told himself, the poisoned circumstances that damned them. The fact that they had met while his wife, Natalie, was dying of cancer determined the tragic outcome. While Natalie lay strapped to a high hospital bed with tubes taped to her arms and monitors recording her life slowly trickling away, he was powerfully attracted to the glittering reporter whose motto "Hey, it's only weather!" had made her everybody's secret sweetheart. He'd been smitten the minute he laid eyes on her. In spite of the fact that he never acted on it while his wife was alive, how could he not be twisted by guilt? Even after Natalie's death, he was still loyal to her memory—an intrepid English teacher with tales of rescued readers. He thought of Natalie with affection even later, when he loved someone else. The guilt never went away. Not even when he and Bonnie were both technically available.

Years later, when he was retired from the police department and recovering from a bad affair with a wild Irish terrorist, it was Bonnie who took him in, nursed him back to health, and, without trying, rekindled the old infatuation. When it burst into flame, they were astonished at the potency of their feelings. The physical part alone was enough to shake them up. Every sexual encounter left them reeling. But that early shadow of Natalie never left them alone. Or maybe it was the shock of their passion. The truth was that Bonnie did not entirely enjoy being so out of control. And, she didn't approve of Jack or his outer-borough style. She had different ambitions than a worn-out ex-cop. Maybe it was all of the irreconcilable differences that had made her proclaim that she needed her own apartment; the unspoken part was that he had to move out.

Dazed, he'd gone back to Queens, and only remembered then that he had no money, no job, and no place to live. He spent some time on strange couches and then went about finding a job.

But he missed Bonnie's voice, and he had grown mute. He missed her habits, so he adopted some (pouring cream in his coffee, reading the *New York Times* and long books end-to-end); he was like a magician trying to conjure up an old trick out of thin air. He even developed her quick temper. There were little explosions on his morning aerobic walk when he spotted an unleashed dog. A pointless confrontation with a homeless man ransacking a garbage bag. The homeless man was rooting in the filth for deposit cans, spilling the contents everywhere, and Jack lectured him; when the man didn't listen, Jack stood him up, and then, with menace, forced him to put the trash back in the bag. Jack knew better. The man was suffering all the wounds and gashes of depression and despair; but so was Jack. In the keenness of his self-pity, he thought that there might come a moment, and it might be soon if he didn't stop brooding and get a grip on his life, when he too would be rooting through garbage for empty cans.

It was a kind of punishment that he had to watch her nightly on the news, with her feathery segment about the weather. But he watched—he couldn't not watch—like some obsessed stalker following his love.

* * *

If he didn't get the job, Jack decided that he'd sell the car. A few thousand—that would hold him another month or two. Of course, without the car he couldn't work. He tried to put the thought aside as he walked into the Expressway Diner. The regulars looked up—a habit, a territorial statement—when he entered their turf.

He was a stranger, but somehow, he was acceptable. Eyes looked him over and blinked, waving him in. They saw a man just past his youth with deep, tormented eyes. Maybe a priest. Or a cop. His brow was unfurrowed and he was average in height and normal in weight, and had the soothing looks of someone on a bus, although the way that he carried himself and the way that he moved suggested an athletic ability. The coat he wore was well woven and the quality was good, but it had been in service for one too many seasons. The suit was stylish, but also bore the signs of heavy wear. It suggested a man of diminished circumstances, living off the last batch of capital. Probably a cop. He had the searching gaze, the skeptical stare, the departmental swagger. And he didn't have the usual baggage of cracked hands and dirty fingernails. A cop. A cop by the slap and tickle of a gun lurking somewhere underneath all that fading haberdashery. Or an ex-cop.

Jack found a table where he could sit with his back to the wall. A habit. He picked up a menu and thought about a fruit cup and a piece of whole wheat toast, but he hesitated when the annoyed waitress loomed over his table, the pad and pencil held like a hammer, and demanded with working-class impatience, "What'll it be?"

It was a challenge. "Black coffee, extra caffeine," he said defiantly. Then he slapped the menu down on the table and hit her with the kicker: "And the Four Deuces."

Her eyebrows rose with respect.

The food came quickly and he ate it quickly because he was hungry, holding out his coffee cup twice for refills. He dropped a dollar tip and it was like leaving behind a silver bullet—who was that man?

Even the sour aftertaste of the food was good and he was glad that he had cleaned his plate and ignored the cholesterol consequences. He was right not to go in hungry.

The receptionist glowed. A neon blonde. She had blazing lipstick, sparkling nail polish, and an iridescent blush that almost throbbed in his face. When she bent over—and she made a point of bending over even when she reached behind her—her cleavage stuck out. Too young for the makeup and the sweater, thought Jack. Way too young. She wet her lips and ran a hand through the long mane of hair, just watching to see the effect; her attitude was almost clinical.

Must be hard, he thought, like a SAC bomber crew on alert, to keep constant check on her allure. Funny part was that under all that effort she was pretty. He could see that, although she did her best to hide it. And there were ominous portents on her desk—two half-eaten donuts along with a Diet Coke. A willful, wanton girl, with pale regrets. She would be fat and sloppy by the time she was thirty, unless she had babies and then it could come sooner. All those waiting donuts, all that temptation—and no willpower. And that sad Diet Coke like some midnight prayer against the dark.

"Yeah?"

He told her his name and said that he had an appointment with Tommy.

Out of her mouth poured Queens: "Whyncha take a seat." She nodded at an orange motel-vinyl sofa with long tears along the arms.

He smiled and turned and examined the displays on the wall. There were framed certificates and newspaper stories, all singing the praises of Tommy Holman. From cop to public-spirited citizen to quick-witted sleuth—it was all there on the wall, recorded in public print and civic plaques. He heard her buzz and announce him. She laughed and hung up.

"He'll be witcha innasec."

Jack would dangle for a moment. That was the game. Tommy liked to think that he was a master of the game. He talked about it during the three o'clock confessions of squad-car partners when they rode together as cops. Lectures in which Holman laid out the paranoid political strategies of a New York City cop on the make. "You never wanna get creamed on a domestic run," he'd say with a cunning that passed for wisdom. "But you better go like shit through a goose on a ten-thirteen." As if Jack didn't know that every cop went all-out when another cop was crying for help!

That's why Jack had become a cop in the first place—out of that fierce tribal solidarity born in precinct locker rooms and in dawn stakeouts. There was nothing like the loyalty of men who crashed through barred doors together with no knowledge of what lay on the other side. The faith in the reliability of your backup was the thinnest, strongest thread he knew. He had been partners with smelly old boozers and bright young idealists. But they all had that in common: dependability on entering the unknown. Cop loyalty. Natalie, for all her depth and under-standing, never grasped it. He knew that the night they were coming home from a movie and were stopped by a trembling junkie who put a knife at Jack's belly. The reflex was perfect. He grabbed the wrist, twisted it so that the blade was useless, and threw the junkie to the ground. Then, methodically, clinically, he cracked four or five ribs with precise kicks.

Natalie was howling out of fear of the mugger and the perceived meanness of Jack's response, and he explained that unless he had to spend some time in a detox unit, the junkie had no chance of help. If he went to court uninjured he'd be out on the street by morning sticking a knife in someone else's belly—someone perhaps less able to defend himself. This way he was helping the junkie and protecting society.

Natalie saw the logic, but was disgusted by the brutality all
the same. And Jack had never been able to justify his action
to her.

The emotional attachments within the department had been
crucial for Jack Mann. He'd grown up in a home parched of
loving demonstrations. His mother was overwhelmed by her six
children, and his father was a sullen, silent man who thought
that his oldest son was childishly dependent. And so Jack developed emotional secrets.

After reading all the tributes and laminated legends posted on
the wall, Jack finally took a seat, listening to the wheezing sigh
of the plastic covers as he sank down. He smiled, thinking of the
self-promotion that went into that library. Not that Tommy was
all bluff. He possessed uncommon physical bravery. He didn't
hesitate to barge through uncertain doors or stand his ground
against armed felons. He didn't wait for backup, either. He just
went in, uttering his famous battle cry: "Fellas, we're the cops;
no one else is coming!"

After fifteen minutes—an interval calculated like some as-
trologer's plot of the most advantageous position of the stars—
the intercom buzzed and Jack was ushered into Tommy's
splashy office. It glittered with gold-trim awards and plaques.
The desk was broad and cluttered with a miniature gun paper-
weight, a penholder with Tommy's old shield encased in plastic,
a lamp made out of a 20-mm shell, a telephone console deco-
rated with CRIME SCENE yellow trim, WANTED posters made into
a blotter, and bookends that replicated John Dillinger's death
mask. "See," Tommy would say in those long-ago seminars in
the squad car, "you gotta have a theme. Know what I mean?
You're a private dick, you show a lot of metal. Gives the customer a sense of security. Something to grab onto. Civilians like
bullets and guns out in the open."

Jack smiled. Maybe he was right. It certainly caught the eye,
got the attention, delivered the message. They shook hands, but

that wasn't enough for Tommy, who came out from behind his battleship desk and grabbed Jack with his gorilla arm and pulled him in for an embrace. They were old partners. Old partners were blood brothers.

"You look good, you son of a bitch," said Tommy kissing Jack on the lips. "You look terrific." He grabbed Jack's crotch and laughed as his old partner blushed and tried to laugh. He clapped Jack on the back, punched him playfully in his gut— feeling for the tone, Jack guessed.

Tommy was starting to lose a little hair, Jack noticed. He kept patting his head, getting the sides back into place, covering the patches that appeared like snowcaps melting on his scalp. He could still, no doubt, lift parking meters out of cement. Tommy was famous for his strength. It was, Jack believed, how he had lost his job in the first place. Tommy had been working Anti-Crime in plainclothes, doing one of those crazy decoy stunts in which you invite bad guys to crack you in the head so that you can catch them in the act, when an inspector brought him up on charges for drinking on the job. Tommy protested that he was playing the part of a derelict and had to have some liquor on his breath, and besides, he'd had two bad whacks in a week and needed something for the pain.

But the inspectors wanted Tommy's badge. He was too flamboyant, he had too many mob friends, too many movie-star friends; he hung out with royalty and politicians and had a garish life-style. It made them uneasy that he'd once spent a weekend in Paris and reported for work the next day. Must be something rancid there. Not that they could prove anything. And the strength! My God, the man lifted parking meters and cars and wrestled football players for fun.

He was denied his gold detective's shield and he was placed on suspension for drinking on the job, and so Tommy had quit the department. He'd found an unusual way to do it. He went to One Police Plaza, handed in his retirement papers, wept like a baby in the toilet, then went out into the parking lot and found the car that belonged to the inspector who had brought him up on charges. It was a Ford compact, and he lifted it with his bare hands and put the rear on top of one of the curbside cement pillars constructed to defend against terrorist attacks after the Beirut bombing.

From his fifth-floor window, the inspector saw a crowd assembling in the parking lot, in the vicinity of his car. He rushed out to find a foot patrolman issuing him a ticket for unauthorized parking. No amount of protest or argument stopped the cop from planting the ticket on the inspector's windshield. There was an unshakable solidarity on the force when it came to martinet taskmasters. Everyone knew what the inspector had done to Tommy and everyone had vowed that, given an opportunity, they would stick it back to him. He had broken the poor son-of-a-bitch cop on a rigid technicality; that deserved some firm payback. Every cop in that crowd around the car—with its ass stuck absurdly in the air, riding a cement finger—smiled at the sweet revenge.

Tommy became a martyr and a civilian who wore $2500 suits, gold cufflinks, a diamond pinky ring, a Rolex watch, Armani shoes, and custom-made shirts. He had an "in."

Jack planted himself in a chair, looked around, took it all in, felt the mass of Tommy's possessions, and shook his head. "You're doing okay, I see."

Tommy was sitting back with his feet up on his desk, but he kicked free at Jack's words. "Bullshit!" he snarled. Then he gave Jack a huge grin. In a low, rasping voice, he said, "I'm doing fucking great! Best thing that ever happened to me."

He laughed, and it sounded to Jack like the laugh of a lottery winner. Of course, Tommy missed the shield. That part was a lie. They all missed the shield. Jack woke up some mornings and, in that foggy moment before clarity, thought that he was still on the job. The strange, painful thing about it was, when he awoke to that belief, he was happy.

When Jack quit the department and went into business for

himself, it was the sense of being on the side of goodness that he missed. The fact that his business never took root was sad, but not relevant.

"So how ya doin' in your shop?" asked Tommy Holman, who knew very well that Jack had no shop.

"Not bad," replied Jack breezily. "I'm an international consultant like Henry Kissinger. The Chinese love me. I do some speaking engagements for fifty thousand a pop."

Tommy laughed.

"Life's shit," said Jack. "I had a leak in the bathroom and the car sprung an oil leak, but apart from that, everything sucks."

"Gee, that's too bad, kid," said Tommy, who was, at thirty-eight, years younger than Jack Mann.

"Yeah, well, life's full of speed bumps."

Tommy nodded, plucked a cigar out of a humidor made from a nineteenth-century police helmet, offered one to Jack, who took it, and began puffing his own stogie to life. "How's the weather broad?"

"A little stormy."

"Too bad," said Tommy, who listened with the wavering attention of a man awaiting an important call. "I heard you broke up. What, the glamorous shit? Show biz? She fuckin' around?"

Jack smiled. Life was broken down along very simple lines for Tommy Holman. Relationships began and ended on the high shoals of lust. All the other strains and hardships were la-di-da bullshit. If you gave a broad a good fuck, that was that. She was home for you. "We are in different worlds," said Jack.

"Yeah, well, how about some coffee?" said Tommy casually, as if such romantic breakups were only trivial disturbances in a man's life.

Jack nodded. He could use coffee, or maybe a drink.

"Listen, sorry, but, you know the girl can't leave the phones," said Tommy, smiling. "You know, business." Tommy peeled a $50 bill from a thick roll. "Look, there's a place right down the block. Can't miss it. I could use a decaf and a bear claw."

"I'm not that thirsty," said Jack.

Tommy's hand was in midair, the fifty dangling from the fingers. A long moment passed. "Fuck it," he said punching the intercom. "I got plenty of business." The neon blonde came sauntering in, flashing white cleavage. "Hey, listen, me and my old partner would like some repast."

"Huh?"

"Coffee, a bear claw. Two, three bear claws."

"You're gonna hafta get the phones," she said cracking the gum.

"I'll handle it."

She took the fifty and said that she would keep the change.

When they were alone, Tommy came around and sat on the couch, pulled Jack over with him and put his arm around his shoulder. "I know you could use some work," he said. Jack didn't deny it. "Now, I'm starting to branch out and I could use some help."

"Me, too."

Tommy laughed and slapped Jack's knee. Then he stopped and was serious again. "I'm getting some contracts—important client—and I need someone discreet. Someone who can move in high circles and not draw a lot of fire, if you get my drift. I need a guy who I can trust."

"We rode together," Jack said.

Tommy nodded. "Yeah, we rode together and now we're gonna ride together again. Listen, this is important. There's a big political year comin' up. Big fuckin' year. There's a lot of security work in that. Protecting people at press conferences, staging things—events—you know the shit. But you know what else these guys do? They tap each other's phones. They pick over old garbage in the past. They find shit about each other. Not that they use it. Not always. Leak it sometimes. Everybody does it."

"I knew I'd be picking through garbage soon."

6

T HERE WAS AN unmistakable mark of doom on the countenance of the man slumped in the leather chair near the fireplace in the library of Gracie Mansion. Pasquale Scotto's face was sickly gray and his eyes had a glazed, resigned look. The great Democratic party mule who had once prowled the city with unchallenged authority and unmatched brawn was clearly dying.

It was hard to imagine that this was the same virile Patsy Scotto who had reigned like a duke over municipal politics. There were platoons of judges, squads of assistant district attorneys, not to mention high police officials and significant commissioners, who owed their careers to Scotto's final consent. The mayor, Billy Cohen, had longstanding obligations to Scotto; there had been a time when Cohen would not make an appointment or contemplate an important move without consulting the powerful Democratic leader. Even now, in the twilight of his career, Scotto was owed a show of respect for all his accumulated services. He knew that it was merely a show.

A glance in the mirror was all he needed to remind himself that his power, like his life, was draining away. The flesh on his jowls hung in drooping sacs, as if death was a slow act of gravity.

Scotto's neck—once the thick conduit for his quick mind—was now stringy and moved without touching the collar of the shirt. Even the hand that held his brandy (a hand that had once settled political destinies by the simple movement of a finger) trembled in the gust of dry fund-raising prattle.

What brought him out into public in spite of his infirmity was a fierce tenacity, a determination to defend his own property rights. He might not be the chief executive of New York City, but he regarded himself as the rightful landlord. Billy Cohen might be the mayor, but no one slept in Gracie Mansion without Patsy Scotto's permission.

He remembered a time, as his unforgiving eyes swept over the mayor's guests at this midwinter fund-raiser, when he could command all the attention in such a room. At public meetings, without ceremony, he told annoying, long-winded senior congressmen to shut up and sit down. In those exact words. And they obeyed. With a roll of his eyes he could grant or withhold support for elected governors, powerful senators, and a range of minor office seekers.

His power was legendary. He had carried in his pocket an inventory of jobs in the police department, the transit authority, the sanitation department, and the post office. He handed them out like so much candy. For these favors he received strict, complete obedience, and, most importantly, disciplined votes. A man who could deliver congressional districts with the dependability of the mail was someone to be respected, as well as feared.

Even he was amazed at his potency. This short, squat ex-dock worker with the vocabulary of a street tough was the leader of the Brooklyn Democratic party—a post that sounded paltry on paper, but had the force of a sledgehammer. Out of the smoke-filled rooms deals were made, alliances formed, Christmas baskets of food delivered to the hungry, coal donated to the poor. Not a bad thing, the party, from Patsy Scotto's point of view.

But times had changed. The party had been reformed.

Bosses had been shoved aside by circus primaries and politically correct handlers. The reformers had marched from conducting business on an honorable street level to squabbling in the gutter. Now the cold and hungry constituents had to depend on a system of social services spread across an incomprehensible bureaucratic landscape.

But Patsy's pockets were not yet empty. Over the years, Scotto had hoarded debts from labor chieftains, clubhouse politicians, and civic leaders. In spite of everything, on election day, he believed that he could deliver his borough, and therefore still held the balance of power in his trembling hand.

Even as he sucked in shallow breaths and sipped the burning brandy, Patsy Scotto gazed around the room with his old back-alley cunning, trying to measure the opposition in this looming battle for City Hall.

It was no secret that Billy Cohen had grown weary of running New York City. The budget was busted, the factions irrevocably split. Nothing worked. Subways broke down, garbage lay uncollected in filthy streets, water pipes burst, streets went unrepaired, cops broke the law, teachers played hooky. Worst of all, the racial tension was unbearable and intractable. No matter which side the mayor took, the other was quick to denounce him. And if he remained impartial, both sides went after him. No, the city exhausted Cohen and he was ready for his next job: governor. He had made friends from Buffalo to Ithaca and would have no trouble getting elected to the political retirement village of Albany.

As for a successor, he had one. John Fasio was waiting in the wings. And Scotto knew it. He smelled it like smoke in the air. Cohen and Fasio were getting ready to present him with a fait accompli. The plan was simple. Cohen would resign to run for governor, then Governor Michael Toedtman (already a lame duck who yearned to retire and play golf) would appoint Fasio to fill the mayoralty vacancy. Fasio would run next time as an unbeatable incumbent.

It would have been an elegant short-circuit of Scotto if the old man had been less alert. As far as Fasio and Cohen making moves on him, well, he could handle that. He wasn't even bothered by the treachery of the plan. He could admire the tactical maneuvering.

Well, such things were inevitable. Before he died, he knew, he would become a political corpse. Soon he would not be able to sit at the corner table reserved for him at the Queen Restaurant in downtown Brooklyn and hold court over the endless procession of fawning office holders and seekers. The councilmen and borough presidents and police commissioners would no longer come to shake his hand and ask his opinion about the tabloid events of the day. A vain thing, but still . . .

And yet it was not a done deal. They needed Scotto's blessing to make Fasio mayor. The governor would never appoint John Fasio as interim acting mayor without Scotto's okay. And furthermore, they needed Scotto to inspire the political infantry. Precinct captains from Red Hook to Rochester would not go into the trenches without the okay from the old man. Oh, they would loyally support the party ticket for the next election, but not with the nudge and push of zealots. It was in the barbershops and barrooms and diners that the endorsements were truly delivered.

Fasio and Cohen thought Scotto would have to go along. But Scotto had other plans.

Scotto trusted his judgment. He had spent a lifetime sizing up people. He studied small things, little quirks, emerging patterns. He could tell who could be trusted and who couldn't by the way a man retold the same story. And he had heard too many self-serving tales from John Fasio to think well of him. No, the man was unreliable.

And then there was Murray Gerber. That one was a true gangster. Between the two of them, they would either bleed the city white or cripple it through incompetence.

It was partly an intuitive decision and partly based on the

shrewd calculation of a savvy veteran, but it was rock solid: Patsy Scotto knew in some essential way that he would have to wreck this plan to make John Fasio mayor.

It was, at bottom, a decision made on the highest principle.

It would have surprised his enemies—who counted Scotto a ruthless man—to learn that he had such ethical standards. Scotto found it convenient to allow that jagged reputation to act as a restraining bodyguard. The embarrassing truth was that he was an honorable man. He had come of age under the moral arc of clubhouse politics when rules existed to guarantee fair and virtuous behavior. To approach justice. Above all, Patsy Scotto wanted to do good. He wanted to appear praiseworthy in the eyes of Rose, his wife.

If the political clubhouse was his cathedral, Rose Scotto was his priest. His every act was weighed by her strict ideals. And she never had to move a muscle to make her views known. During his rowdy days, when he would stay up half the night fighting for the appointment of a judge, he would come home to the same attached house he had bought when they were married sixty-odd years ago and regale her with stories (he carried them home like leftover cookies). He'd explain about this one's treachery and that one's ruthlessness. She would listen and he would watch the liquid laser eyes form an opinion: this one was a fool, that one was a villain. She was seldom wrong. It didn't matter that he was a widower; Rose had died ten years ago. He spoke to her picture over the fireplace.

No, he wouldn't allow Fasio into Gracie Mansion. How could he ever explain it to Rose?

Billy Cohen's midwinter fund-raiser was an apparent success. It had drawn the usual crowd—real-estate barons, media tycoons, corporate hustlers, sharp lawyers, hungry politicians, spin doctors and handlers, along with the standard pool of fixers and strivers—all of whom would write four-figure checks before the evening was out. In spite of the ongoing march of feminism (along with the accession to power of one or two congresswomen and commissioners), females still occupied an inferior and essentially ornamental role in the business of the city. They were the lush second wives or the brittle business dates or the adoring postgraduate flatterers who whispered praise into the ears of the men of accomplishments.

These were the people who clustered around the chair near the fireplace where Patsy Scotto blinked and spoke in a wet, raspy voice. "My father used to bring me into this same room when Jimmy Walker was mayor, which was before I was even born."

He still delivered his outlaw act for his fans. He could lift a telephone and be put through the White House switchboard—his name still on the operator's list of calls to be accepted without question—nevertheless, he posed as the perennial desperado. Every time he opened his mouth, he uncovered the blast furnace of his indiscriminate rage. Even now, in his farewell appearance, the flame licked at his lips.

"I hated the place. I could 'a' been out stealin' apples. But my father, he drags me down because he wants me to see the son of a bitch. So's I'd know."

He opened his eyes. The chemotherapy had not dimmed that light. Scotto looked around and exchanged something with Gerber. A fierce, knowing look.

Then he closed his eyes and leaned back in the chair again. "Fuckin' thieves," he muttered, and he could feel the thrill move around him; they always liked it when you spoke mutiny. It came from both sides of his family. He was half Irish rebel and half Italian anarchist. His Catholic mother hid guns in her skirts before she had to flee Dublin to marry an Italian exile in New York.

Scotto brought the shaky outlaw hand holding the glass of brandy to his lips. He spilled a bit, but managed to get down most of the fuel for the furnace. "Ah, they're all smelly bastards. Always were."

He rolled his eyes in the direction of the shut door behind which Mayor Billy Cohen was supposed to be conducting the business of the people. Scotto knew that he was in there plotting a corrupt little coup. The trouble was that he didn't know how far along they were. He had been on the other side of that door often enough to know that by now it could be all over for him and his corner table at the Queen Restaurant.

"I never liked the crooked fuck," said Scotto, and he saw Gerber shiver. Good, he thought. He knows I'm still dangerous. "Jimmy Walker," he said, smiling. "All that fancy glitter! All that expert polish! That effort! The fuck never did an honest day's work. Assholes!"

Now he was lying back in his chair, some spittle coming out of the side of his mouth. He sat up. "You know what that fine gentleman used to do? He used to take society ladies into the pantry and they'd give him a blowjob. Charming Pilgrim daughters, with their husbands outside and a cop standing guard at the door; they'd give the mayor of New York City a blowjob!"

Scotto was still offended by this ancient defiling of the political temple. The Catholic moralist had come face-to-face with the political desperado and religion had won. He slumped back in his chair. "And the honest union men who spent a day pickin' up the garbage or riding scows in the harbor and swingin' a balin' hook, all the time, they're waiting to see if there's gonna be a strike. His ass is on the pantry table rolling in the dough and they don't know if they're gonna be able to put bread on the table!"

Scotto saw a woman in her thirties—somewhere near the top of her profession, judging by the swank of her accessories— shake her head and say in a low voice to Gerber, "I didn't even know he was still alive."

Gerber looked at the old man, then back at the lush woman and shrugged. "He's not."

"My father was a garbage collector," continued the old man. "Now they're waste engineers. But he collected the garbage.

Hated the fuckin' mayor. Told him so. Said, 'You're a no-good society prick and you wouldn't last an hour on the back of a truck.' My father was a Sacco-and-Vanzetti union socialist anarchist. So, Jimmy Walker, he looks at my father, eyes him up and down from his worn-out hands to his ripped shoes, and he says, 'You're right, but you wouldn't last a second in this jungle.' "

Everyone laughed, including Murray Gerber and the lush woman in her thirties.

"That Lindsay! You know, Mike Quill got him perfect. Called him 'Lindsley.' Made him crazy. Insult their Protestant names. That makes them crazy. 'Lindsley.' Perfect. You know, you gotta be more than right. You gotta be smart. Wagner, he was smart. Knew everything about the job. Where the bodies were buried, and why they had to be killed. You don't wanna go against that guy. Most of 'em had problems. Most of 'em were fools, and maybe that's the worst problem. Biggest schmuck of all was Koch. Never saw a Jew so dumb."

Some of the Jewish pols and shakers flinched, but it was habit, and they assumed that there was a certain amount of anti-Semitism built in. It went with the Irish-Italian Catholic roots. Just like Jews were always counting Jews.

"One thing I liked about Koch. He had a belly like mine." Scotto looked down to where he had once had a medicine ball. It was all shrunken now. He still didn't quite realize. He swallowed more brandy so that the shrunken belly would have company.

A plainclothes guard came out of the mayor's study and caught Murray Gerber's eye. The plainclothesman moved his head to indicate that Gerber and Scotto were wanted in the mayor's office. Scotto was not ready to budge yet.

"I remember LaGuardia. He was some piece of work. They said that he was nice, you know? Like he had no balls. But he was a big ballbreaker. There was this time that Roosevelt, he sends some Haaa-vard type up to break some bad news about the budget. I mean, we're dying in a depression. A real depression. People takin' dives off buildings. So LaGuardia takes this overeducated schmuck into a private room where they're all alone, because he sure don't want no one to overhear, and he says, 'Listen, pal, it's winter, you know? It's cold. Your man, he just got elected and he's sleeping in the White House. I got people sleeping under newspapers. I got people living under bridges. They call 'em 'Hoovervilles.' But you know what? They're gonna change the name. I got a better one. You tell that lame fuck in Washington that if he doesn't get me some money to put a roof over people, I am gonna go sleep in the park myself. And I am gonna put a big sign on my blanket. You know what it's gonna say? It's gonna say 'Hotel Roosevelt.' ''

"Well, LaGuardia got his money."

Scotto had a laughing cough. Murray Gerber went over to him, leaned down, and offered his handkerchief.

"Haaa-vard!" said Scotto, struggling to his feet, pushing away Gerber's arm. There was a bubble of murmurs as Scotto and Gerber vanished into the next room. The lush woman in her thirties turned to another stranger and asked: "You think any of that is true?"

Mayor Billy Cohen's den had masculine touches sprinkled everywhere. Leather chair, a big globe, dark colors that soaked up the light, floor-to-ceiling bookcases (in disarray because someone once told him that dedicated readers pored through four or five books at a time, and so he left impressive biographies scattered on the exposed surfaces of his library). The rugs were thick and there was an aroma of pine left over from Christmas, along with the musk of whiskey and cigars. The most striking feature was the many pictures of Teddy Roosevelt; he had sketches of Teddy charging up San Juan Hill, hunting bear in Yellowstone Park, smiling toothfully with a rifle. And he had a framed quotation from the "Rough Rider":

> It's not the critic who counts, not the man who points out
> how the strong man stumbled, or where the doer of deeds

could have done them better. The credit belongs to the
man who is actually in the arena; whose face is marred by
dust and sweat and blood; who strives valiantly; who errs
and comes up short again and again; who knows the great
enthusiasms, the great devotions and who spends himself in
a worthy cause; who at the best, knows in the end, the
triumph of high achievement; and who, at the worst, if he
fails, at least fails while daring greatly.

Whenever someone he even suspected of feminist sensitivity
came upon the quotation, Billy Cohen was overly careful to
point out that the masculine pronoun was a fashion of the times;
it could as easily have been "if she fails."

The mayor was at the door and ushered Scotto into a comfortable chair, then made certain that the old party leader had
a snifter of brandy at his elbow.

Scotto nodded in appreciation, accepting the mayor's solici-
tude. Scotto had picked Billy Cohen because of such gestures,
along with his looks. Billy Cohen was a tall man with a thin,
patrician appearance. His battleship gray hair was thick and
parted near the middle. He wore a charcoal-gray suit and his
necktie was splashed with red globs that matched the hankie
flying from his breast pocket. His custom-made suits always
blended with his neckwear and handkerchief. He was sixty-three
years old, but his face reflected only a certain calm satisfaction
with nature's design. Scotto had been so affected by Cohen's
appearance that he had never stopped to question what, if anything, lay behind such perfect poise. He put him into Congress,
and thought about the Senate, but after he got to know him,
Scotto decided that while he looked the part, Cohen was really
too stupid for the great body and gave him City Hall.

Slumped on the couch was Cohen's codefendant, John
Fasio. Scotto nodded. He glanced over and saw Murray Gerber
where he expected to find him—not far from the elbow of his
master, his arms folded across his chest. That one! "Get me

something to eat, kid," he said to Gerber, who looked at Fasio. The Queens borough president nodded. "It's the medication," said Scotto to Fasio, as if that were the real explanation for the command. "I've got to keep something inside what's left of my stomach."

"Murray doesn't mind," said Fasio.

Gerber unfolded his arms and asked what he should fetch. "Bread," said Scotto. "And a piece of fruit. Carrot sticks. Anything that takes fifteen minutes to put on a plate. Oh, yeah—a beer."

Murray nodded and left.

"Nice boy," said Scotto. "Checks with you before he takes a shit, does he?"

"Murray doesn't shit. At least, he hasn't checked with me," said Fasio.

Scotto laughed a belly laugh, then focused on Fasio. Took a second to answer. "You think he's okay?"

"I think so."

"He listens to everything. Takes it all in. Like a fuckin' sponge."

Cohen had taken a hard look at Scotto and decided that he was a lot sicker than he was willing to let on. It wasn't just the color; there was the shaking hand, the weary eyes, and the lack of vigor. Easier to deal with, thought Cohen, who had always been intimidated by Scotto.

"I knew him when he worked for your father," said Scotto, still referring to Murray Gerber.

The mayor had gone back behind his desk, where the lamps were placed in such a way as to mask his face in shadows. His hands were folded on top of the immaculate desk. Big Bill Cohen was impatient to get to the point, Scotto knew. Soon there would be pressure for him to get out and circulate. Nobody wrote checks without seeing the bride.

"Patsy, you feeling good?"

Scotto shrugged. He had never let himself get too close to

Fasio, had stayed out of it when he went after borough president. That absence had been construed as an endorsement. It wasn't. He just hadn't been willing to take out the knives. Besides, it was useful to have the memory of Big Jim's martyrdom neutralized by his son's active presence in the party. As long as it stayed local and small. Not when it crossed the bridges and tunnels and came into Manhattan. Not when he went after Gracie Mansion.

"You look good," said Fasio.

"Bullshit!"

Cohen leaned forward, his face touching the light. "Listen, Patsy, you know what I want."

"Remind me, Billy."

Cohen shook his head. "I think you know."

"I got an idea," Scotto brightened, sitting up in his chair. Fasio leaned forward.

"I think you're too big for this place." Scotto looked around at the Teddy Roosevelt memorials, at the dark colors and flagrant books. "You know what I mean? Fuckin' place—you can't move. It's suffocating. I think maybe you should be in Albany. They got a real mansion, you know?"

"You think I should run for governor?"

Scotto fell back in his chair. "This guy, he's a piece of work. Knows my own mind before I do. You don't have to whack him in the head with a two-by-four. He gets the point, one, two, three."

Billy Cohen rose, walked slowly over to Scotto's chair, poured some more brandy, topping the old man's balloon glass, and said thoughtfully, "I'd be a good governor."

Scotto nodded vigorously. "You would. You would be one helluva fuckin' governor. You'd have a high school named after you. Maybe even a mall, although the way the economy is in the shithouse, I don't think you'd want a mall. But a great governor. Maybe I'd vote for you myself."

"You would?" Fasio said cheerfully.

"Well, maybe. But it's your duty to run." His voice grown raspy and moist from the brandy, he went on:

> *Tonight I quit these walls,*
> *The thought my soul appalls,*
> *But when stern duty calls,*
> *I must obey.*

"That's from *The Pirates of Penzance,*" Scotto said with satisfaction. Had Pasquale Scotto had the poem prepared, or was he truly more educated than he let on? Fasio couldn't tell.

"The will of the people," said Fasio, nodding his head gravely. Then, he turned to Cohen and said, "I don't see how you can refuse the call of duty."

It was progressing along the lines that Pasquale Scotto had expected. He had foreseen it exactly. The cancer had not devoured his political instincts.

"I can always sense the will of the people," he said.

Billy Cohen had taken back his chair, was absorbing the implications of Scotto's assessment. He had thought that he wanted to be governor to retire from the people's will; now he was being persuaded that there was something more to this. Perhaps fate. Maybe he was responding to what he detected on some higher level of consciousness. Perhaps he was acting on chaste motives, instead of exhaustion. Maybe he was that sensitive.

"It's a very grave responsibility," Cohen said.

Scotto had to suppress a laugh. He knew that Cohen had been sending his trusted lieutenants throughout the state for months. Upstate leaders from Schenectady to Ithaca had reported back to Scotto that Cohen was testing his reputation for a run at the governorship. Scotto had been too sick to pay attention before, and it hadn't mattered much. But with Fasio and Cohen conspiring together . . .

"You can't miss," he said. "All the declared candidates,

they're assholes. You got a bald attorney general, a cranky feminist Dracula who couldn't even get the female vote, a right-wing fanatic who should wear a sheet. I'm tellin' ya, there's nobody. You got experience, you got a record, you never been caught stealin'. And you even look like a governor. You could be a governor in the movies, even, and that's a lot harder than getting elected."

Fasio and Cohen laughed, although Billy Cohen was listening carefully, waiting for the punch line.

"As far as I'm concerned, you can start shopping for a warm coat. It gets a little chilly in Albany."

There was a silent toast to the new governor as each raised his glass and emptied it. But in that remnant of his stomach that worked like a smoke alarm, Scotto experienced a sour bubble. There would be trouble from that other item on the agenda.

"There's one problem," Fasio said evenly, examining his glass.

"Just one?" Scotto replied. "That's a fuckin' miracle."

"One big problem."

Scotto nodded, knew what was coming, tried to act surprised.

"When Bill announces his candidacy, he's gonna resign."

Scotto didn't say anything. He was pretending to think about this strange twist in the plan. He had to look calm.

"He doesn't have to," he said.

"No," said Billy Cohen, as usual slightly off in his timing, rushing in too fast with the cooked-up strategy. "But if I do, the governor names my successor."

Scotto nodded. "True, that's one way of doing it. 'Course, the fuckin' law doesn't say that. The dumbshit city council president is next in line."

Billy Cohen was in fast with the next step. "No, no, no. Not if we get the governor to call for a special election and appoint someone in the interim. An interim incumbent would have a terrific advantage."

"You got somebody in mind?"

They both looked at Fasio, who grinned.

"Listen, Pat, with me in Albany and John down here, we'd get a lot done. There wouldn't be any question of cooperation. We'd get a lot done."

"Uh, yeah? Whatdja want done?"

Cohen started to speak, but nothing came out. He blew air into the sky. "Oh, uh . . . everything."

What stuck in Scotto's sore gullet was the certainty of John Fasio's slippery ethical code. Maybe it ran in the family. And if that family skeleton came out, the whole local Democratic party machine might fly to pieces. It was a very tricky subject.

"You want this job?" he asked Fasio, nodding at Cohen. His voice had the inquisitive sound of a wronged lover.

Fasio nodded. "I'd be a good mayor," he said.

Scotto moved his hand. "So Billy here would resign and run for governor, and meanwhile, you'd be mayor and run on your own. I can see that a lot of thought has gone into this."

"It seems reasonable," said Billy Cohen.

"You know how much money it takes to run for mayor?"

"A bundle," said Fasio.

"Ten million. Probably fifteen because you, you're nobody. No offense. No name recognition. A little, but not enough. You got fifteen million dollars, Johnny?"

Fasio looked up. "I think I can put together a war chest."

"Really? You been cheating on your expense account?"

Fasio smiled. Cohen laughed.

"Why not?" Scotto said. "What the hell. I got one lung, half my gut is gone, my arteries are like overcooked pasta and I sleep next to an oxygen tank. What's so fuckin' crazy about you two running the state? I think you make a winning ticket."

"You don't know what that means to me," said Billy Cohen.

"You know we wouldn't do a thing without you," said Fasio.

Oh, right, so how come you did everything so far without me?

There was a knock on the door and Murray Gerber returned with two platters of food. On one was an assortment of vegetables. On the other were beef and salami. Scotto grabbed the meat platter and gobbled up a thick slice of roast beef. Gerber noticed that the color had returned to his face.

The roast beef was wonderful. Scotto decided to check with Rose before he cut off John Fasio's political legs.

7

IT WAS JUST after three in the afternoon and Bonnie Hudson marched at her usual brisk pace from the newly renovated subway station at Columbus Circle eight blocks north to the headquarters of the Atlantic Broadcasting Network on Sixty-seventh Street. She couldn't get away from the subway station fast enough. There was something a little scary and maybe even heartless about what they'd done to the subway stop. For one thing, the scale was off. It sat out in the middle of a plaza—a stagnant tract whose centerpiece was an abandoned convention hall. Instead of inspiring a sense of space and prospect, the plaza made her feel exposed and small.

The subway had been rebuilt with steel and glass and tile, and draped over most of the graffiti-resistant surfaces were the blemishes that couldn't be erased: the soiled, sour, sullen drift of homeless people. They wilted in corners, spread out under cardboard blankets, slouched along the walls, and gave off a stench of volatility and menace. The paper cups they used for begging were left like accusations near the exits and entrances and Bonnie could feel their smoldering, indicting eyes follow her as she raced by.

In a few blocks she was in Manhattan's intellectual heartland, an older, windblown section of the island sprinkled with musty bookstores and discreet emporiums that sold strange items of uncertain but wildly fluctuating value: an Indian teapot that would fetch $2,500 from a collector; glass candleholders from the eighteenth century worth all of the inventory of some of the newer, brighter bargain shops. If Manhattan was Baghdad-on-the-Hudson, this was where you would find Aladdin's lamp.

There were also the inevitable video palaces and the health food temples and all the other symptoms of the quicksilver mercantile trends that passed through the city like a winter virus. But the frenzy of the newcomers was not rooted in the solid, Gothic style of the Upper West Side neighborhood, which suggested an older, sturdier tone.

It was Monday, February 3rd, and Bonnie was an hour early on her first day of work. She advanced like a soldier, bracing for the worst, watching the deep shadows of the skyscrapers for sudden, belligerent movements of the crack-dead street people. She was a veteran New Yorker and knew that the predators lurked everywhere and could lurch out of nowhere. The best defense was to walk tough. To throw off a preemptive glare, like an eyeball security laser beam.

Abruptly, Bonnie stopped. She was struck by something even more ominous than the streets of Manhattan: the probability of blowing her cool. No sense showing her new masters at the television station that she was overanxious by reporting early. She changed direction, avoiding the coffee shop directly in front of the station, and headed west across Sixty-seventh Street to a tavern called The Idiot Box. It was a rusty bucket kind of pub and as she pushed through the door and hit the warm, moist, stale air, she heard sarcastic, edgy voices cutting through the smoke. She felt at home. The bar was filled with a stock family sound—cranky journalists. Pawing at the sawdust floor were off-duty rough-hewn technicians and the pampered on-air talent (some of whom still wore their studio makeup, having run across the street for a quick one).

And hunkered down at a table across the room she spotted Jake Neal, a friend from the old days. He had been recruited six months earlier to lend the weight of print journalism to the wisp of television news. He had become, of all things, a business reporter. Bonnie and Jake had spent years in the same heavily shelled trench during the newspaper wars. When he knew Bonnie, in the seventies, Jake was a late-blooming hippie with a long list of real and surreal complaints. In those high-minded, optimistic days he wore dirty jeans and a ponytail, in spite of the fact that he was going bald at a very young age.

The thing that appealed to Bonnie was his inflexible subversive attitude. Jake had a rare talent for avoiding work, disappearing at every crucial moment from the City Room. After ducking the heavy-lifting details, he would lecture the cub reporters on the correct occupational protocol; according to Jake, working-class reporters were obliged to bring down capitalism, one step at a time. He envisioned a long march of industrial sabotage. He, himself, claimed to be eating away at the portfolios of the ruling class from the inside, although Bonnie would have said that there was a large measure of self-indulgence propelling his philosophy, since sneaking off to the movies in the afternoon had a suspicious component of pleasure.

But she had to admire him—no one could beat Jake at dodging an unwanted assignment. After a while, the newspaper gave up. He was exiled to the vagrant and obscure "style" section of the Long Island newspaper, where his muttering discontent was unheard. His sole responsibility was to produce a single celebrity profile each week. Entombed there with him were three bitter and disappointed editors. One was a former communist poet, another was a burned-out novelist, and the third—the man in charge—was a pale, malignant bean-counter who spent his days plotting and scheming to get noticed by the hot cityside editors.

It went without saying that they all hated Jake, but not as much as they detested each other. And so each attempted to wrest control of the section by leaving behind an imprint on the celebrity profile. The communist poet insisted that every celebrity subject make a political utterance, preferably seditious. The constipated novelist demanded to know what book had the greatest influence on the subject (hoping that one day his own lonely book would pop up as someone's artistic inspiration). And the chief of the section had one single, unchangeable demand: he wanted to know what high school the subject had attended. Why he wanted to know the identity of the high school remained a complete mystery. Naturally, Jake speculated about it during the long lunches before he sailed off to his daily matinee. Perhaps the chief had some unfinished business. Maybe the pinched and arid senior editor was on a quest for a long-lost love. But that was unlikely. More probable, he was searching for someone who had known him as a high school geek. To show off his late-blooming professional muscles.

Nonetheless, Jake Neal behaved with total dedication to each demand, as if he understood implicitly the heavy meaning that lay behind each loopy question. He asked, they answered, and he recorded what came out of the mouths of the perplexed celebrities. And, for reasons beyond anyone's comprehension, it worked. The celebrity profiles became, themselves, a celebrated feature of the Sunday newspaper. Jake received award after award and while the fact did not serve to rehabilitate the disappointed editors, it left him beyond their reach for discipline.

In time, for reasons that were never clear, Jake's load was lightened. Bonnie was transferred to the style section and named his assistant. In the stainless, tasteless coffee shop on the first floor of the newspaper, Jake delivered to her his concise lecture about how to perform a celebrity profile. The indoctrination consisted of a single sheet of paper. He took it from his jacket pocket and smoothed it out on the table. It was a checklist of twenty-two questions. She stared at the wrinkled, smudged list. It was a complete celebrity interview kit. It had all the required data: age, physical description, ambition, proudest accomplishment—

hopes, fears and dreams. And there was room for one quote. Just one. Not a long one, either. Not in a five-hundred-word article. Not if you were going to include the three blind mice of politics, literature, and high school.

"What if they give you more than one quote?" Bonnie had asked in all innocence during that decade-old lunch hour when Jake was watching the clock and checking the movie timetables so that he wouldn't be late eating away at the purses of the bloated plutocrats. He looked up from the entertainment section of a rival newspaper and replied emphatically, "I tell them to shut up."

Jake had a foolproof system. He didn't want to be disturbed, having gone to all the trouble of working out this scientific method of getting his week's work done in half a day. The interview would take him half an hour, tops. Anything more was padding. He ran down his checklist, discouraged any attempt to embroider, flatter, or probe too deeply, then returned to the office and blasted out the copy before lunch. He devoted the rest of the week to keeping up with the entertainment industry (which is how he justified the movie receipts on his expense account).

Bonnie could not accept such a simple thesis. On each and every celebrity interview, as she plunged into her new job with her customary zest, she wrote down at least forty quotes. She transcribed them painfully into her personal computer. And when it came time to write the profile, she found that she had room for only one. Not a long one at that. By the time she inserted the age and pertinent book and former high school and the color of the hair, etc., they all read pretty much like one of Jake Neal's assembly-line Model A's.

Ten years later, the anarchist hippie Jake Neal was wearing a three-piece suit and a rep necktie, and his head wobbled as if it were trembling on a loose spring. Too much liquor, thought Bonnie. She knew that it was a moral strain being the business reporter for Channel 9 News, given his old anarchist proclamations, and Jake would have to douse himself with alcohol daily to rid himself of the guilt. She noted that he was also trying to poison himself with her very own high-fat diet. He had before him a dish of oil-soaked potatoes, thick hamburger, and salty pickles. Everything swam in a puddle of ketchup. She was tempted to swipe a chip.

"Well," said Bonnie plunking herself down across from her old comrade, "how's life on the ash heap of history?"

At first his face twisted with a sort of sloppy anger, but then it fell into a smile as he recognized the voice and the face and the frame of reference all at once. "Bonnie!" he said, tipsily proud of his ability to marshal so much concentration and lucidity. "Bonnie Hudson."

"True. All too true. So, how's the business reporter?"

He hunched his shoulders and looked at the ceiling, which was a mistake because it made him dizzy. "I thrive; I have a gift," he said, regaining his poise. He nodded. "Plus, I have worked hard—very hard—to master this new discipline."

"As I recall, your financial ability was pretty thin. You had to go deeply into debt to make the price of a subway token."

"Ahhh! That was in my younger, less frugal days."

"Now that I recall with even sharper clarity, you had trouble with math. I remember asking you for change of a dollar and it took you ten minutes and you still got it wrong."

"I did?"

She nodded. "You gave me three quarters and five dimes."

He dipped his fingers in the ketchup and fished out a potato. "I got better."

"How?"

"Well, for one thing, I watch 'Adam Smith's Money World.' I read *Business Week*. And, in fact, I ask my cousin, Larry, who, in addition to being a blood relative, is a kung-fu CPA black belt killer in the field of finance. Actually, Larry's a genius. He talks, I listen. He says all the financial experts are full of shit when they discuss business cycles and market dips and global interest-rate fluctuations. Nobody knows what they're talking about when you are dealing with something as fundamentally mystifying and occult as economics; it's a crapshoot." He stopped and his eyes brightened. "Speaking of crapshoots, is it true that you tried to break the bank at Atlantic City?"

He threw back his head and dropped another bleeding potato into his open yap.

"It's a complete lie. Atlantic City and I are just good friends. Rumors. Never bet on a rumor. Tell me, Jake, how do you pull it off—I mean the economic-expert bullshit?"

He shrugged. "The old-fashioned way: one good quote."

"That's it?"

"On the tube, we call it a sound bite. One good sound bite. Doesn't have to make sense. In fact, better if it doesn't. Sounds deep. Doesn't even have to be true. Just has to have the sound of sincerity and reckless disregard for conventional wisdom." His elbows were on the table now, and he stared at her intently. He had sobered, seeing his old friend from the celebrity profile days—a woman of guileless wit and substance. "That's the whole story, my child. Nothing complicated. You always want complications. Good thing you didn't decide to become a surgeon."

She laughed and shook her head. "You don't know what the fuck you're talking about, do you? I mean, selling short, futures, margin calls—it's all bullshit, am I right? You wouldn't know a CD from an LP."

"Me?! What about you? You are a meteorologist? You don't know the first thing about climatology, shifting weather patterns, global effects from sun spots or alterations in the jet stream, fallout from active volcanoes, intricate forecast anomalies. You seriously expect me to believe that you have aced the study of ambient changes in weather patterns resulting from subtle movement of the Gulf Stream? C'mon, Hudson, you don't fool me. Fucking magic, right? You read the weather wire service copy. I read the business wires. Nothing unethical. Not even dangerous. I always take care to make my opinions—if that's what you want to call them—scornfully ambiguous. I am fanatically and carefully on every side of every trend."

She shook her head. He was always a little bit of a quack. "At least I tell the folks if it's raining."

"Me, too! I always try to get the rainwear out when the market's bad."

"You know when the market's bad?"

"Of course not. For that I depend on Felix Rohatyn."

"He knows?"

"Nobody knows. That's the beauty. There's nobody to call me a liar."

"Except me."

"Hey! We do our best, given all the variables and reservations. Do you know, Hudson, that I'm up for an award? It was a piece I did last year on the probability of uncertainty in a confused and unpredictable market."

A roaming waitress brought Bonnie a beer and she drank while Jake held his mug in ketchup-stained hands. They were quiet for a moment and then she asked, referring to the television station and its management, "How is it here?"

He shook his head. "Ohhhhhhh!"

"Bad? How could it be bad?"

He blinked, bent lower to meet her gaze, and replied, "How could it be good?"

"Harvey's bad? How could Harvey be bad?"

"Harvey! Oh, he's a prince. Sometimes he's an asshole, but that's his job. He's management. They have to be assholes, even when they're a natural-born prince, which we both agree that Harvey definitely is."

"You don't sound convincing."

"You know, you're not the first person to tell me that. I don't sound convincing. Especially when I mean it. Listen, Bonnie, I like you. You're a prince. And I know you like Harvey. But he does what he's told. He works for Thatch and all these crypto-

British assassins who own everything. Harvey's an overseer, that's all." He shrugged.

"Oh, Christ!" she sighed.

He reached over, after cleaning his hand, and patted her lowered head.

"Not to worry, child," he said. "They will not trouble you. I happen to know that for a fact."

She looked up. "What do you know?"

He tilted his head, an act that revived Bonnie's memories of his outcast charm. "You are golden. You have been summoned to lift the station's ratings. They need a boost. That's you. Our ratings suffer. They languish below average. This is like failing to get vital signs in an emergency room. That's what television studios are, you know—emergency wards. Everybody running around trying to stop the bleeding, people dying left and right, and the doctors don't know what the fuck they're doing." Then he paused and looked at her and smiled. "You don't have to worry. Not for a while."

"How do you know this?"

"I eavesdrop. I listen in. I have friends in swank places who have heard your name sung like a medieval antiphon."

"You're full of shit, Jake."

There was a surge of something at the bar and she turned to see what the commotion was about. It was a rush of new customers, a change of shift at the station, which wrought a change of shifts at the bar. Jake was due back. He ducked his head a little, stuffed some food in his mouth, said that he had to go. Editors were in motion, which invariably set off a tide among the lower orders of workers.

She squinted. "You're still hiding out?"

He shook his head, then smiled. "Not as much. This is television. They have cameras. You have to show them your face—at least, you have to display yourself enough to remind them that you're on the payroll. The worst part is, you have to seem eager." He frowned. "I'm afraid that despair shows up under the makeup."

"Poor Jake."

And then he was gone.

"Something to drink?" asked the waiter as Bonnie's new boss, Basil "Thatch" Conway, glanced at his watch, then turned to gaze out of the window at the arches and fountains of Lincoln Center. They were in his private dining room at the station, where she had just been introduced to her new boss by Harvey Levy. She and Thatch were, in their separate fashions, taking the measure of each other. He did it by turning away—showing his wandering attention. She studied him, drank him in, tried to read the fine print of his polished insult.

But she saw more. Thatch Conway was a tall man who had the attributes of youth. He was thin and sleek in the way that successful men sometimes remain thin and sleek—an extra gift of wealth, as if the skin and hair lived up to the fine clothing textures in which they were encased. His cuffs were held together by gold studs and his tie was pure silk, and his shirt had the smallest possible monogram where a pocket would have been.

But there was no way to tell his age. She knew that he was a year or two past fifty, but the lines of character and age were still dormant, lurking somewhere under all that coddling and indulgence; there would come a day, she knew, when they would surface and he would seem to age overnight. It would be sudden. One day he would be young, and the next he wouldn't. But there was no sign of it yet, and he drank his whiskey with the smooth and elegant movements of a veteran stage performer.

"You, ah, do the weather," he said in his faraway voice, a device by which he maintained distance from those he was not yet prepared to allow close.

"I can do other things," she said.

He turned quickly and looked at her, full face. Harvey Levy

had warned him about this one. She crackles, Levy had said. He was right. Thatch could smell the burning tinder. He smiled at the memory of his own firebrand days.

"Yes, of course, actually, I heard that you have other ambitions. Unfortunately, we need you to do the weather."

He realized that Bonnie was ignorant of the larger picture; she didn't know that he needed her tested popularity to boost the appeal of his holdings, to woo the bankers for his next move. He craved a cable franchise. There was a large pot of money available in the franchises. Whoever controlled the installation and services reaped a windfall—and not only from the sale of programming. There were other important benefits: influence and power. Buying Channel 9 was only the first step in his larger scheme of gaining a foothold in high American society. He wanted entry into the important American media markets, not just some piddling local station where he could cadge dinner invitations to Gracie Mansion. He had his appetite set on meals at the White House.

It would, furthermore, be delicious revenge on his jeering wife, Nellie, who never tired of reminding him that she was the daughter of a British royal duke. She was a titled member of the grandest aristocracy on earth—another detail she was fond of mentioning. Of course, there had been a time when he was a catch—a boy genius in the Fleet Street newspaper set. He had inherited a small newspaper from his father and had found a formula that appealed to the English public. He took over dying newspapers and magazines, lowered the overhead by bullying the unions into submission, then completed the fiscal conquests by making the editorial product tawdry. The secret of turning a profit was a generous show of female flesh, not to mention a regular (if dubious) scandal. It was high tabloid journalism and it lent him the air of a buccaneer. For a time, Thatch Conway was a famous rake in London. Until he got bored with the chase and made the mistake of choosing the wrong woman.

Her ladyship Nelda Smyth-Poindexter regarded her rogue

husband as a coarse merchant. Someone without standing. Who else would give up British citizenship so casually? She never failed to make it clear that he was socially beneath her. For a long time he wondered why on earth she had ever married him, but then he realized that it was another in the long, tedious sequence of her antisocial acts of defiance. She had married Thatch Conway in order to fling him in the face of her horrified family.

For some reason, her scorn mattered, and he wanted to fling something back. America was an open window, an inspiration, aglow with possibilities. He was glad to leave her behind in London with her smoldering contempt. He didn't give a damn about British citizenship, only success. And that was stateless.

"I've always found the weather . . . somehow, very reassuring," he said, thinking that Bonnie's spunk would be unacceptable at any decent London studio. Still, it was part of her appeal. Americans like feistiness. Thumbing your nose at the boss was considered brave. He thought it was rude and foolish. "You know, speaking of weather, it is the one part of the news that's not really grim—unless one has to report a flood or a hurricane. It's a real service, alerting people how to dress for the day, whether to bring an umbrella. And, it is something for which one shoulders no blame. I've always found that part . . . soothing."

"I've always found it a little windy," she shot back.

He could see how Bonnie's spitfire personality could annoy and crack the tolerance of a supervisor. Levy had tried to warn him about her flinty personality, but Thatch said that he could handle her. After all, she was a girl in financial distress. She needed a job. She couldn't afford to give him a lot of trouble.

"What is it that you wish to do?"

She sputtered, turned to look around. The waiter was watching, as if she might break into spasms. Harvey had vanished completely.

"I wish to do news," she said managing to keep her voice under control but mimicking his accent. He ignored the affront.

"Yes, that's fine. Weather's part of the news."

"No. Not just weather."

"Something more. Yes. I see. Well, why not do something odd, you know, like that fat man Willard-what's-his-name does? You know, with old people. People who are having their hundredth birthdays. 'Course he's got that sewn up—the hundred-year-olds—and the truth is that old people are wrinkled. Still, a gimmick is always good for some viewers. But, you know, why not go the other way? Show babies. Mr. and Mrs. Jones have a bouncing baby girl. Hold up a picture of a cute little baby. That would work very nicely, don't you think?"

She shook her head. Then she brightened. "Hey, what if I hold up a naked picture of Fergie? Or, better yet, each night I hold up a picture of a different royal and tell something really scummy about them."

He tried to laugh but it came out more like an alarmed cough. "They warned me about your sense of humor."

"Okay, I was kidding about the naked Fergie if you were kidding about the babies. Listen, Mr. Conway, I simply want to get back to some honest reporting. I'll do the weather, but I feel wasted without a press card."

Then it struck him. "Oh, you mean like going after police shootouts and chasing fires? That sort of thing? That wouldn't be a problem, so long as you take care of the weather portion."

"Will you tell Harvey?"

He had no such intention. He started to pull away. "Well, we have to think about these things. There certainly could be more for you to do than simply deliver temperatures. And, let me say, I certainly would like to welcome you to our little family; I'm sure that it will all work out." He excused himself, heading to the far end of the room, where there was a door that opened into the sanctuary of his private office. His back was as sleek as his front.

8

Lunch?" asked Jack Mann's partner.

Jack looked at his watch. It was 12:30 and his sidekick, Jerry Bandolino, was already licking his chops. Bandolino was a forty-nine-year-old ex-cop with a bad eating habit. He'd been glancing at the time for half an hour, moving up and down on the balls of his feet, back and forth, side to side, like someone who had to find a bathroom.

"You hungry already?" asked Jack, without taking his eyes off of the building across the street. "You just had breakfast."

They were near Chinatown, down on Canal Street, standing with proprietary license in the heated doorway of an office building. The building manager took one look at the two of them, thought, "Cops," and walked away and left them alone.

"Chinese?" suggested Bandolino.

A veteran street cop instinctively aligned his menu with his surroundings. When he was going out on an assignment, that was invariably a cop's first thought: where to eat. You pulled a job on Mulberry Street in Little Italy, you ate Italian; in Astoria you ate Greek; downtown near City Hall you had the fancy South Street Seaport; in midtown you got the silver pushcarts under yellow umbrellas looking like a long line of steaming beachfront cabanas; in the East Village you had the Second Avenue Deli or one of the other dairy or Hungarian-Jewish restaurants that stuck out under the flood of third world immigrants like the masts of sunken ships. To the food experts who patrolled the streets of New York, the city was a smorgasbord of spicy lunch counters.

But Jack Mann and Jerry Bandolino were on a stalk and this was one more confirmation of Jack's original opinion: Bandolino must have been one lousy cop. The primary edict of tracking someone is that there is no lunch. Especially when the guy doesn't know that he is being followed. He could very easily slip away without telling you.

Jack seldom ate on the job. Apart from that general rule, he was wearing his cop eyes. He tended to eat sideways under occupational stress—one eye on the door, one eye on the street. Food got in the way. The other thing was, he wasn't hungry. In that regard, he was a freak, since the average cop regarded his meal as a sacred contractual entitlement from God. And Bandolino looked devoutly hungry. Not even today's half-frozen rain put him off his feed.

"Whyncha get us a couple of heros," said Jack, handing Bandolino a twenty.

One thing about Holman—he was generous with the expenses. When he put Jack on the payroll, he gave him an envelope with fifty twenties and told him that they would straighten out the accounting later, when there was time. Ask if you need more, said Holman waving an arm expansively. Somebody with deep pockets wanted a lace-curtain surveillance.

Bandolino was disappointed that he was going to have to take his meal on the run, but he deferred to Jack, the senior member of the team. He knew that he was only along to provide muscle. He rolled his shoulders in a kind of acquiescence.

"There's a place near the corner," said Jack, pointing to a Greek deli.

"Whatdoya want?"

"Anything. Ham and cheese."

"Mustard?"

"Yeah, okay, mustard."

"What kind of cheese?"

"Swiss. Anything. Let's just make it quick."

"Beer?"

Jack gave him a stern look and said, "Diet Coke." He almost added, "Don't take your eyes off me," but he didn't want to heap too many insults on the linebacker-sized former cop. The procedure was rudimentary, and even an ape like Bandolino had to know that he ought to keep Jack in sight.

Jack didn't have to wait long to regret not spelling it out clearly—the moment Bandolino ducked into the Greek's coffee shop to pick up the hero sandwiches and the soft drinks, the target subject emerged from the building off Canal Street. The subject stood alertly in the doorway of the apartment building for a few seconds scanning the street up and down (not that he suspected that he was being followed, but more out of ancient, ingrained habit) then tucked the brown briefcase under his arm, lowered his head, and plunged toward the west side of that pinched end of Manhattan where he had parked his car. He was moving too fast for Jack to go back and get Bandolino. There was no choice—Jack crossed to the far side of Canal Street and kept his man in sight. The street on which the subject moved was choked with pedestrians and fish stands and exotic vegetable displays and he picked up the bob and weave of the man's head as he pushed aggressively through the mob. You couldn't just walk down the south side of Canal Street; you had to pick your way through a dense congestion of shoppers and tourists and street hustlers and hawkers.

He and his target were heading west past Broadway and Jack suddenly had an alarming thought: did Bandolino leave him the car keys? He did a quick pat-down of himself and was relieved when he felt the keys in his jacket pocket. He kept pace with the target—walking in the secure tailing position, about twenty feet behind the line of sight. If the target looked to the side, or over to the north side of the street, he still wouldn't see Jack. If he looked back, the tendency would be to skip past that little blind spot.

Jack turned once and saw Bandolino standing on the corner, his brush-cut head swivelling in panic. In spite of his alarm, Bandolino was taking big bites out of a hero sandwich as he made full searching sweeps of the panorama. It would have been stupid to try and signal him—the target might notice. Maybe Bandolino would remember where they left the car, thought Jack. But he doubted it. The last time he saw Bandolino, he was stuffing the last three inches of the sandwich into his moving mouth and scratching his patchy head with the hand that held a bag with Jack's sandwich and the soft drinks.

Then Jack's attention returned to the target and he saw Murray Gerber's head whip around in his direction. He ducked into a check-cashing store for quick cover. Gerber probably didn't catch him, he thought. He'd have to be a bloodhound to be that swift. Jack had been too fast, and there was too much territory for Murray to survey, for that rapid a lock on Jack.

He came out in time to see Murray glide out of view, now heading north. Jack tried to maintain cover by keeping pace with fast-moving groups, blending into couples or bunches of men on their way to lunch. And he was not conspicuous. That was his greatest asset in plainclothes—the sheer everyday, unremarkable nature of his appearance. He was an ordinary-looking man of ordinary height and ordinary style. It was only when he spoke and switched on the light of his fugitive intelligence that he became remarkable. But in his prosaic camouflage of the common man, he kept his distance from Murray Gerber, who moved swiftly in and out of the lunchtime crowds in the heart of Chinatown.

Murray Gerber sensed something. He couldn't name it, but somewhere in the early warning nerve endings that had been vibrating in various stages of alert for most of his adult life he knew that he was being followed. He wouldn't look around. That would be dumb. Whenever he could, however, he did check the reflections of the pedestrians in the shop windows, and he stopped once to pick up a newspaper. He took that opportunity to make one quick snap glance behind him. Just one. He saw nothing. It was enough.

He crossed rashly into the traffic, which was, at that hour on a Friday, moving east and west at a crawl, as trucks and cars prodded each other into a tunnel or onto a bridge in order to escape the city. He ran in front of a truck and the driver slammed on the brakes—Murray was instantly counted as one more urban lunatic, betting everything on the prompt reactions of a total stranger, just to beat a traffic light. But then you had to be a desperate, long-shot gambler to live in the city.

People turned at the blare of the truck horn, glanced at the possibility of a violent street-corner drama quivering on the horizon, and turned back again to their own irritating passage when they saw that no one was down, no punches were thrown, no blood was spilled. The waters merely boiled at their usual high temperature. Murray slipped gracefully through the grinding progress of the motor traffic and darted up north, away from his car, heading for the relative serenity of Sixth Avenue.

An uptown bus passed and Murray picked up speed; he ran half a block, turning sideways, finding holes in the pedestrian congestion, until he leaped aboard the bus just before the driver shut the door. He didn't flash his city badge of office, which would have entitled him to a free ride, but also would have called attention to himself. He dropped one of the tokens he always kept in his pocket into the fare counter, took a transfer, and headed to the rear of the wheezing bus so that he could be near the exit. He was always conscious of leaving himself an escape route.

He had no idea who was there behind him. It was not someone he saw—but something he felt. He had picked up the raw, primitive scent of a tracker. It was in the air. He was never without some pilot light of fear and caution when he was on one of his clandestine operations. But this was something sharper, more focused, more heart-pounding.

A sleeping junkie was spread along the back row, taking up six seats and creating a belligerent no-man's-land for the rest of the passengers, who stood a few feet away and glared at the elongated berthing gluttony of the derelict. Murray wanted to push the man's legs off the seat, but he couldn't break his cover. He was a stealth passenger on a bus inching uptown on the broken streets, past the work crews from Con Edison, the New York Telephone Company, the water department—all forcing the traffic to squeeze left and then right in a continuing moving funnel that made everyone feel like they were being pushed painfully out of a tube of toothpaste.

It had been a frantic, hectic morning. He needed a moment to relax. If there was someone back there following him, he had shaken them off. No one could have made that stormy crossing of the street and the race for the bus—he would have noticed. Murray needed a moment to unwind. He had spent an hour in a dueling argument with Councilman Sam Morris, who couldn't get it through his thick head that the environmental impact study would put off the municipal incinerator for a year. Minimum. Sam didn't want to go back to his people with only Gerber's word that Fasio had agreed to the extra time for the study. Not that easy. Not after such a rugged fight against construction.

Gerber had to get tough. He told the councilman that Sam had no choice but to take his word for it. Cautiously, he hinted about other considerations, suggested that Fasio was toying with the mayoralty. What was an incinerator in Bayside, compared to that? Then he got angry at himself for revealing too much.

"Just make sure you buy ten tables for the dinner at the Hyatt," Murray told the old councilman, who nodded obediently. The money was nothing. He would pass off the $10,000 cost of the one hundred tickets to the attorneys for the home-owners' committee. It was worth that much to buy goodwill for the incinerator delay. In fact, that part was reassuring. There was a soothing comfort in the familiar corruption. In Queens politics, an exchange of favors was the permissible political barter. That was the way it worked. That's the way business was always conducted. The lawyers and lobbyists laid out a sacrificial carpet of football tickets, charitable donations, campaign gifts, and vacation treats, and in return, they got Murray Gerber. They got consideration, they got access, they got tangible and intangible benefits. They got indefinite delays. Corruption was a very pacifying dogma to an old Queens councilman.

One thing that Sam didn't get was face-to-face assurances from Fasio, himself. Every time Councilman Morris indicated that he would like to be able to go back to his Bayside clients and assure them that he had it from the horse's mouth, Murray Gerber gave him that annoyed, twisted look he bestowed on dim-witted clerks and slow-paying building inspectors. Deniability, he explained with his fluent eyes. A councilman, of all people, should know that the man has to have the ability to deny!

Still, he knew that Sam Morris suspected that Murray was running it by himself. Not that it made much difference—the effect was the same. Sam would have liked to have something on Fasio, and Murray was determined to prevent that.

"So I hear he's really gonna run," Sam Morris had said, grabbing Gerber's arm as he tried to leave Cunningham Park, near Murray's apartment in Fresh Meadows. They had met there in the crisp dawn when only joggers were out.

Murray had smiled, one of those absent, mirthless expressions intended to convey more meaning than it actually delivered. A cold smile to fend off further questions.

After he left Councilman Morris in the park, Murray raced to Canal Street and Becky's overheated apartment. He planned a frenzied hour in bed with this insatiable widow, whose consulting work for the parks department gave no hint of a bottomless appetite for sex. She was not good-looking, not young, not desirable in any obvious way. But in bed she was all the things Murray Gerber had ever craved or dreamed about. It was as if she had burrowed into his subconscious and acted out all his immoral fantasies.

The moment he entered the apartment, she opened her housecoat and showed him her lush, gently drooping breasts, and thicket of exposed pubic hair, then slammed the robe shut to heighten the tease. They didn't speak, except in shallow breaths. She bent over, as if she were taking something out of a dresser drawer, and showed him her moist naked eagerness. He was so overcome that he uttered something hoarse and she sauntered over to the chair where he sat with his pants open. She smirked and put a hand on him. It was a jolt. Then she swooped down on him, took him between her breasts, licked him, placed him in her mouth. She squirmed against him and moved up and put him between her legs, making him for a moment unable to exhale. She moved so smoothly and swiftly, switching him back and forth and all around, that he was delirious with her musk and touch and shameless enthusiasm. He banged against her teeth, kissing her mouth, then took her breasts, one after the other, then sat her down and dove between her legs while she moaned and ranted so loud that he was certain all the neighbors were listening at the walls.

By the time he lifted her off her feet and carried her to the unmade bed, he was hysterical and half mad with lust. He was naked and he didn't even remember undressing. She was muttering and screaming and pulling at him and bending over him and he had never been harder or more crazed with aching lechery.

And when it was done, they gave each other slanted looks, as if revealing so much so intensely made them bitter enemies.

Gerber heard a tickle of rain and sleet against the side of the bus as it maneuvered through the stammering traffic. He could see pedestrians fighting the wind with inside-out umbrellas, clutching fluttering hats, faces red from the cold.

He hated the days when Fasio arranged to meet him in the city, claiming that they were sunny truants stealing a day off from school. It was always a lie. He'll be waiting, thought Gerber. He'll be sitting at his back table in the French restaurant, sipping his third glass of wine, sinking into one of his black moods.

The bus lurched forward, having found open ground between the bottlenecks. Suddenly the standing passengers were all thrown back, falling against each other, apologizing cheerfully because at least they were moving.

Jack found that he could keep up with the bus on foot as long as it kept squirming its way uptown. In fact, if he wasn't careful he'd outdistance it. He didn't want to get even with the bus because then Gerber would see him out of the window. Gerber did not miss much. Jack had needed only one look to know that this was someone dangerous, someone to avoid.

He didn't know why he was supposed to follow the assistant to the borough president. It was a little irritating. When he was a cop working for the city, he had never had to question such things. His occupation was honorable by its very nature. He could always justify his assignments by telling himself that he was on the side of the angels, fighting crime. He was one of the good guys. It didn't even matter if he got hurt or killed. He would have fallen in a virtuous battle. He preferred that kind of clarity.

This was different. He didn't know who he was working for or why. Holman had held up a traffic cop's hand when he'd started to ask. Just follow him, he'd said. Make sure you find out who he sees. Find out what you can. Nothing more specific than that. Stay with him until I pull you off. The main thing is, don't compromise the surveillance. He can't know that he's being followed.

Jack knew that Bandolino had no curiosity about the job.

They were following Gerber, and he didn't care why. Jack thought that his partner must have assumed that it was something that he would store under the general heading of "routine." Everything from swiping apples to freeloading meals to shaking down contractors fit under that broad topic. He was being paid and fed, and that was enough reason for a man like Bandolino.

Jack had studied the file, had spent three long days in a trailing surveillance, so that he knew Murray's morning routine. He had been waiting in the park, hidden behind a pile of winter salt, when Murray met the councilman. Jack watched from a distance, while Bandolino waited in the car eating an egg sandwich. He was too far away to overhear or even see clearly. But the unusual meeting was disturbing, nevertheless.

The trip to Canal Street felt better. That fell within the range of city business. It was even reassuring to know that Gerber had private yearnings. But then there was that clandestine farce of shaking off the tail. Why was he so careful and so devious?

Sleet hit Jack like pellets in the face and he flinched. Well, what the hell, he thought, sobered by the cold, wet slaps, what did I expect? It's a job. Nothing illegal. All I'm doing is following a guy. But this guy happened to be the executive assistant and bodyguard to the borough president of Queens, and there were very disturbing possibilities lurking around that relationship. Jack considered John Fasio one of the good guys. Like most everyone else in Queens, he thought that Fasio lent a certain youthful exuberance and a touch of humanity to the office, which had been, before his arrival on the scene, a bloodless, sleepy hideout from serious government affairs. Fasio was honest, forthright, and had the glow of someone clearly headed for bigger things.

And he had that tragic mystery lurking about his name. Jack had heard the sad business about his father—Big Jim Fasio. Everyone knew the story. Or, at least they had heard some epic version of the tale. In a heroic act of political sacrifice, Big Jim

Fasio had taken the blame for someone else's crime to save the party from a ruinous investigation. That was what the party workers wanted to believe. The twenty-year-old debt remained unpaid, but a big credit ended up in the son's account. A lot of the old timers believed that John Fasio was owed special treatment for the father's selflessness.

So why was Jack following John Fasio's right-hand man?

The bus found the opening in the traffic and jumped forward. Jack thought of running to keep up, but then he was knocked back by a bicycle messenger. "Wake the fuck up, dumb shitass motherfucker!"

Well, he thought, the kid on the bike had a point, although he himself would have put it a little more elegantly. He stepped back on the sidewalk and was instantly splashed by a passing cab. A woman crashed into him with her umbrella. She was a nice-looking woman in an expensive raincoat. Bendel's, he guessed. "Asshole!" she said. He marched on.

9

WARDROBE HAD LOST his blazer, and Jerry Kantor, the anchor of the two o'clock newsbreak on Channel 9, suspected treachery. The reason his first guess was perfidy was that the backup jacket was also missing.

"I'm not going to wear it," he said, looking in the mirror at a substitute jacket Wardrobe had scrounged from Jake Neal's office. It was two sizes too large and made him look puny, which he was. Kantor was very touchy about his size. Until the new management took over at Channel 9, he had been a sportscaster and had taken a lifetime of ribbing from the mammoth NFL linebackers who drifted into sportscasting once their playing days were over. Now he had his eye on the important evening anchor chair, and every time he did the two o'clock newsbreak, he regarded it as an audition. He was adamant on the jacket question; he was not going to make himself look ridiculous by wearing a blazer that fit like a horseblanket.

The trouble with that unbending attitude was that the station had a policy of using identical sky-blue blazers with a Channel 9 logo on the breast pocket on all of their newscasters. It gave them a perky, user-friendly look on the air. At least that was what the consultant who recommended the uniform style told

Thatch Conway and Harvey Levy when he was selling the idea. He further made the claim that the blazers—by actual word count—made the newscasters more talky on the air. Thatch believed it, or, rather, believed that, by spreading that expensive opinion around, it would become a self-fulfilling prophecy. Bonnie, who was making what Harvey called a "nice adjustment" to her new weather job (in the same way that intensive care patients are upgraded from serious to fair condition), had taken to wearing her sky-blue blazer at staff meetings; it helped her speak up, she said.

Harvey Levy, the managing editor of the news division, summoned from a nap in his office to resolve Kantor's blazer crisis, saw that the jacket didn't really fit, but he suggested that they bring in someone from Wardrobe who would fix it. Pin it up, just for the newsbreak. They'd hunt down a new blazer by the main evening newscast.

Kantor shook his head. "What if comes undone on the air?"

"Jerry, it's a fifty-two-second spot," argued Levy.

"No," said the pint-sized unyielding anchor.

"Okay," said Levy after studying Kantor for a moment, not wanting to push this into a head-on clash between management and labor. The man had a point—he would look slightly ludicrous, even if they got it adjusted. Too much shoulder and lapel to stuff under a few straight pins. They could put two guys down under the desk, crouching off-camera, holding the wings of the jacket to keep it from puffing up or flapping loose. But that was dangerous. Someone was bound to call one of the gossip columnists with that little tidbit. It was too juicy and wicked a glimpse into the superficiality of television news to pass without comment. And Kantor had made enough enemies with his insincere humility to guarantee wide circulation of the jacket story.

It was getting close to air time. Four minutes. Technicians were starting to pace and fret, to get that dancing look in their eyes.

"Okay," said Levy, "I won't insist."

"Thank you," said Kantor, grabbing his custom-made suit jacket, which, he was convinced, made him appear more substantial, more trustworthy, or, at least, a judge of fine tailoring.

"I'll get Frank to anchor the newsbreak," said Levy, motioning to a new young reporter.

Kantor stopped cold, his right hand in the air halfway into his suit jacket, frozen for an instant in a modified Nazi salute. Then, like someone hitting a rewind button, he removed his arm from the sleeve of his expensive tailored suit jacket and swam back into the oversized blazer. "See if you can do something," he told the man from Wardrobe, who began quickly pinning the cuffs of the jacket. "I'll do the break," he said to Levy.

The soundman, Max Gross, placed the microphone on Kantor's tie. "Boy," he said, retreating from the bright anchor desk, "nobody can find their jackets today."

"What? What do you mean?"

"Thirty seconds. Quiet on the set! Cue One."

Kantor was certain. Someone was doing a number on him. But not just him. What did Max mean? Maybe there was a prankster who stole all of the jackets . . . a plot . . . by Channel 11 . . .

"Four . . . three . . . two . . ."

"Good afternoon, I'm Jerry Kantor for Channel 9 midafternoon newsbreak," he read from the scrolling prompter. "The Democratic presidential candidates were in New Jersey today, all seeking the Garden State's support for the upcoming primary. A shooting and a stabbing this morning at the High School of Performing Arts in Manhattan. Fortunately no one was seriously hurt. School officials said that the shooting was the result of a dispute between two acting students, both of whom wanted the same part in *The Odd Couple*. The gun used by the senior was a prop and only fired blanks. The competing senior stabbed his rival with a trick knife. More news and Bonnie Hudson with today's weather after this . . ."

A voice from the control room came over the set, a reminder

that vast, unseen powers were always in play: "We're off the air. Commercial. Thirty seconds."

Kantor looked up and saw Bonnie fidgeting with her jacket. It looked a little tight for her.

"Twenty seconds."

He had a suspicion . . . nothing that he was ready to say out loud, not with certainty.

"Ten."

Besides, he couldn't get up to check, not now when he was sitting just right on the wings of the jacket to keep it from bunching up.

"Three . . . two . . ."

The finger pointed at him. "Now for the weather with Bonnie Hudson. What did you think of that last story about the violence in our schools, Bonnie?" he said by way of making small-talk noise.

"I think it proves that, thank God, our kids are practicing safe mayhem," she replied with mock solemnity.

Then she turned to face the camera. "Now for the weather. Those of you who've been outside know that it's cold and rainy with periods of sleet, which will be followed by periods of winter colds; those of you who haven't been out, stay home. Gonna get colder tonight, but that's what happens when the sun goes down and the earth turns into a cold, stark ball of unfriendly ice." She smiled and went on. "Tomorrow's kind of a toss-up between light snow, more rain, and lousy temperatures. February, folks. Winter. No good will come of it."

She turned to the map—a concession on her part. Harvey Levy had extracted a formal promise that she would refer to the map at least once during every newscast.

"You got all these Canadian air masses moving down, and that will bring the temperature down to the high thirties."

When she turned to the map, Kantor saw the little smudge on the back of the jacket. It was his smudge. He had intended to have his jacket cleaned, which is how he recognized the spot.

But he'd postponed it because the mark was on the back and he was always facing front. Now he saw that stain on the back of the jacket Bonnie was wearing. It was his jacket. No doubt.

Jerry Kantor was supposed to announce the evening newscast with a chirpy promise of full and complete details, then show thoughtful diligence by rifling through a stack of pages upon which, presumably, urgent news had come clacking into the newsroom from distant poles and disputing nations, as the credits rolled and the scene faded. But that's not what he did.

"You took my jacket!" he cried, forgetting they were still on the air, and spilling the urgent pages that were stacked on the anchor desk. He held up the long sleeves of his own tentlike substitute—a pathetic demonstration of humiliation.

Bonnie turned, pleased, in fact, to be called away from the cluttered map, swarming with unfathomable highs and lows. She smiled. "Did I take your jacket?" She tugged at the sides. "You know, I thought this was a little snug."

He stood up and the camera pulled back—an automatic reaction from technicians trained to follow movement—so that both Bonnie and Jerry were covered in the two-shot. Kantor was swimming and flapping and sputtering inside his tent, which was coming loose from the pins, and Bonnie—seeing his agitation—was taking her jacket off to give it back to the anchor. "Here, you can have it," she said. "Did you know there's a bad stain on it?"

"What do we do?" shouted Sloan Mathews, the news director, who was in the control booth. He was asking Harvey Levy. "We've got nineteen seconds to go."

A television eternity.

Harvey Levy's mouth was open. The scene was not altogether registering. Sure, something strange was happening on the set, and although it was not quite happy talk, it didn't qualify as a brawl or a full-scale riot. But it was all so surreal and far beyond the things that he planned or foresaw when he designed his shows that he was slow in responding.

"Harvey! This is going out live over the air!" said the director, a bearded, intense man brought in by Levy as a signal to the staff of the shift to youth in the prevailing wind.

"Yes, I know, but what is it? Do you think he's serious?"

Maybe this was Jerry Kantor's version of a gag. Harvey knew that Kantor had a tin ear when it came to wit and was wooden when it came to human contact. Levy couldn't be absolutely certain that this wasn't some clumsy attempt by Kantor to become just one of the guys. God knows, he'd never been able to manage that as a sportscaster.

The red phone from Thatch's office was beeping, and sound technicians and lighting experts were in a pantomime of fits, collapsed with mute laughter at the spectacle of Jerry Kantor flinging off his jacket and going after Bonnie Hudson.

"Yes?" said Harvey into the red phone.

"I have important business to attend to, Mr. Levy, and I was glancing at the monitor in my office. What is going on?"

"The jackets, Mr. Conway. It's working. We're getting more words."

"I realize that I'm new to American cultural peculiarities, but it looks to me like they're having words, as in fighting. Put a stop to it at once."

Thatch hung up first. Harvey signaled to Max Gross.

Jerry's face was red. "That's mine, you miserable, little . . ."

That's when Max Gross cut off the sound.

All the phones were ablaze, and Sloan Mathews was screaming at Harvey Levy, "The FCC will have our ass, Harvey!"

He wasn't sure. It could be treated as a kind of borderline prank. But then, everyone would remind themselves that this was, after all, Jerry Kantor, who was incapable of frivolity.

"Go to black, go to black!" said Harvey Levy in the control booth, and he began plotting damage control. There would be a bubble in the ratings. That would help him a bit with Thatch, who was absorbed with his "special project." It would certainly appear as a clip on the other broadcasts. Maybe they could use it, advertise themselves: "The show bursting with spontaneous emotions and temper tantrums!"

He knew that he'd better go out and convince Jerry Kantor to go along with the official version that he'd just dreamed up—that it was all a good-natured misunderstanding; that he really adored Bonnie Hudson and that it was he, Jerry Kantor, who had played the joke on her!

The question on Levy's mind, one that he didn't want answered, was how much of it did Bonnie plan?

The restaurant was on Madison Avenue, off the street, down a few steps. First one pair of steps, a stammer, then another pair. Just four steps, but the pause gave the impression of a long descent. There were two sets of doors, which also heightened the sense of transition. A small distance, but it left the street far behind.

The maître d', Robert, was a smooth gentleman of the old school who had come to America from the south of France half a century earlier. There was the whiff of the silver-haired roué about him, with his silk foulards and handsome profile and the succession of women of a certain age who appeared after the lunch hour and waited patiently with calf eyes for a whispered word from Robert. In spite of having spent the bulk of his life in New York City, Robert had not lost his thick French accent, which was a commercial and social asset. He was waiting just inside the door, his hand out, a brittle smile on his face.

" 'E is at ze usual table," he said in a voice one pitch above his usual mastery. "Would you like to leave ze briefcase?"

Murray shook his head. He needed it. He handed Robert his overcoat, then started for the rear. The restaurant hummed with soft, sibilant conversations. There were couples murmuring intimately over balloon glasses of expensive wine. A father was directing a luncheon for his teenage daughters and his wife. He ordered in French. The teenagers giggled when the waiter replied in English. There was one table of three men, leaning back in their chairs, smoking cigars and talking investments in an expansive, callous fashion. Their mirthless laughter was like great slabs of beef. Waiters in black jackets and low aprons moved with condescending speed from the kitchen to the tables, bearing plates of steaming fish, scalloped potatoes, and fragrant beef. They listened to the customers, took down instructions on their small white pads, then walked away with half-lidded, half-disguised disdain. They did not approve.

It was a long, narrow restaurant, with Paris street signs on the walls, and frosted glass partitions. The room was broken in two by a bar bulging out from a side wall into the middle, the wood dark and well polished. In the back, one booth was partitioned from the rest of the restaurant. There, shielded on three sides from view, sat John Fasio, his face lit by a huge aimless grin. His tie was undone, his shirt stained, his hair askew. His hands floated above the table where a near-empty bottle of Valpolicella stood.

"My friend!" he said, then held out a palm to indicate a place for his assistant.

Murray slid into the seat across from Fasio and accepted a glass of wine poured by his boss. Then he took out a sheaf of papers from his case and laid them out on the table. Fasio looked down and shivered.

"You okay, boss?"

Fasio nodded emphatically. The dips were exaggerated. But he was not drunk. He was overwrought.

"You probably think that I had too much to drink on my day off, don't you?"

"Nah, uh . . ."

Fasio shook his head with fervor. The voice was not slurred, yet the notes between words wandered. "Not so," he protested. "True, I have had a glass or two, maybe three, but, as to my actual state of sobriety, I would put it at eight or nine on a scale of ten."

"Did you eat something?"

"That's an Irma question. Very good question. Very responsible. Of course, when she asks, she wants to know the fat content of what I have eaten. That, along with whether it's unsaturated, not whether I'm saturated."

Murray took a piece of bread and a slab of butter. The bread was fresh and the butter smooth. It could have been a meal.

"You know, Detective Gerber, I was sitting here thinking." Fasio drew his hands together as he became earnestly pensive. "I was remembering why it was that I became a lawyer. Did you ever wonder that? Why you became a cop?"

"No, I just happen to like guns."

"My father, Big Jim Fasio, once took us all to Gettysburg. Ever been there?" He didn't wait for an answer. "Big Jim was really a lover of land. He should have gone into real estate. He'd've been rich." He looked over at his assistant and smiled. "If he got out when Bush got elected." He took another sip of water and continued. "He took us to Gettysburg, and it was summertime. July. He wanted the season to match the battle. We went for a tour of the battlefield and then we walked across the land. Marched, really.

"Oh, what a march! The long, long advance up to Little Round Top. The heat! My God, the heat! And the ground underneath my feet. I was eleven, maybe twelve, and the ground felt like it was shifting underneath me. We walked along the Wheat Field and the Taneytown Road, stood where Robert E. Lee stood . . ."

"Yeah, I went there once," Murray interrupted, his mouth full of bread.

"You did? Well, my father appreciated facts. Earth. And that was very good land. He knew the value of it. Paid for with a lot of blood. Priceless. Maybe the most expensive land in America." He shook his head. "That's not my point. No! My point was, why I became a lawyer. See, my father did what he did for noble reasons. I believe that."

He poured more wine in Murray's glass, then his own, and

with the bottle empty, signaled Robert for another. "My father believed in land," he said after Robert had uncorked a fresh bottle, filled the glasses, and put them both down for a luncheon of the duck special. "Soooooo . . .," he went on after Robert left, "I accept that. He got into politics because . . . well, who knows. Maybe he saw some relationship between being a citizen and the stewardship of land. Well, you knew him."

Murray felt the blood rush to his face. They had never discussed Big Jim. Implied between them was a range of understandings and affection, none of it needing to be explained. Murray Gerber had been part of the plainclothes squad assigned to the local party headquarters, where Big Jim had been given an office, after a bomb threat. It was a season when bomb threats were taken seriously, a season of political assassinations and dirty tricks. When the threat ebbed, Murray took a leave from the police department and became Big Jim's gofer. Eventually, the job increased in scope until Murray was arranging meetings, providing private security, and offering advice. Not much more was known by John Fasio. He accepted it at face value. Murray was a loyal soldier, then a loyal friend, right up until the day of his father's suicide.

"He was a good man," said Gerber of Big Jim.

Fasio nodded. "I know that. That's why I became a lawyer. I decided on the law after he got into trouble. You know, they have all these divisions of the law—torts, contract law, corporate law, appeals. But that's bullshit. I was in it for criminal law." He leaned toward his assistant. "That's where you get into the fucking ring. That's open cuts and thumbs in the eye and knees in the groin. That's go-for-the-fucking-throat law. That other stuff is just candy. Fuck civil suits. I wanted to defend desperate men falsely accused. I wanted to save, actually, my father."

The food came and they ate in an abrupt silence. Murray was not hungry, but did his duty just to shut the boss up.

"Not bad," said Gerber, soaking up the gravy with another chunk of country bread.

"Tell me about the dinner," said Fasio, pushing his plate away. There was nothing on it but the bones.

"It's taken care of."

Fasio pulled a cigar from his inside pocket, bit off the end, and lit it. "How, taken care of?"

Gerber shrugged. "Sold out."

Fasio laughed. "You mean, the whole fucking dinner? The entire ballroom? All eight hundred seats?"

"That's right, boss."

Fasio got out his pen and notebook and wrote something down. "That's $80,000. You sold out eight hundred seats in, what, a week?"

"A lot of people want you to be mayor."

"Who bought the seats?"

Gerber took a sip of wine. "Civic leaders. Clubs. Homeowners. Tenant committees. You know, people who are active."

He could see Fasio's brow folding up in thought, wondering how far he should carry this line of questioning. Listen, he should tell him, you wanna run for mayor, you gotta raise some money! You gotta have paid professionals running the volunteers, he thought. That's how Big Jim got into trouble—trying to manage a big-league operation while holding down a full-time job at the same time. Otherwise, stay home.

Gerber was wrong about what Fasio was thinking. Fasio was bothered by the fact that the dinner was originally scheduled to benefit a homeless shelter, but they couldn't get enough subscribers. They had been about to cancel the date for lack of interest. But when Fasio gave Gerber approval to use the date for a fund-raising dinner for his as yet unannounced mayoral campaign—under the guise of paying off old debts for the Queens Democratic party—it had been fully subscribed in a matter of days. A few phone calls. That's all it took.

Fasio sighed and pocketed his notebook. He put on his reading glasses and picked up the papers authorizing a further study for the Bayside incinerator, which had lain like ice next to him throughout the meal.

"Murray," he said, holding the cigar and the pen out of the way, "tell me the truth, am I doing the right thing? I don't know if I have the stomach for this."

"For what? You're gonna be the mayor. You don't even have to run. You're already in."

Fasio was quiet. Very quiet. The waiter came by with coffee. Fasio had drunk too much wine, Gerber could see. He had drunk himself sober.

"And if I didn't sign this authorization for that extra study for the incinerator?" Fasio asked.

"What about it?"

"You think we'd get so many Bayside homeowners to come out and support me if I was blowing smoke in their backyard?"

Gerber didn't have to argue. The arguments had all been made in Fasio's head long before he showed up. Made, and won. He had started out paying for the damn cup of coffee in the mornings. He'd jumped out of the car, plunked down a couple of bucks, and taken the coffee and the bagel. Then, one day, he'd gotten a little lazy. He'd stayed in the car and let Murray get the coffee. He'd closed his eyes and didn't look to see if Murray paid or not. He didn't want to know.

Fasio signed the papers. His eyes were open now.

10

DETECTIVE FIRST GRADE Sam Jackson operated the buzzer that controlled the iron portal into the executive wing of City Hall. He decided who came and who went. He was the gatekeeper.

It had been a sleepy morning, with the mayor out of town testifying before a congressional committee on urban problems, and the veteran detective hit the button with only cursory attention to the familiar faces coming and going into the mayoral suite of offices at City Hall. There was the usual brisk procession of stylish clerks, fussy secretaries, overbearing deputy mayors, and overburdened commissioners, trailed by clouds of lofty deputies and overstrung flunkies; they all moved at flank speed, as if theirs was the most urgent of city business. And all were resentful of the momentary pause before Detective First Grade Jackson pushed the release button, believing each and every one that they were exempt from security rituals. By two in the afternoon Detective Jackson had had his third cup of coffee, but still felt the heavy listlessness that went with boring indoor duty at an overheated post.

Beside the gate, leaning coquettishly against the wall, were the pretty girls—political moths—who always seemed to appear

on the fringe of events. This time it was two grade-school teachers whose class was being given a tour of the great rotunda, with
its council chambers and nineteenth-century paintings and his-
torical desks. Just now the class had been taken over by the
parent volunteers and was having an afternoon snack, and the
teachers were on a break. Jackson was not surprised to find that
women with their own relatively impressive social status were
susceptible to the perfume of big-time politics.

"You ever had to, you know, defend the mayor?" asked the
smaller, thin-boned teacher, trying to sound nonchalant.

Detective Jackson thought, next she'll want to touch my gun.
It was a strange thing—the unlikeliest people were dazzled by
sheer brawn. He remembered when he had worked a dinner
honoring basketball players. Art patrons and fashion leaders—
women who never spoke above an arched eyebrow—became
tongue-tied and giddy adolescents in the presence of the awe-
some seven-foot-tall men. They approached the players and
found some reason to brush against their solid flesh.

It was the same with politics. There was a raw intoxicating
magnetism to those who wielded power. The gun and the shield
and the proximity of excitement and authority, as well as a hint
of risk, put even sensible citizens into a kind of mild public
swoon.

"We're really not allowed to talk about it," replied Detective
Jackson in his modest rock-star voice.

The other one, the not-so-pretty one, was covertly thrilled.
She turned away to conceal it.

"Let me ask you," pressed the small-boned teacher, "isn't
this a terrible responsibility? I mean, how do you know who's a
kook and who's normal?"

The secretaries and clerks and important administrators,
meanwhile, were passing through the gate, hiding knowing
smiles.

"You get to know," said Detective Jackson, as if he were
revealing a meaningful secret.

The teachers nodded solemnly, keepers now of privileged intelligence.

Suddenly, Detective Jackson's partner, Chuck Malone, came out of the suite's communications center in a state of hightened alert. His suit jacket was on straight, his posture was stiff, his face had that flat, Marine Corps parade-ground look. Behind him, an energetic bustle, like a fresh wind, stirred in the executive offices. Malone leaned over and delivered the word in an official whisper: "The man is on the move. Ten minutes."

That meant that Mayor Billy Cohen was back in the city, riding in from LaGuardia on a police helicopter. Malone always made it sound like the countdown for a combat assault.

Nevertheless, Detective Jackson sat up in his chair and checked the surface of the desk as if he was about to undergo a white-glove inspection, took one last swallow of the cold coffee in the soggy paper cup, then turned to study the file of supplicants and callers waiting for appointments with the mayor. They were lined up like suspects on the hard wooden bench outside the locked gate.

The teachers felt the gust of sudden change. They were sensible enough to realize that now they were underfoot and withdrew to find their class.

Detective Malone stepped outside the gate and went down the line, making eyeball contact with the seekers, displaying a calculated, deterrent fury. Malone always thought he could detect the hot spots. He was, as he had once been, a watchful cop on a beat. Like all good cops walking a beat, his first priority was establishing neatness and order.

Behind him, Detective Jackson could hear the pitch of phone conversations change as the business of the city shifted into a higher, more imperative gear. The mayor was five minutes away now. Detective Jackson dropped the almost-empty coffee container into a wastebasket, spilling some on the front of his gray civilian slacks. Damn! Always near the crotch! Why was that? A man could not splash any liquid without it heading like some laser-guided force to the most embarrassing part of the trousers.

Never seemed to happen to Malone, he thought, annoyed. That man always had a geometric gig line and spotless turnout. He was a marine, a plain fact that he always managed to bring out to Jackson. A combat marine who had survived Khe Sanh and expected the world to honor his service by eternally passing in review.

"What happened, your diaper break?" Malone whispered into Jackson's ear when they switched places and Jackson got up to empty the wastebasket.

Jackson bent closer to whisper back, "No, I got excited watching you walk the walk."

"The man is here," announced Connie Tufo, one of the female detectives who had assumed flanking posts at the entrance.

Jackson could see the reporters rush out of Room 9 across the rotunda to swarm around the mayor. They were like a defensive football line going after the ball, piling on the mayor with their microphones and cameras and pads. Not that they ever had a good question, Jackson thought. They asked things that were obvious or silly, or intended to provoke. They were not in the business of illumination or abetting.

Not that Detective Jackson had a high opinion of the mayor. "You'd think he had something to say," said Jackson, shaking his head.

"You mean, like the meaning of life?" said Detective Connie Tufo, who had a sharp, biting comment about everything.

"They're all assholes," said Malone, who, when he had the gate, constantly gave the boys from Room 9 a hard time. It was something left over from Vietnam. He still resented them for what he considered their treasonous disloyalty. Blamed them for the loss of the war. And so he forced them to wear their press cards, examined the pictures as if he hadn't seen them a thousand times before, and took mulish pleasure out of seeing them redden as he broke their balls.

Jackson had a more accommodating view. The reporters were not uniformly thick-witted and unsympathetic to police demands. Some were, but then there was Don Franklin, the bureau chief from *New York Newsday*. He was a slower, more thoughtful member of the press. He didn't lunge into the pack, he didn't complain about his treatment, and he didn't think his press card entitled him to anything special. Usually, Detective Jackson saw Franklin standing in the back of the hectoring mob, half turned away so that he could hear better, bent over a pad and taking notes. He did his job, and he smiled at Jackson as if they were conspirators.

Maybe they were, thought Detective Jackson. Maybe he liked Franklin simply because he was black. Lord knows there are few enough of us around in City Hall, he thought. He could count them. There was Nat Berry, the mayor's executive assistant, but he was a little shy about being too black. He slapped the hand and called you "Bro," or "Homey," but he backed off and talked Yale shit when Billy Cohen was close by. Had his nose up the man's ass. But, then, how else would he get where he was?

The mayor was outdistancing the reporters and heading for his office. Detective Jackson hit the buzzer and Malone and Tufo were there at the bottleneck, making certain that no unauthorized pests snuck in.

"How are ya," said the mayor barging through, not waiting for an answer. Nat Berry, who had been waiting for the mayor's return, came out of his own office and followed him.

Behind the doors of his office, the mayor deflated. The energy went out of him like air out of a balloon and he sank into his chair. He flung his hat and topcoat on the couch; his secretary, Bella Gertz, gathered his things without complaining and put them neatly in the closet. After putting the message slips on his desk, she left like a whisper.

"God, I hate Washington," said the mayor, who was always offended by the experience of being handled with dignified scorn. The fact that he was the chief executive officer of New York City, the cultural center of the nation, the mecca for business and capital, cut no ice on the Potomac. The national legislators treated him like another country bumpkin, a rustic, one more mayor from one more open urban sore looking for a handout.

"Washington's a nice place to visit," said Nat Berry.

The mayor looked up quickly. It was a joke. He was always astonished at the speed and subtlety of his chief aide's mind. The surprise was, of course, a measure of his racism, but he was aware of his racism and ashamed of himself for being constantly shocked at Berry's sparkling intelligence. He couldn't help either part.

Berry was a young man, not yet out of his thirties. His father and his grandfather had been doctors—a profession open in modest part to blacks. Thus, Berry belonged to that rare elite of third-generation black achievers. He was an Ivy Leaguer. Yale. He appreciated wine and food and opera and was embraced by whites, and therefore, mistrusted by the strident Afrocentrists.

But the thing that made him less than threatening to Billy Cohen was the plain fact that Nat Berry was endearingly plump. Somehow, it absolved Berry of all the alarming possibilities whites always managed to conjure up about spiteful blacks. No lean and hungry look about him. They had the wine and food in common, which was a great comfort to the lonely mayor.

"Hard time?" asked Berry, laying out the mayor's agenda on the clean desk.

"No, not really." There was a trace of exhaustion in the mayor's voice. "At least not any more than usual. You know, they wanted to know about my needs, and then they proceeded to tell me I wouldn't get them."

Berry was only half listening, trying to get the items lined up on the desk in proper order. He had been instructed to operate systematically—to deliver things to Billy Cohen in a coherent fashion—because the mayor was not a patient man.

"I hope there's nothing much today," said Cohen.

Berry scanned down his list, then looked at the stacks of municipal business: an increase in parking fines (which never helped the illegal parking problem—putting a car in a lot regularly cost as much as taking a chance on a ticket); a tax code amendment allowing an investment company more exemptions in order to keep them from moving to New Jersey; a zoning variation to prevent Donald Trump from erecting another eyesore; an executive order to jolt the police department into hiring more blacks. "This stuff can wait until tomorrow," he said.

"Fine, fine," Cohen said gratefully.

Then Berry glanced at the appointment list. "You've got a dinner tonight."

Cohen nodded grimly. There was always a dinner. Some club or charity or business group or religious sect on the make was always throwing an annual event in which he had to sit through two hours of brain-numbing speeches filled with soaring platitudes and insincere flattery, consume dried out chicken, and make a badly conceived speech of his own.

"Who?" he asked with resignation.

"St. Ann's Building Fund."

Cohen looked puzzled, then brightened. "Brooklyn?"

"Right."

"Okay. See if you can get me in and out so I can miss the other speeches. What do I say?"

Berry reached into a case and brought out a few pages of large-type printed text created by a speech writer. "Here. Just how happy you are that they're putting on a new addition, and it doesn't really hurt the public schools, and it's people like you white dogs who are the backbone of the city."

Cohen took the speech, read through it with his half-glasses. "You could deliver this better than me—especially about the white-dog shit. They'll probably think I'm white."

"Not if I'm standing next to you."

They had grown close enough to make such droll remarks

about racial differences, but increasingly the jokes left Cohen feeling uneasy. He thought Berry might be disparaging him in some cunningly coded ghetto fashion.

"What else, what else?" said Cohen, tossing the speech on his desk.

Berry sighed. Shook his head. "Just Scotto."

Cohen groaned. "What about him?"

"He has to see you." He looked at his watch. "Should be here in half an hour."

There were standing orders to pass Patsy Scotto into the inner sanctum without delay—a leftover courtesy—and Detective Jackson buzzed him through, nodding and saying, "How are you, Mr. Scotto?"

"Ten minutes from hell," replied the testy Brooklyn leader, who walked falteringly into the mayor's office, attracting only mild curiosity from the rank and file of passing pols and journalists. No one suspected a mission of any urgency. Not anymore.

He tried to make himself comfortable, but his leg hurt, his chest ached, and he was bad tempered. He waited until they were alone, and then he accepted a whiskey from Billy Cohen.

"I don't think it's a great idea, especially with your stomach," said the mayor solicitously.

Scotto waved his arm like a claw. "Listen, Billy, with my health, anything that keeps me awake is a fuckin' miracle."

Billy Cohen drank with him for the company. It was almost four in the afternoon and the mayor wanted to rest up back at Gracie Mansion before the dinner.

"I ran into the governor," said Mayor Cohen.

"Oh, yeah, how are his hemorrhoids?"

"He doesn't tell me everything," said Cohen.

"It's that Albany weather. Cold." He shivered. "Did I warn you about that? I mean, it's cold. Even for governors."

"Stop trying to charm me into it."

"I'm serious. That job keeps the proctologists employed."

Scotto was teasing gently, but letting Cohen know that he didn't approve of the Albany move.

"I've got an iron sphincter," said Cohen.

Scotto emptied the glass of whiskey, shook off a refill, and got down to the point. "Lemme ask you something. You think that Fasio's solid?"

"What do you mean?"

Scotto shook his head. "I mean everything." He held up the glass. He had changed his mind. He needed a refill. "It bothers me," he said. "Big Jim . . ."

Cohen waited. He took his time and poured the old boss another drink.

Scotto waved a hand, as if he was trying to catch something in the air. "I'm telling you, Billy, the guy doesn't seem right."

"You're not going to visit the sins of the father . . ."

Scotto was mad. "That fuckin' weasel assistant, you think he's not bent?"

"Gerber?"

"I'm not talking about Cardinal O'Connor. That little shit, Gerber, he worked for Big Jim . . ."

"I'd stake my reputation on John Fasio," said Cohen.

"Oh, you are. That's for sure."

Scotto looked sad. He couldn't tell Cohen what was really bothering him. Digging up the past. Rummaging through old scandals. Bringing back to life the unpaid blood debt.

The red phone rang. It was the hot line. "Excuse me," said Billy Cohen, leaping to pick it up. He always lunged to pick up the hot line. He expected . . . nuclear war. It was the old shock of John F. Kennedy. The bulletins. The interrupted programming. The bloody widow. It was no longer possible to see the word "bulletin" or to hear the red phone without experiencing a petrifying moment. There had been many bulletins and many shocks since then, but that was the one he raced to grab—as if he could stop it.

"This is Lieutenant Melon at PC One. We have an officer down in Harlem, Mr. Mayor."

There were standing orders for PC One—the police commissioner's command communications' network—to notify the mayor whenever a cop was shot. It was always their second call.

"Yes? What do you know?"

"Looks like a drug bust gone bad, sir."

"Undercover cop."

"Yes, sir."

"How bad?"

"Not clear yet, sir, but we don't think it's a fatal. He's red blanket to Presbyterian Hospital."

"Keep me updated."

"Yes, sir."

He hung up and gave Scotto a quick rundown of the conversation.

"Crack is gonna destroy us," said Scotto solemnly. He held up the glass for some more whiskey. "That Perot had the right idea. You rope off the neighborhood and go in with SWAT teams." He shrugged, dismissing the constitutional misgivings. "It's the only way."

Cohen laughed scornfully. "You try it. Al Sharpton'll be out with all his legions. Even I'll picket you."

"Yeah, well, fuck you. Sooner or later, people'll accept the fact that there's no other choice. You either put up or shut up."

He leaned back and drank his whiskey, and Billy Cohen could see the exhaustion in his face.

The clock said 4:05.

Scotto saw the eyes flick toward the mantel and knew the meaning. "Lemme talk to you about Fasio, Billy. I know all the good things about him. He talks to the people, whoever the hell they are, and he feels the pain, whatever the hell that is. But I got a bad feeling. He's wrong."

Cohen moved closer. A confidant. "How do you mean?"

Scotto looked around the room, as if he could find an example, as if searching for an answer. "Sometimes," he said carefully, "in this business, you just know something. It's a funny business. You go into a room with a guy and you hafta be able to tell whether or not he's a good guy or an asshole. And there's not much to go on. Some gut feeling. I got a gut feeling about this guy. Always have. He's young—I don't care about that. I like that. But, I'm tellin' ya, he's wrong."

"I like him," said Cohen, sounding unusually forceful.

Scotto smiled. *He stands up to me now that I'm breathing on one lung. In the old days my word was good enough.* He said, "What about the people on Staten Island? They don't like him."

He meant the neoconservatives of the outer boroughs who were betting on a bright new candidate, Gary Ahearn, a tough-talking former Staten Island district attorney who was pro-life, pro–death penalty, and advocated—if his speeches were any clue—putting every criminal away for life pending a trial. Ahearn was a blow-dried Dan Quayle clone. A Rush Limbaugh zealot.

Cohen shrugged. "Ahearn will fold. Listen, Patsy, Fasio's good. He has great crowd appeal. Great on issues. Great on a one-to-one basis. This guy could go really far."

Scotto put up his traffic-cop hand. "Where's he gonna get his cash? That's the real question. Where'll he be gettin' all those big bucks to put up the big fight? He's not getting it from the party. As far as I know, he doesn't have a large annuity from Big Jim. Where the fuck will the money be coming from?"

Cohen got up, paced. "I really don't know." He stopped, turned and faced Scotto. "But I believe he's honest."

"Nobody's honest. Not when that damn tickle starts and they want the office. Look, all I'm suggesting is that you be careful. You wanna know a lot more about him before we toss away your reputation."

Cohen rolled things over in his mind. "Are you gonna oppose him? At the fund-raiser, I got the impression you were on board."

Scotto finished the last of the drink and put down the glass deliberately and asked, "Where's he getting his money?"

It was a good question, and Cohen didn't really know. Scotto could see in his eyes that he didn't know, and that was what he had come to find out.

The red phone rang and it was Lieutenant Melon at PC One again. "The cop died," he said.

"How?"

"He bled to death. Internal bleeding."

The mayor hit the panic button, which was located on the inside of his desk drawer. Nat Berry came in from a hidden door on the side of the mayor's office. Detectives Jackson, Tufo, and Malone at the gate cleared the lobby so that the mayor could make a clean, quick exit. A policeman killed in the line of duty required a visit from the mayor. It was more than a sign of respect—it was a commitment.

The mayor's driver, Detective Donald Fine, was down in the basement security office having a cup of coffee when a lieutenant took the call from upstairs. He sent Detective Fine out running to start up the official limousine.

Scotto left City Hall as he had arrived—almost unnoticed. In the flurry of ceremonial disquiet, he walked a little faster to get out of the way, and because he had things to do.

11

I T WAS NOT something that she dwelled on—or even considered worthwhile—but Bonnie Hudson shone on the air. She
was one of those rare people who glowed with a noticeable and
appealing intensity in the eye of the television lens. And when
she spoke, the words spilled out of her mouth in bright arcs of
light. She was a natural.

"So, what we can expect tomorrow is a blast of very chilly
air and some wet stuff with it, which will cause the ever-baffling
subway tie-up. No one knows how this happens, since the
weather takes place, on the whole, outdoors. Subways do not.
One of nature's mysteries. It just happens. Along with the customary highway flooding, which will cause the predictable back-
ups and a flare-up of tempers. However, it's not all grim. There
will be a long, cozy weekend for those of you struck by sudden
traffic congestion and mass transit flu."

There was a momentary lull as the rest of the staff waited for
the next little candle.

"Thank you, Bonnie, that was very enlightening," said Jerry
Kantor, the anchor, in a starched and disapproving tone.

"Hey, it's only weather!" said Bonnie Hudson with a casual
flip of her shoulder toward the map, which was winter-soggy
with displays of rain and sleet.

There was a pause. Jerry Kantor bid the audience good night on behalf of himself and the staff, and then there was a long, rolling silence in which the camera lingered on the staff, and people watching felt the weight of a million eyes. And then the red eye on the camera blinked and went out.

"Okay! We're off the air," said the voice from the control room. "Nice broadcast, folks. Bonnie, you are one noisy warm front."

That was Jerry Kantor's signal. He had been sitting impatiently in the anchor chair, chewing on his lip and puffing himself into something close to active indignation over Bonnie Hudson's seemingly indifferent delivery of the weather report. Kantor regarded himself as a father figure on the set, being the senior anchor, and thought that a good talking-to might bring Bonnie around to his no-nonsense approach to the job. He wanted his news segment—and he thought of the news segment as his—to be an island of grave and solid information in the television sea of frivolity. He wanted a professional newscast.

Jerry Kantor was genuinely perplexed by all the glib and glitzy turns that television journalism had taken during his twenty-year career in the business. He had been trained to believe that television news was serious business and should be approached with deep respect—to be performed more or less without humor, like an undertaker. Which is why his manner—a kind of gut-wrenching concentration on street battles, toxic waste, and political abuse—was alarming to the viewers, who preferred something more glimmering and reassuring. He didn't know that his ponderous earnestness had set in motion a clock on his career.

"Bonnie," he said, reaching for the pipe he kept in his jacket pocket, "could I talk to you?" He had the look in his eye—the one Bonnie had seen in lay preachers blinded by their pious and fervent vision. In spite of everything, there was something likable, or at least faintly charming, about Jerry Kantor. It was, she supposed, his guileless zeal.

"Sure, Jer," she said lightly. She was in a fine mood, now that she had gotten permissions from Thatch Conway and Harvey Levy to go out and report, as long as it didn't interfere with her job as a weather forecaster. Conway was so pleased with the uptick in the ratings and Bonnie's robust reception by viewers that he had even authorized a police press card in her name. The only thing Bonnie had to find now was a good story to cover.

The television studios had the murky, unfinished atmosphere of a theater backstage. Props and lights and bits of furniture were scattered in the shadows. Voices echoed from the balconies. Nothing seemed settled or permanent. There was a brightly lit lounge off the main dressing rooms where the staff took their coffee breaks and consumed their brown-bag lunches. It was a glassed-in room with no place to rest—all white walls and sterile art with stiff plastic chairs and cold Formica tables and chemical snacks out of colossal vending machines. Even the trash was kept at an antiseptic distance. The bin was lined with a heavy-duty plastic bag, which was at the moment stuffed with discarded wrappers of candy and cookies. The lounge reminded Bonnie of a lifeless spacecraft or an operating room.

She let Jerry fetch her tea; it came out of a machine and into a paper cup that bent in from the heat and steam. A little liquid spilled on his hand, and he flinched. He put the pipe in his mouth, but there was no tobacco in the bowl.

Kantor was a tall man with angular features. He had spent many hours gazing into mirrors, contemplating the twists and interesting edges; in spite of that, he had come to no definite conclusion about himself. He had, at the age of forty-six, decided that nature had bestowed upon him a magnificent visage. He felt that he should try to live up to his face.

"You know," he said chuckling, pulling his chair closer to Bonnie, "your weather segment is really quite . . . uh, . . . cute. Really."

"Thanks," she said.

"No, no, I mean that," he said.

"Of course you do."

He paused and looked at Bonnie. She spoke in such convo-
luted coils of meaning that he never knew when she was being
sincere or when she was humoring him.

"Well, I do believe that," he insisted.

"I know. That's what I said."

He was again at a loss.

"Okay. But, now, don't take this the wrong way . . ."

"I'll try."

There it was again. He squinted, his on-camera, determined
diligent look. So hard to puzzle this one out.

"Bonnie, I think we could turn this broadcast around if we
all pitch in together."

"I see."

He brightened. "Do you? Do you really?"

"Yes, of course. You want us to be on the same page of the
playbook."

"Exactly." He was relieved.

"You want me to pitch in."

"I wouldn't want to pressure you."

"Not at all. After all, this is a family. A team. We're all in this
together."

"You do believe that, don't you?"

"No."

"I didn't think so."

She shook her head, then asked, "By pitching in, do you
mean, like having everyone over to dinner? Or, maybe we all do
high fives after the show? Or are you suggesting I start some kind
of softball league?"

He laughed. She was joking. He was almost certain. He took
the unlit pipe out of his mouth and held it.

"No, what I had in mind was that we do a more conventional
style of weather forecast. You know, tell about the highs and the
lows and the pressure systems. Use the satellite pictures—that's

what they're there for—and the moving clouds and then tell the audience what they all mean."

"You think they really want to know?"

Whenever Jerry Kantor wanted to sound wise, or, at least, deeper than usual, his speech took on a slightly British tone. It was not something he was conscious of doing—in the same way that he was not fully cognizant of turning away from the camera and presenting his best profile to his audience—but out came the Empire, all the same, whenever he was trying to impress anyone.

"Oh, yes. I do. I like to see the explanation. And the way you do it—well, it's very amusing. I'm told that our viewers enjoy it and the ratings are improving. But, you know, dear, it's not really a proper weather report, is it?"

"Actually, I believe that it is," replied Bonnie, unconsciously mocking his Britishisms. "I deliver all the usual weather facts and trivia. Temperature. Expectations. Consequences. If you'll examine the segment closely, you'll see that I really do everything that the other weather people do. You may be put off by my so-called style. Frankly, so am I. I happen to take the weather very seriously. Very seriously! You'd be surprised. But, Jerry, I really do do the weather, if you catch my drift."

Then she felt a little mean and bent closer to try and make it clear to him. "Look, Jer, I do the best that I can. Really, I do. But, frankly, I hate the weather. I've never been very fond of it. Knowing about it, I mean. Knowing too much. Rain and snow—I like to be surprised. Go outside and there it is—a fresh fall of snow, all crisp and new. That's what I like.

"But, you know, I'm getting out of it. I don't do this, not really. I'm not in it just for the thumping. I'm not just gonna stick to the weather. I have my eye on other things."

He was dazzled and slightly suspicious. She was going on like a madwoman. Could it be pills? "Yes," he said ambiguously.

She raced ahead. "Thatch said that I could cover regular stories. I even got a press card."

She held up the white laminated card shaped like a police shield. It had her picture on it.

He was shocked. To Jerry Kantor, there was a system and order in the television world. A weathergirl should not put her finger in other pies. It violated his sense of the fitness of things. "So, you'll be doing regular stories, like upbeat features about people and their hobbies? That sort of thing?"

"God, I hope not. No, the truth is, I wanna go out and sink my teeth into a real juicy story. I was once a pretty good police reporter, you know. Covered murders and crime and politics and the Mafia. For *Newsday.*"

"Of course." He was horrified. He didn't believe a word.

"I'm not kidding!" she said, not surprised that he didn't know her reputation. "I won some awards, for Christ's sake!"

He had stopped listening and was trying to think of ways of steering her back on course. He had suggestions. "What about using, you know, those little magnetic characters like they have on the other weather segments. You know, cartoons of you in, say, rain gear, or snow shoes?"

"Jerry!" she said flatly.

"Why not?"

She saw that this was not a profitable path to follow. Jerry Kantor had limitations: to him, news came in over teletype wires from distant points, and how it got onto the wires in the first place was a complete mystery. Jerry had not spent time in police shacks listening to radio calls and chasing fires. He was a television reporter and had spent his youth reading sports results. As far as stories were concerned, he would never touch one until it had become an official version.

"I think the cartoons are very warm—humanizing," he said. "You see all the others doing it—Willard, Storm, Scott, Al . . . they all do it. It's just a nice little touch that amuses the viewers."

She looked at him for a long moment, causing him to squirm. Then she said coldly, "What if I suggested, for example, that you wear a fire hat when reporting on a big blaze? Or a police helmet for a big arrest or a shootout?"

He scrunched his face, an indication that he was deep in thought. He was considering it. A fire helmet. A police hat. To Jerry Kantor, it was worth considering, unless, of course, it damaged his image.

She took the idea away from him. "No, Jerry, I am afraid that I won't do that. I want to do some serious work."

He reached across the table and took her hand. At first she flinched, then realized that it was his father-figure acting, and relaxed. "You know, Bonnie, this station is having a very tough time, economically. We are picking up, thank God, but there is a recession on and the revenues are down, and unless we get some help, we will be sold. I've been at some stations that have changed ownership abruptly. It's not pretty."

She nodded. She didn't give a damn about the station's finances. That was Thatch Conway's worry. As long as he met the payroll, she was content. Her duty was to find a story. She needed a good table-thumper, and she was going out to Queens to find one. She had worked the police courts on Queens Boulevard when she was a reporter for *Newsday*. She should be able to find something out there.

The homefront was sapping John Fasio's energy. He had thought that bringing his mother into his house would be a simple mathematical procedure. He would add a single person to a ten-room house in which both he and Irma rattled around in lonely solitude, and the addition would fill the cracks. It was a small addition, he thought. All to the good. Someone else for Irma to fuss over. He hoped that it would relieve the pressure. But it had the opposite effect. Celia's arrival seemed to compress everything. Home life became like one of those nightmares in which a trick room collapsed and squeezed and crushed everyone inside. Two of them alone were not enough to fill the void left by their dead son, but the addition of a third person was suffocating.

They brushed against each other lightly in the passage of their daily lives, leaving deep emotional welts and passionate bruises. And it fell to him to be the mediator of all the petty disputes.

"She won't let me in the kitchen," said Celia, speaking of his wife.

"Well, Ma, it is her kitchen."

That was a mistake. He saw the look that crossed her face. Shock. Pain. Confusion. His mistake. He thought that they were talking about the kitchen, but the subject was something far more sensitive and far less within his grasp.

"Lemme talk to her," he said, tenderly.

"No," said Celia, deflated.

"I'll explain . . ."

"No! No."

They spoke in half-finished sentences, as if by starting to speak, they had lit dangerous fuses that burned themselves out before reaching the explosive conclusion.

"She doesn't . . . ," and the latest grievance or insult trailed away.

"How about I get you a VCR for your room?"

"I can't even get the cable."

"There's no cable."

"What're you talking about? I always get the cable. The MTV, the TNT, the old movies . . ."

"That was at the home, Mom. In Westchester. We don't have cable hookups in Queens."

"That's crazy! I need the cable."

His mother was beyond his reach. She drifted between coherence and frustration like some lost traveler. "Your father liked my pasta sauce," she said, returning to the kitchen issue.

"We all like your pasta sauce," replied Fasio. "Thing is, Ma, that Irma was making something . . ."

He saw the anger. She was the mother. She had parental rights! She didn't remember yesterday's heartache at the Golden Years home. Only today's sorrow. Nobody wanted a housekeeper, a stranger, in the house.

"You have to do something about your mother," Irma would say late at night as they both lay in the dark, sleepless with the predicament.

"You got any suggestions?"

She wept. That was her suggestion.

"Irma! What can I do?! She's my mother."

She pulled away. "I want to go to Rome," she said.

In the aftermath of their son's death Irma had become spiritually enslaved. She mumbled prayers and went to mass daily and visited the gravesite of their son weekly, where she sobbed openly for an hour. It was not enough. A belief had taken root in her mind that if only she saw the Pope, if she was blessed by His Holiness, it would start some healing process.

"We can't go now," he said of the trip. "Christ, I'm running for mayor!"

As she lay in her furious silence, he could sense her reproach. His ambition stood between her and the pilgrimage. Stood between them. Far into the night and on into the early morning, when they fell asleep from sheer exhaustion, she cursed him in silence.

He had no choice. He was running for office. It had been decided after he pulled his mother out of the home in Westchester County. That very next day, he had complained about the home to the county social service supervisors and had been treated with delicate scorn. As if he was trying to bully overburdened and virtuous agencies with his puny political clout. The Golden Years home had a good reputation, said the high-ranking Westchester County official in a brittle voice, then he hung up.

That last act was the thing that settled it. Wounded pride. He could afford another home, a better home, but he wanted revenge. He had Murray to take care of the money. But what about all the poor souls who didn't have an executive assistant to manage the $200-a-day financing necessary for a decent residential home? he asked himself in a fury of self-justification. He would take care of the people without means when he achieved higher office. That would be his first priority. Plus feed the hungry and shelter the homeless and comfort the afflicted. In his way, he was not so different from Irma in taking comfort along desperate spiritual lines.

John Fasio managed to convince himself that he had nothing but pure and noble motives for seeking the mayoralty. It was an easy case to make, now that he had perfected his pragmatic arguments. It was an old trick. Murray Gerber had come into his life to arrange his affairs, to balance his checkbooks, to smooth the rough going. A matter of arithmetic. Just turn your finances over to me, Murray had said after the boy's death when he saw the lopsided balance sheets and unpaid bills. The other part of the bargain was that he couldn't ask too many questions. All he had to do was to open a checking account. Once or twice a month he handed Murray a check—$500 here, $1000 there—and instructed him to pay the vacation package, the car payment, whatever. He would ask, "Is there enough money in the sludge account to cover my mother's home?" Murray would always nod and say, "Plenty." It never ran short. But asking—"Is there enough?"—gave his numbed conscience an easy exit.

Finally, Fasio stopped asking questions about the checking account that acted like a circus car full of clowns. He slid into the warm water of Murray's comfortable management. He didn't get out of the car in the morning to make certain that the coffee was paid for. He had too many appointments to keep, too many legislative packages to read, too many calls to take to have time to handle the financing of his mother's care, his home, or the campaign. He told himself that an important political leader had to delegate the everyday care-and-feeding responsibilities to assistants, people like Murray Gerber. And if he knew, somewhere deep in a shriveling memory of scruples, that he was sitting with his eyes shut in the passenger seat of a runaway career, he refused to dwell on it. Better to get angry at Patsy Scotto for holding a grudge against his innocent dead father.

Fasio raced through his morning routine. The exercise. The healthy breakfast. The nagging. The complaints. The futile attempt to establish a ceasefire. It had become a relief to go to work early and stay late. He couldn't wait to escape the bitter silences and strangled complaints.

"We got a problem," said Murray Gerber as they headed for lunch at the Pastrami King across from the Borough Hall on Queens Boulevard. Fasio had spent the morning assuring the Democratic club leaders that if he became mayor, he would remember his first loyalty: his home borough. He had been on the phone, had met some in the office, and had sent out little handwritten notes to keep them calm. Political shifts invariably caused tremors and aftershocks and worry, and it was the business of a political leader to quiet the waters. Fasio was good at that sort of thing. He told small ribald jokes and guaranteed the standing of the local leaders; he had the gift of sounding sincere.

"What's the problem?"

"You got the dinner. It's all set. It's fully subscribed. That's good."

"So, what's the problem?"

They were on a traffic island, halfway across the boulevard. Lunch-hour traffic was swift and unforgiving. They were between corners; they waited for a break in the flow.

"The problem is, there's only about $100,000 in the bank."

Fasio laughed. "That doesn't sound like a big problem. A hundred big ones." He laughed heartily. "That could be Irma's trip to Rome with Paris thrown in."

Gerber took the unlit cigar out of his mouth and looked his boss in the eye. "John, we're talking about a big-time campaign. A hundred thousand buys you one storefront office," he said over the crash of the traffic. "That does not get you into any kind of major-league municipal race."

There was a crack in the traffic and Gerber ran ahead. Fasio followed. He had always thought of money in terms of paying the mortgage, buying groceries, taking a trip to Rome. Little bites of a few thousand dollars to pay bills, to fend off creditors. He still was not thinking of it in great chunks of hard cash. Yet he'd told Cohen and Scotto he'd raise fifteen million.

Running for office the usual way was easy. The party took care of such things. That was the way it worked. If the party endorsed you, the party organized the campaign. He had vague, imprecise knowledge of the details. Budgets were fixed, goals were set, the usual contributors were tapped for the ever-increasing donations. Money was there when needed.

But this time it was different. He wasn't running for office yet, and he was campaigning over Patsy Scotto's head. He had to prove to Scotto that he was a serious candidate and that meant raising serious money. A couple of million, say. Once he had that, he could expect help. But not until then. Scotto was not ready to help him. And Scotto held the party purse strings.

Fasio felt Scotto's animosity. He told himself that it was a grudge based on a competitive foundation—one borough leader against another. A lion in winter defending his den against youth. But that didn't convince him. It must be Big Jim, he told himself. Scotto still holds my father's punishment against me. That's when he got angry.

My father was innocent!

First things first. If he was going to run for mayor, he had to raise a lot of money. As Fasio sat in the Pastrami King wolfing down the sour pickles that Moe the waiter placed in front of him as soon as he saw him, he had no idea how he was going to manage it. Such things were done through dinners and fund-raisers. He knew that people passed checks in secret handshakes, but exactly how to arrange it . . . how to suggest it . . . how to make it known

. . . of that he was ignorant. The technique required a burglar's skills. There would be debts incurred, favors owed, obligations assumed. He knew that much. Businessmen, civic leaders, clubs . . . all these he would have to contact, and make his pitch. It was a dirty, sordid business, but it could be done. He was certain of that.

Down went another pickle as Moe rushed to the table, sweating with his plates of food and armload of beer. He tried to shift his attention to his lunch. He'd been looking forward to it.

Murray would know how to go about it. Murray knew the ins and outs of everything. Fasio started to relax.

He ate his six-inch-thick corned-beef sandwich without tasting it. He dipped the fried potatoes in the ketchup and inhaled them one after another. He emptied the beer in large swallows.

Gerber watched and took his little nibbles, allowing the borough president to absorb the implications of what it would take to raise lots of money. Sooner or later, Gerber knew, Fasio would have to turn the job over to someone who knew how to use the government machinery as leverage. Murray Gerber.

12

T HE OLD BUICK LeSabre coughed and sputtered and growled as Jack Mann mashed and tickled and hammered the gas pedal. He almost laughed. The car was like an old dog, taking on the mood and mannerisms of its master. Usually, the Buick was a good-natured, lazy old mutt, dozing along parkways or snoozing in the garage. But at the moment, it was acting like a mean junkyard mongrel, snarling and nipping at the rear bumpers of every other vehicle on the road. Which is pretty much how Jack felt after a bad morning with Tommy Holman.

"You okay?" asked Jerry Bandolino, who was being whipped back and forth in the passenger seat as Jack punched the car through heavy traffic. They were heading west on Northern Boulevard toward Manhattan, under the thunder and flickering sunlight coming down through the slats of the overhead train tracks.

"Me? I'm great," said Jack, scattering a file of pedestrians. "Why, is there something wrong with my driving, too?"

Taking a tongue-lashing from Tommy Holman was one thing, but criticism from Bandolino was too much. He knew that Bandolino had heard the uproar through the closed door of Tommy's office earlier that morning. Not that Bandolino would have speculated about the substance of the fight. Bosses fight. That's as much as Bandolino knew. That's all he wanted to know. That and the fact that they signed the paycheck. Period.

In fact, Bandolino's name had figured prominently in the argument. It began just before they'd started out to shadow Murray Gerber again. Tommy took Jack into the private office and said, in his flat, sarcastic voice, that he didn't want a repetition of last week's screwup. This time, Jack couldn't blow the surveillance. Tommy had not forgiven Jack for leaving Bandolino behind when he went to follow Murray Gerber alone. He blamed Jack. When Jack pointed out the tactical difficulties— that, in fact, if he had waited for his partner to come back with his hero sandwich, he would have lost Gerber anyway—Tommy just shook his head. He stuck a cigar in his mouth and said that Jack should never have let his partner go for lunch in the first place.

The worst part of Holman's insulting lecture was that he was right. Jack agreed with him. That's what made it impossible to swallow and why Jack fought so hard against accepting it. Jack offered a pathetic defense. "Yeah, you wanna try comin' between Bandolino and a meal?"

But even as he said it, he felt low. He was not only supporting a weak position, he was being disloyal to his partner. Not that he was developing more than a kind of pet affection for the hulking ex-cop. Still, a partner was a partner and you didn't sell him out to save your own ass. But it was too late. Tommy sensed a moral crack in Jack's case. "He would have listened to you," said Tommy finally, irrefutably, with a whiff of insufferable virtue.

Again, the smug son of a bitch was right, thought Jack. Bandolino had accepted Jack's seniority. He would have obeyed an order.

"Jesus!" said Bandolino as Jack turned the wheel of the car quickly, swerved, and briskly peeled away from the embarrassing chaos he had created at the intersection.

He was acting crazy. He knew better. He blinked and eased up on the gas.

"So, Jerry, you go out with a pension?"

Bandolino was holding the front strap with a white-knuckled grip. His face was pale.

"Huh?" He was not prepared for the nonchalant mood shift.

"When you left the job, you take a pension?"

Bandolino shook his head no, but said, "Yeah, disability. Fifty percent."

"Disability!" said Jack, nodding.

"I got shot."

"No shit?!"

"Yeah, I was cleaning my gun. The foot."

Jack nodded. Cop sympathy. Accidents happen. Work with weapons and some percentage of guys are gonna shoot themselves in the foot. Especially the ones who are a little clumsy, or, even more prosaic, a little afraid of the gun. That was a big thing about being a cop. You had to conquer the gun.

He remembered training at the police academy; the day they got the gun was a dramatic turning point in everyone's life. They were no longer civilians. The gun made the critical difference. It conferred upon them nothing less than the power of life and death. It was a decisive transformation.

That first day with the gun, he rode home to Queens in a car with three other police recruits. Boys, really, just out of their teens, and wide-eyed with the sudden shock of power. All the way across the Queensboro Bridge and through the streets of Queens, he turned the weapon over in his hands. He ran his fingers across the smooth, unyielding metal surfaces, felt a tingle as he listened to the decisive mechanical click of metal striking metal, gazed into the black, bottomless pit of the barrel, waiting for it to erupt in his face. Had shivering visions of fire and death. He would later wonder what the passing strangers in other cars thought that day in Queens when they saw the bright-eyed young men in the car all fondling brand-new pistols, their faces shining with excitement.

He went straight to his room when he got home and spent the rest of the day playing with the gun. He touched it and held it and watched himself in the mirror as he aimed it, wielded it, saw how he looked, judged this new image. He opened the box of bullets and his hand shook when he loaded and unloaded the gun, getting the feel and heft of the weight. And then he did something almost undefinable. He put the barrel in his mouth, not so much a sexual thing, although there was a grain of that lurking somewhere, but saying, in effect, I am not afraid of you, gun!

One day in a locker room he heard someone else admit that he had gone over the same ground—conquered the gun by putting it in his mouth. It seemed that everyone did it. A common thing, a rite of passage, a denial of the weapon's potency. Otherwise you couldn't carry it on your hip for the rest of your professional life. It was too much lethal power to be worn so casually! It was bound to take a toll.

"I was home, and the wife was out," said Bandolino. He shrugged.

Jack remembered now. Bandolino had been married and his wife had run off with another cop. One day he came home and she was gone and he tried to eat the gun. Only he missed, or maybe just dropped it and ate up a toe. It was a famous story for a while, but because Bandolino was such a pale, dull character, the story did not attach itself to his name. It became just another cautionary police tale told in squad cars after midnight when cops told each other ghost stories: this is what happens when you're out defending the citizens—your wife runs around with another guy. Another cop woe.

They were a tribe. Cops knew what other cops knew. They passed the legends along around the campfire of the crackling police radio in the night as they huddled against the shadows. They had all that, as well as the gun and the last resort of the bottomless barrel in common. And so there was always a last-ditch secret sympathy for another cop.

Of course Jack had further reasons. He had the fresh wound of Bonnie's loss. And she was everywhere. No matter how fiercely he tried to fight her off, he could never completely escape. Every night she was there on television to remind him (and everyone else in the tristate area) to wear an extra sweater or bring along an umbrella. Every night, he was reminded of the spools of charm he knew firsthand when her mood spilled out on camera, witnessed the same spitfire temper when the jocks in the sports department tried to belittle her gender and she displayed her upper-body strength by a scathing quip. And every night, there was her complicated smile and jaunty signoff: "Hey, it's only weather!" It always felt like a kiss. A lost love on television never went away; there was another rerun every night. And so he had the country-blues heartbreak music in common with Bandolino, too.

"How's it now?" he asked.

Bandolino looked down, although he couldn't see his foot. "I still limp a little," he said.

Traffic had bottled up at the entrance to the bridge. Jack rolled skillfully through the gaps. There was a tow truck ahead and Jack fell in behind it. He got past the fender bender that had slowed the movement. A weary-looking cop handling traffic at the scene recognized, not specifically Jack or Bandolino, but the scent of the police fraternity, and waved them through.

Jack experienced a feeling of relief, almost like a fresh breath of air, as they rolled over the stammering metal grillwork of the bridge and into the vivid heart of Manhattan. He knew just where to find the target, and he wasn't going to let Bandolino run off to get lunch.

Murray Gerber was too lowly in the political scheme of things to be counted as a significant visitor to Channel 9. He arrived unnoticed. Just one more guy among the many wide-eyed pilgrims who came to see for themselves the glamorous inner workings of television. There was a tour and he trailed behind, then announced himself to the guard at the executive elevator. As he waited for the car, he watched the tour group march on, saw the faces of the visitors light up, then sag a bit when they passed a familiar soap opera star. The stars were always smaller in person. Learning the secrets of magic invariably left the audience a little sad and a little deflated. Reality was always so puny.

He arrived like a spy, which he was, but an up-to-date, modern spy. And like a modern spy, Murray Gerber hid in plain sight. That was what you did in the brazen nineties.

Still, the meeting—latent with possibilities on both sides—had to be conducted delicately.

Harvey Levy was waiting for him in an executive dining suite on the twelfth floor. Levy had reserved it. There were drinks and ice at the bar and a tray of sandwiches on a table, but no one to serve, no one to disturb or eavesdrop on their conversation.

Gerber saw the uncertain impression he made in the reflection of Levy's eyes. Such a small, rumpled man—how could he control a huge undertaking? That was always Gerber's impact on people, and that was precisely what made him so effective. It was an intentional diversion.

There was an instant aversion on both sides. Gerber could feel it in the air.

"So, I hear that your man is going to be the next mayor." It was a declaration, not a question.

Gerber laughed. "My man is terrific," he said with imperfectly suppressed pride. He shrugged. "The truth is, he's going wherever he wants to go. I can guarantee that."

"Actually," said Harvey Levy, turning to smile at Murray Gerber, "so is mine. Drink?"

The exchange did not break the stuffy atmosphere. Each thought the other coarse, insubstantial, unworthy. Levy poured himself a scotch and water and another for Gerber and they sat in soft comfortable chairs looking out of the window. A barge moved up the river, the cargo covered by a large canvas sheet. Cars crossed the George Washington Bridge and a helicopter owned by a radio station swooped up and down, monitoring traffic, issuing up-to-the-minute bulletins on tie-ups. They could hear nothing in the room except the gentle rattle of ice and their own anxious, heavy breathing.

It was a lavishly expensive room, with oil paintings of ships hanging on the deep, dark wooden walls; thick, rich carpets on the floor; and flowers billowing out of porcelain vases. And yet there was a sterility to it that suggested it was better empty, without people. Gerber could detect no one's hand in the decor. It was an executive room to suit any executive. A handsome, though transient, throne.

Levy asked offhandedly, "How is it going? I mean the campaign."

Gerber's eyes rose to the frosted ceiling. "It's not really a campaign, you know. Not formally." He shrugged.

Levy wanted more, was trying to extract information, feeling his way along the muddy bottom of unknown waters. But Gerber was an expert in evasion.

"You were a cop?" Levy asked.

"And you were a newspaper hound."

Levy nodded happily. "True. Too true. An inkstained wretch. Born on deadline." He glanced over to see if this was making any impression at all; Gerber was peering into the bottom of his glass. "I guess I'm feeling just a little nostalgic," said Levy. He looked at the dwindling liquid in his own glass. "The liquor."

Gerber nodded. "Yes, well, I do see. I, too, have a profession. In fact, I still see myself as a policeman."

"Do you?" Levy said with a touch of scorn.

Gerber nodded and held up his glass for a refill. Levy topped both glasses again. "A policeman," said Levy. "They say once a cop, always a cop."

"They do."

"Why is that, do you suppose?"

Gerber thought about that, staring through the whiskey at the light. "I believe being a policeman—being a good police-man—is a gift," he said, inviting Levy's derision.

"A gift? You mean, like something conferred from on high?"

Gerber nodded. "A natural thing. By nature, I mean that a natural-born policeman has an uncluttered knowledge of what's right and what's wrong."

"By nature? He comes by this 'gift' naturally?"

Gerber nodded slowly. "That's what I believe. It's the only way. The laws they write on paper are only attempts to capture the things we know by nature." He snatched at something in the air. "Like catching an insect in flight."

Levy laughed out loud. Gerber smiled. Something was dissolving between them.

"Of course, having the uncluttered knowledge does not mean you will always act according to the strict written rules."

Levy slapped him on the knee.

"I tell you, we are blessed to have had—even for a little while—an honorable occupation," said Levy. "You know, I can almost see your point. Once I was an honest newspaperman, earning an honest dollar. Now I am the ringmaster for a whole tent of television clowns. I seem like the man I was then, but, of course, I've grown up. I have an uncluttered view of what a real journalist should be doing, but it's simply not possible any longer. Yes, I see what you're talking about."

"It's a hard thing," said Gerber, bending closer to his new friend. "I was once a true guardian of the people. I kept the streets safe." He shook his head.

Levy nodded emphatically. "And now?" he asked.

Gerber shrugged and smiled. "No longer possible."

They sighed and drained their glasses again.

"So, how does Mr. Conway like America?"

Gerber saw that Levy understood the meaning, the backing away of plain talk. After all, he should grasp the fact that Gerber was a man who made a living by extracting raw confessions from handy felons. To him, words were instruments, like hammers and spikes. He was going to be careful how he struck one against another. "He doesn't miss England? His citizenship? His wife?"

"He loves it here," replied Levy. "The openness. The freedom. So much opportunity. Of course, he's still getting used to our laws."

Gerber nodded, held the glass for a refill. "Yes, it's different in England. D-notices and government-run stations."

It was not possible for Gerber to know if Levy was in a position to negotiate for Thatch Conway. But he had to assume that he was the designated intermediary, just as Levy had to assume that Murray Gerber was operating with the consent of the borough president. Still, if they spoke to each like men advancing out on very thin ice, a growing confidence—bolstered by the liquor—was developing between them. They gazed out of the window overlooking the Hudson River, taking another measure of each other, like sailors re-shooting the stars for a fresh longitudinal and latitudinal fix. Gerber couldn't tell about Levy. There was an air of authority about him, and the gist of common sense in his voice.

"He has great expectations," said Levy of Conway.

Gerber nodded. "Yes, well, so has my man. Great expectations. Wasn't that an English book?"

"Dickens."

"What?"

"Charles Dickens. He wrote *Great Expectations.*"

"Movie."

Both men were thinking at blazing speed while speaking in mincing little steps. By now they were enjoying themselves.

The sandwiches were stale, but Gerber didn't mind. He nibbled at the smoked salmon on white bread without crusts.

"You see how much Perot spent on paid media?" he asked, putting a toe out to listen for a crack.

"A great sum," replied Levy.

Gerber shook his head. "They really should reform the system," he said. "All that money."

Levy laughed. "It pays my salary. But there's a lot of room for reform."

"Well, there's reform and there's reform. We have a broadcast television system that used to work well. Now cable, that's a different thing."

This was the business end of the meeting. This was why Murray Gerber had risked exposure and compromised his safety to come here: this was his great opportunity. Cable television, he had seen, was a ripe fruit. Everyone was clamoring for cable—he had even heard a Slavic youth say during a man-in-the-street interview in Hungary that the reason he wanted the Cold War to end was so that he could get MTV. It was now being spliced into Budapest, but the outer boroughs of New York City still didn't have it.

There were so many operators, and so fuzzy were the jurisdictional boundaries, that applications were bounced between Washington, Albany, and City Hall. And still nothing got done. Because of the federal deregulation that kicked in during the Reagan era, the operators of Manhattan's cable systems had incrementally jacked up rates and were getting rich on the pay-per-view movies, sporting events, and old black-and-whites. These seemingly boundless profits only whetted the appetites of the operators for the outer borough franchises.

Only the franchises were in a kind of political gridlock. The Federal Communications Commission had only a distant supervisory role, and couldn't mediate the conflict. After all, Reagan and Bush were dedicated believers in letting the marketplace set the prices and terms for business. That left it up to the state to decide on the operator. But the New York bureau of franchises granted licenses based on the recommendations of municipalities, and New York City was a jungle of competing interests. The municipal interests were salivating over the lucrative franchises. While citizens' groups pleaded and whined to have some system—any system—installed the cable operators lobbied and pushed to influence the local watchdog agencies. Sitting on the local watchdog agencies were local politicians who found during the long dispute that they never had to worry about campaign financing. There were always generous contributions from would-be cable operators. And so it served the interests of the politicians—some of whom even held stock in some cable operations—to delay and dither over granting a cable franchise.

In Queens, John Fasio had decisive leverage over which company would wire the borough. He appointed the members of the watchdog agency, he had a powerful vote of his own, and he could, by a series of administrative fakes and drives, push one application along and bury another.

Thatch Conway wanted a cable franchise in Queens.

Levy leaned over the table and whispered, "Let's cut the bullshit."

Gerber smiled. "Have a cigar." He pulled two slim cigars from his inside pocket.

"My guy is very impressed by your guy," Levy said, sucking on the cigar. "He thinks he should be mayor."

"Well, there are two million people in Queens," Gerber said, leaning back in his chair. "We have to consider their interests. My guy always has the interests of the public uppermost in his mind. He thinks it's criminal that it's taking so long to bring cable TV to his home borough. His own mother can't watch a movie."

Levy nodded, pondered, then said meaningfully, "Mr. Conway was telling me only today that it was a shame that even the best candidates had to build up a big campaign chest to run for high office."

"Nothing like a good cigar to cut through the bullshit," Gerber said.

Bonnie came tumbling out of the cab and landed in Jack's arms. Her heel had caught in her long scarf. He grabbed her just before she fell onto the cold sidewalk in front of the Channel 9 studio.

"You know," she said, looking up in his half-smiling face, "I have a sneaking suspicion that you engineered that."

"Yeah, well, I was tired of me falling for you," he said. "The tough part was keeping a straight face while I waited."

The security guard had come out of the building by then and was looking skeptically at Jack, who continued to hold Bonnie in his arms.

She was early, and they went for coffee at the diner across the street from the station. As they sat together, old juices stirred. At the same time, old hesitations closed off any chance of a natural conversation. They had left Bandolino outside watching the studio building.

"You're doing great," he said, unable to swallow.

"You look awful," she replied.

"Well . . . it's only a lingering symptom of grief. Just another drive-by regret."

"Jack!"

"Sorry, sorry! No grief. I'm great. Better off. Do not miss the pantyhose in the tub, the quest for authentic French-roast coffee. Not a thing."

"Good," she said, smiling hugely. "Glad to hear it."

"Yes, I'm even working. That guy outside"—he indicated the jumpy Bandolino—"is there to help me."

"Do what?" she said, looking at the size of his partner. "Contract killings?"

"No, he gives me my medication, prevents me from leaping off tall buildings . . ."

"Cut the shit, Jack!" She was angry, getting up.

He took her arm and reassured her. "Okay, okay. I didn't know you'd be here. I mean it. I know you work here—hard to avoid that—but I'm on a job."

She sat, smoothed her gloves, and finally looked up. "What's the job?"

"I can't tell you."

Just then, Murray Gerber left the building, and Jack threw five dollars on the table, took one last liquid look at Bonnie, and started after him. He wasn't going to lose him again.

Bonnie watched Jack go. Cops, she thought. There was something eternally fierce about them. Something . . . and then she saw who it was that he was following. Why would Jack be following John Fasio's gofer? She had seen Gerber's scowling face a thousand times; he was always there behind Fasio, sending out evil rays. Then she thought, what was Fasio's gofer doing at Channel 9?

13

C OUNCILMAN SAM MORRIS's house stood at the end of a lonely dead-end street overlooking the quilted chop of Long Island Sound. It was an old Victorian building, with a long porch that wrapped around the house, and great bay windows that leaned out over the rough platform like contented after-dinner spectators.

The aged planks of the house groaned in the wind. The water of the bay lapped gently against the nearby bulkhead, and the seagulls squawked and swooped low over the water in a graceful search for food. The rhythm of the wind and the tides and the faint cry of the birds had a natural, tranquilizing effect on the people who lived along that portion of the waterfront.

It still grew dark early in March, and Sam Morris turned on the lights before he began his evening routine. It was his habit to prepare his wife's dinner on Tuesday evenings. He would sit at her bedside, chat while she ate, brush away the crumbs from the sheet, and then read to her. These days she fell asleep to the consoling performances of Agatha Christie.

He was still flushed and vexed after his frustrating fight with Murray Gerber. He had called Gerber to complain about the pace of the incinerator study. Gerber was brusque, too busy to speak about the contracts for the study, which were already going out. Sam Morris wanted the damn thing put on a back burner. But Gerber didn't want to listen. Sam made the calculations: if the tempo remained the same, the complete study and findings and recommendations could be on the mayor's desk in about a month. Approval could also be quick—a matter of weeks—then contracts could be awarded and the incinerator under construction by summer. The summer nights would be shattered by the throb and tumult of hurried timetables.

It was all a dizzying turnabout for Councilman Morris. He had reminded Gerber that the Bayside homeowners had paid too much money and spent too much emotion to allow this to happen without some kind of upheaval. Not to mention his own steep bill for throwing away his integrity. When he added up the legal contributions, the under-the-table envelopes, the "consultant fees" paid directly into Gerber's account, Sam Morris and the homeowners association had put up $212,550 to stop the damn incinerator. That should have been enough, he thought.

But he'd run into a stone wall. Gerber's voice announced with frosty irritation that the borough president could not interfere with the duly designated duties of the site-study panel, nor could he disrupt the necessary progress of the municipal sanitation department. In fact, the whole business was out of the hands of the borough officials and had already been passed along to higher municipal authority.

It seemed as if the damned incinerator was going to be built—that much was clear from the cold stiff-arm he received from the mouth of Murray Gerber. Something had happened. Something had changed. Morris could no longer rely on their initial understanding. He couldn't count on the agreement— bought and paid for—to slow down the incinerator. The deal had been struck in gold! Money had changed hands. Now Gerber was going back on it.

What was so odd, so impossible to fathom, was that Fasio wasn't interested in his money. But that didn't make sense either.

John Fasio had to need his money. He was plunging into the race for mayor. Everyone knew that! You couldn't do that without some deep pocket to pick. And even more to the point, everyone in Queens knew that Patsy Scotto—the senior member of the party—was holding back his support. He was sitting on the party's assets, claiming that it wouldn't be fair to take sides so early in the contest. This forced Fasio to find other resources. Sam would have thought he'd be more sympathetic to the Bayside homeowners.

Where *was* Fasio getting his money? Was this whole business about accelerating the incinerator schedule merely a ploy to extract even more money from the Bayside homeowners? A jolt of fear to up the ante? At least that made sense. If that was the case, there was still hope. He still had a chance to slow down the incinerator itself.

Either way, he knew that he had to get to the bottom of it. Fast.

Sam Morris decided that he was not going to go down without a fight, without making a big stink. "Okay," he'd told Gerber in that bitter late-afternoon phone call, "if that's your attitude, I'll take it up with John, personally. And if I can't get John to see it my way, maybe I'll go to Billy Cohen and Patsy Scotto!"

There was an ominous silence on the other end of the phone. "I don't think that's a great idea," said Gerber finally.

"Well, why the hell not?" shot back Councilman Morris. "He's part of this, isn't he? That's what you kept telling me. This is not me talking, you said. This is John Fasio, you said. I'm just here because he cannot be implicated, you said—"

"Hold it! Just hold it!"

"Don't tell me to hold it! I went way out on a limb over this. I made promises to people. I put my reputation, my career, on the line! And, as you know, my people came up with two hundred and twelve thousand, five hundred and fifty dollars to stop this damn thing! That's a lot of fucking money!"

"Calm down, for Christ's sake! Calm down! Listen, Sam, we can work this out." Gerber's voice had taken on a tone somewhere between alarm and appeasement. It was a sound that warmed Sam Morris.

The conversation thereafter was full of oblique references, unstated implications. No other mention was made of the payoffs, the deal, the quid pro quo. But it was there in the subtext. It was present in the bulky silences and the dense insinuations.

"Yes, I'm calm. I'm very goddamn calm. I'm so freaking calm that I intend to wait until tomorrow morning before I speak to Borough President Fasio. I can wait that long."

He was still exhilarated by his own ringing passion. It felt like it used to feel when he was the young crusading Sam Morris— the lawyer advocate who got into politics for important, noble reasons. No, it felt even better than that. He felt like PFC Sam Morris. He was a brave belly gunner on a B-17 who flew combat missions over Germany in World War II and refused to change his dog tags. He left the *H* for *Hebrew* under the marking for religion. They warned him that if he was forced to bail out, it would go harder on a captured Jew. But he was crazy with courage in those reckless days. And that's how he felt when he'd spoken just now to Murray Gerber. He'd let all of his anger and defiance show.

"You can mark me down for 10:00 A.M.," he had said.

"Okay, Sam," Murray Gerber had agreed. "I'm putting you down for a ten o'clock appointment. But don't be late—he has to see the mayor for lunch."

The manager of the retirement home on Staten Island employed a crisp professional smile. He was a scrubbed and well-groomed man who wore a dark pinstripe suit and kept his hands folded tightly in his lap as he spoke to John and Irma Fasio.

"I can virtually guarantee that your mother will be very happy here," he said in that deeply unctuous manner of an actor reading a part. "She will be with people of her own generation and, believe me, that is a very important thing. Having spoken to her, I can see what a dear, dear woman she is."

His name, Carl Smith, was printed on a plastic disc pinned on the pocket of his jacket. He was young, but balding, and he laid the last strands of his dark hair across his scalp like a bed sheet. John Fasio guessed that he was thirty-five, but he couldn't be certain. He was one of those ageless men who look mature and stuck in middle age from youth on.

"What about the doctors?" asked Fasio aggressively.

He found that he resented Carl Smith's manner and his eagerness and even his willingness to oblige.

The manager reached over and took a blue folder from his desk. It had Fasio's mother's name on the cover. The manager folded over a few pages, fumbled with his reading glasses, and nodded.

"As you know, Mrs. Fasio has some minor problems when it comes to orientation." He shrugged. "It's not a big problem, yet." He looked down at the folder. "Eventually, I am afraid that she will need help."

John Fasio felt the gummy euphemisms of the manager stuffing his ears. It made no difference. He had no choice. The fights at home had worn down his resistance. He had given in and accepted the fact that his mother and wife could not live under the same roof. He had stopped blaming Irma for the miserable, contentious atmosphere; he had seen firsthand how his mother lashed out at everything. She was impossible.

Celia had grown more and more strident, more and more demanding, more and more peevish . . . over nothing—the use of a certain towel, buying her own vegetables, cooking her own food, choosing the television shows. For her own defense, Irma had been forced to adopt a willful, stony obstinacy with her mother-in-law. There were times when nothing else worked and Celia had to be treated like a spoiled child.

"Our doctors are the finest," said Mr. Smith.

Irma had put on her own glasses, as if prepared to read the medical reports along with the manager.

"She likes to cook," she said of her mother-in-law, perhaps searching for a good trait.

The manager said that there were cooking classes which many of the guests enjoyed, but that cooking in the rooms was forbidden. Many of the guests were unreliable with sharp instruments and fire.

So she would be put back in a room, thought Fasio.

"Our visitation policy is totally lenient," said Mr. Smith, consolingly. "You can visit as often as you like. And, may I just say what an honor it will be to have your mother as a guest."

Fasio looked up, his eyes burning.

"If you'll forgive me, many of my staff live in Queens and they all speak so highly of you."

"Thank you," said Fasio, his voice croaking.

"Not that we don't give all of our guests special treatment, but, well, we all hope that the next mayor will visit regularly."

Fasio thought Mr. Smith's smile might slide off of his face.

"It's only a rumor," said Fasio, turning away.

Fasio read the plaques and testimonials on the wall, smelled the boiled potatoes and fish dinners as they were wheeled on their high metal trolleys to the rooms. Through the glass panels beside the door he saw his mother walking with an attendant. She had started out her tour of the home allowing herself to be helped, with the attendant's hand under her elbow. But now she was upright, marching down the corridor, talking with a robust chirping, driving, decisive displeasure. At home, she was bent and quiet and merely cranky.

"What about church?" he asked sharply.

Mr. Smith's smile changed to a look of long-suffering concern. The manager must have been accustomed to this—the grown, middle-aged children who are filled with guilt and remorse for the terrible sin of casting out their parents, taking it out on the nearest Mr. Smith.

"There is a weekly van for those of our guests who are still able to make the journey to St. Mary's on Victory Boulevard," he said. He didn't say what happened to those unable to make the weekly trip.

"She likes daily mass," said Fasio.

The manager looked troubled. "Maybe we could work something out," he said.

There was nothing else to discuss. The home was clean and seemed well-staffed. It was saturated with the kindness of indifferent strangers. There were hand-drawn pictures on the bulletin boards. Bright, sunny scenes with wooden stick-figures —pictures like children draw in kindergarten. And John Fasio felt a swollen ache in his heart over the inevitable.

"We have to think about it."

"Of course."

"We will let you know."

"Of course. Take your time."

They drove home in silence. John behind the wheel, Irma in the passenger seat, looking out of the side window as if she would never pass this way again, and Celia in the back, choking on her black anger.

Murray Gerber didn't know whether he had to go through with it. But he had to be prepared. He parked the borrowed city car in a mini-mall where it would be lost among the dinner and theater and shopping crowds. He hadn't wanted to bring his own car—it might be recognized, especially in this neighborhood. He wore dark clothing, but not conspicuously dark. Just winterwear. It did not seem odd that he kept his head down when he walked, especially on a cold evening when there were pellets of sleet in the wind.

It was half a mile to the bay and Murray Gerber walked the distance with authority, but quietly. Not many people were on foot in this part of Queens—the buses and trains were too infrequent and hard to reach—still, he remained inconspicuous.

The shades and curtains that moved along with him closed behind him. One or two dogs barked, but Gerber kept to the lighted streets and acted as if he belonged.

He rang the bell and pounded on the door of the old Victorian house for a long time before Sam Morris finally answered. The councilman looked frightened when he saw Gerber standing there on the porch, in his black peacoat and knit cap.

"I was upstairs," he said by way of explanation for the delay, blocking the entrance. "I was reading to Gerry." He held up a book.

Morris looked past Gerber, as if he expected to see Fasio waiting in a shadow.

"We have to talk," said Gerber, nodding to indicate that he wanted to go inside. "We have to discuss things before you talk to John."

"I didn't hear your car."

"No, one of the precinct guys dropped me off. He'll pick me up when I call for a ride."

He could see the worry drain out of Morris's eyes. If the local precinct knew where he was, then surely . . . Morris stepped aside and let him into the house. "You know, Murray, I really don't want to cause any trouble," Morris said.

"No, I know that, Sam." He tried to sound sincere. "I just don't wanna find my balls in a wringer."

They settled in the living room and Morris poured his guest a drink. Gerber was grateful for the whiskey. He looked around. It was a cluttered room, with high-backed couches and tables filled with old pictures and books scattered everywhere.

"Let me just tell Gerry that I'll be a few minutes."

"I'll fix myself another drink," said Gerber.

Morris was gone for a moment, but it was enough time for Murray Gerber to wipe his fingerprints off the glass, put it away, then clean the surfaces he had touched. He was waiting for Sam Morris when he came down the staircase. He still was not certain that he had to go through with this.

Morris looked more at ease when he came down. Maybe it was the story about the precinct car, maybe the fact that Gerber had no concern about him going upstairs alone, maybe just the sheer implausibility of his fears, but he sat down on the couch, the strain gone from his face.

"The incinerator . . . would go right there." He pointed to a virgin stretch of beachfront visible in the fading light outside of the window.

"Look, I know that we had a business arrangement," began Murray Gerber. He was standing, looking down. "I know that you put a lot of time and a lot of effort into this . . ."

"Two hundred, twelve thousand, five hundred and fifty dollars, to be exact."

"Yes, I know. A lot of money," replied Gerber, who had already calculated a ten million dollar annuity from the cable television franchise.

"Money that went from my pocket to yours, and, presumably, to John," Sam Morris said pointedly.

"A fair contribution."

"What?! Contribution? To what? A place in Provence?"

Gerber didn't say anything for a few seconds. "We counted most of it as a legitimate campaign contribution. One interest group among many."

"Did you? Did you list it with the IRS? On your long form, Murray?"

This was not getting him anywhere. "Sometimes, Sam, things change."

"That's right, and it seems that I am on the receiving end of some very unfair changes."

There was a time when he'd been working out of a precinct in Manhattan when Murray Gerber had felt the same pressure to act. He had been in charge of a small pad for the uniformed cops. Not much. Couple of hundred a month. Hardly worth bothering about. But a new cop on the job was ready to report the pad to Internal Affairs. It would have been a disaster. Investigations. Disgrace. Prison.

There was a meeting of the uniformed officers involved in the pad and it was decided that something had to be done.

Only no one could say what it was that had to be done. Murray Gerber knew.

That night when he went out on patrol he carried an extra pistol. The "drop" gun. He waited until the new cop was alone on a dark street, and he came up behind him and shot him once in the head at very close range. It was his first kill, and his hand didn't even shake. He threw the drop gun in a sewer and let someone else discover the body, which was reported as one more heroic victim of the city's random violence. The other cops in the precinct—those who were on the pad and guessed at what happened—treated Murray differently after that. They gave him a wide berth of respect, or maybe of fear; he couldn't tell the difference anymore. It didn't matter—he welcomed it.

"Sam, listen to me: there is no way that John Fasio can stop that incinerator. It's gone too far. The sanitation committee on the board of estimate is pushing for an answer. The oversight committee is reporting 'foot-dragging.' You know what that means? If John tries to throw any more blocks in the way, there'll be an investigation. It'll mean his ass. I know about our deal. John did everything that he could. There's nothing more that he can do. Not without getting everyone in trouble."

Sam Morris nodded. PFC Sam Morris, who was credited with two ME 109's, shook his head. "Fine, Sammy. I just have to hear it from his own lips," he said firmly.

That's when Murray Gerber saw that he had no choice. He took out the long dirk he had hidden in the sleeve of his jacket. The knife had a ten-inch blade, needle thin. Hypnotized, Sam Morris watched, caught in the fascinating headlight of Murray's swift and lethal movements. The arm that held the blade was cocked, then the knife came plunging through his shirt, driving past the skin, grazing a bone, and pierced his heart. Councilman

Sam Morris looked down, eyes ablaze, as blood spilled from his still-pumping heart. His last thought before he lost consciousness was that it looked like an oil well—he had brought in a small gusher on his chest.

Murray Gerber watched him die, made certain that he had no time to cry out. Then he doused the lights and made sure no one was looking in. He walked slowly up the staircase. When he opened the bedroom door, Gerry was in bed, her eyes wide with terror.

"Is Sam here?" he asked approaching the bed, throwing her into confusion.

Then he put his left hand over her mouth and drove the dirk through her scrawny body, holding the parchmentlike skin, which kept slipping away at first. She died quickly; a few twitches, a gasp, and she was gone.

Methodically, Murray emptied the bureau drawers onto the floor, took whatever cash and jewelry he could find, went downstairs and repeated the process. He was surprised. Sam Morris had eight hundred dollars in cash in his desk. Before he left, he removed the oversized shoes he had worn to throw off investigators and replaced them with his own.

He walked outside and broke one of the bay windows so that the glass would fall inside to complete the stage setting of a burglary.

He hid the bloody oversized shoes under his peacoat. Then he walked back to his car unhurriedly. He drove to a landfill in Brooklyn, where he left all of the compromised clothing and the dirk. Then he went home and slept. He had plugged the leak. It had taken a dirk, but it had to be done.

14

THERE WAS SOMETHING in the political wind—like the April nip that signaled the change of season. Pete Hawkings sensed it, but then he was a veteran newspaper hound who had worked in the banged-up press room of the Queens borough president's office for the last twenty-two of his sixty-four years. Old newspaper hounds could always smell change.

Suddenly, fresh young television reporters were making regular morning stops in the press room, acting as if they belonged to this distant, forgotten outpost of the business. The electronic media stars were asking questions about Fasio, poking around for a story. What kind of guy is he? What's he ever done? Is he really gonna be appointed mayor? What, exactly, is a borough president?

Uninformed, ignorant, lazy questions. Television questions. It was a built-in defect of the job. Television reporters drifted from city to city, market to market, with no deep understanding of the territory. They invariably operated as if they had just landed in Beirut, wondering if there was someplace clean where they could get a decent sandwich, if the water was safe to drink, and if the natives were friendly.

The print regulars—the four full-time print reporters from

the *New York Times, Daily News, Post,* and *Newsday*—treated the forays of "the media" with the same cool deference that poor relations display to rich relatives. There was a certain amount of respect for the power (and they, too, were influenced by the perfume of fame), but they were mostly annoyed by the television stars. After all, when they left, the regulars would still be banished to the two-fare zone on Queens Boulevard.

The regulars spent their days digging through official gibberish like coal miners, poring through dense bureaucratic reports, looking for something worth printing. They hounded irritated officials, they scanned small, shrill local newspapers for signs of scandal. They read like entrails the flow of petitions and complaints from eternally outraged citizens' groups. They listened to the long, twisted tales of raving obsessives. That was their job. And sometimes it paid off with a juicy yarn. Mostly it didn't.

But the electronic media never stayed in one place long enough to dig out a story of their own. They expected to reap without effort all the benefits that came from the heavy lifting of the print reporters. Theirs was a gilded glide over the surface of events. How could the print soldiers not resent them?

When Bonnie showed up at lunchtime on that crisp day in April, Pete Hawkings was not surprised. After all, she was no stranger. She was one of the guys. She had spent a few seasons behind one of the metal desks reclaimed from the garbage heap by the gypsy scavengers of the press corps. When she was a lowly beat reporter for *Newsday* Bonnie banged away at a salvaged typewriter with the best of them, phoning in the two-paragraph stories about some pet new repaving program or the renaming of a street, or the launch of a new sewer.

And Pete Hawkings almost forgot—despite the differences in age—how much of a crush he had had on Bonnie.

"You still look better in person," he said, keeping his feet propped up on the old desk. He didn't smile, but he nodded, and that was a big welcome.

"Not you," she replied, tossing her beret on the wobbly hat

rack that had been there since the thirties when men always wore hats. "You look like shit in person. No offense."

"Yeah, thank God I'm not on television so I don't have to look at myself."

All the others had gone out to lunch and Hawkings had caught phone duty. Someone had to stay behind to deflect the editors searching for slackers. He was glad he had done so. Bonnie looked a little haggard, although on her it looked good. It was the boyfriend, he thought. She paid a big price for that famous saucy independence. Too bad. He liked Jack. He always thought that he was a good guy. Too good for a cop. All that tough sensitivity. Hawkings was willing to bet that Jack Mann was looking a little haggard these days, too.

"Tired of the Tee Vee?" asked Hawkings, dragging out the initials to signal his opinion of it.

"Hate the Tee Vee," she said, rifling through the pile of press handouts left like candy in a wire basket. She didn't expect to find anything. It was an old habit. Then she fished down into her large tote bag and pulled out two sandwiches and two cans of diet soda. She handed one of each to Hawkings.

"So," she asked, nibbling on a ham and cheese, "whatdoya hear about Sam Morris?"

He looked up, shrugged. "I hear his council seat is open," replied Hawkings, diving into a fresh turkey on rye, licking a spill of mayonnaise off his finger. "Hope this is not that diet shit mayo."

"High-cholesterol mayo," she said reassuringly. "Clogs up the arteries before you finish chewing. Guaranteed."

She looked around. The old headlines were still on the wall: "Headless Body In Topless Bar," "Ford To New York: Drop Dead." They were yellowing and curling at the edges—clever and irreverent headlines that mimicked the sarcastic, sour pose the reporters struck in public. They were, in fact, far more conventional and sentimental than they let on.

"Did you fuck yourself up like that in Atlantic City before or after breaking relations with our ruptured cop?" he asked.

She frowned. "You never used to ask dumb, thoughtless questions, Pete. I remember that from press conferences—there's a man who knows when to keep his mouth shut, I thought with tremendous admiration."

He stared down at his sandwich. "I've been keeping bad company," he said, looking up sheepishly. "Politicians who are not politic. Sorry."

He took another mouthful of food, wet it down with Diet Coke, then bit into a pickle which sprinkled brine over his coat. He picked up a napkin and went to work. Hawkings was a sloppy eater and usually left lunch traces over his jacket. He spread the napkin strategically on his lap.

"Let's talk about something more lighthearted," she said. "Sam. What's the word on him?"

"Sam Morris," he said brightly. "You know, I liked Sam. A putz, but I liked him. Sometimes, even a putz can be all right. Did you know he was in the war? World War II. A tail gunner or a belly gunner. On a bomber over Germany. Doesn't mean anything, not to a punk like you, but it meant something to me. I don't know how much, but something. Imagine. Sam Morris, that putz! Over Germany! Well, I liked him and now he's dead."

"Me, too. I mean, not a lot. But some. Liking, I mean. True, he was an asshole, but he probably didn't start out that way. Not over Germany, anyway. And he did have a soft spot for upper-middle-class semi-rich people like himself. You gotta admire a guy who goes all out for the overprivileged underdog."

"C'mon, Bonnie! You know, you don't give an inch. God, I always forget what a rough character you are."

"No, come on! You want me to be a melodramatic schmuck. I'm without sentiment. That's what you like about me: I'm a nasty bitch."

"Yes, you are. I forgot. I just get fooled by a nice set of melons."

They ate for a while, soaking in the company, as if to remind themselves what it was that they appreciated about each other—a certain resonance of common sense and congenial beliefs. They grew mellow all over again.

"I need a story, Pete."

"Yeah? What happened to the weather? People are always talking about it. That's what I hear."

"It's driving me batshit. I need a real story. I just smelled something with the Sam Morris thing."

He shook his head. "Do Fasio."

"Everybody's doing Fasio."

He nodded, finishing off his sandwich. "That's because he's a good story. The fucker's gonna be mayor. I'm tellin' ya. In less than a month. Open secret. Cohen's gonna quit and Toedtman's gonna name Fasio to take his place. Everybody's on it."

"That's why I don't wanna do it. I hate elbows. I hate politics. God, I hate just about everything. No, I need something else. Something I can really sink my teeth in. You know. My own story. What's wrong with the Sam Morris thing?"

He finished his sandwich and wiped his hands. The phone rang and he let it go twice before picking it up. "No, no . . . He's in the clerk's office," he said into the receiver.

There was no phone in the clerk's office. No way to check up on someone having a long lunch. Sometimes he said that reporters were in meetings, and sometimes they were buried in files in the clerk's office. Always, he said that they'd be right back. In a pinch, if the caller insisted, he'd say that he was going to look for them, then he'd lay the phone on the desk and nap.

He looked at Bonnie. She looked not well groomed (she never looked well groomed) but appealing. Something solid there, he thought. He didn't know what broke her up with Jack Mann, but she was undefeated. He shook his head again. "Forget Sam Morris. It was a cheap, ugly murder," he said grimly. "Someone broke into the poor bastard's house and killed him and then murdered that helpless wife of his in her own bed.

Someone murdered them both for a few hundred bucks and some cheap jewelry." He shrugged. "Happens every day. Push-in murders, drive-by murders, carjacking murders, mindless murders, pointless murders, senseless murders, just plain murders. We got a hundred different kinds of murders."

"Yeah, but this was a city councilman. A friend of the mayor and the borough president. A guy who flew missions over Germany. How come they haven't found anyone yet?"

He shrugged. It was a big shrug wrapped in a tight gesture. "You know how it is. Sometimes they don't find anyone. And if they do, they find the wrong someone. Nah, this is not your good juicy story. Cops aren't even taking it that big. Disbanding the special task force. Fasio, there's your good story."

"How come?"

"What?"

"How come they're disbanding the task force? I mean, even if it is a push-in or a burglary, he was a city councilman, a prominent citizen, and his wife was a helpless cripple. Somebody with a heart should want to nail the perps. You'd think he'd rate a little more time than this."

"They're not gonna give up. They'll keep some homicide guys on it, but you don't wanna waste a fifty-man task force on a push-in murder in Bayside." He shook his head. "Waste of manpower. This kind of thing, the perp doesn't go away. Stays in the area. He'll turn up again. You don't leave the gold shields out on this. Shoe leather isn't gonna solve it. Uniformed cops will break this one. Sooner or later, they'll pick up some cranked-up junkie for something else and he'll tell them about this other time when he broke into a house near some water and had to defend himself against this old guy and his crippled wife. He'll ask for a break if he tells them everything and they'll put him away for a long time. No big mystery."

She shook her head vigorously. "You're wrong," she said.

"That's what I like about you, Bon. You mince words. You

know that? You really have this confidence problem. Listen, say what you think, okay?"

"Don't give me that shit, Pete. I've seen you get your back up when you know you're right. What about the time they tried to blame that kid for a rape just because he was black?"

"They always try to blame a kid because he's black."

"Okay. You know exactly what I mean."

"Yeah, but you're wrong."

"Maybe." She still held a piece of her sandwich in her hand. She looked at it, surprised that it was still there. Then she threw it with a crumb of disgust into the overflowing garbage can. "You know why I hate Tee Vee?"

"Because it pays your rent?"

"Yes, of course, but in addition to that. Because I watch it every night and it tells me nothing. No, that's not exactly true. It tells me the same old exhausted news, over and over and over. I learn nothing. There are world events—revolutions, wars, elections—but on television, it becomes haggard and old in half an hour. Isn't that amazing? How do they do that? Something big happens, and I'm dying to learn about it, and they wear me out in those tiny little shell bursts of things I already know."

"Whatdja expect? Tolstoy? Nobody gives a shit about nothin'. That's my take on it."

"Bullshit. I don't believe that cynical crap. Listen, if I'm hungry for details, so is somebody else. So are you. There are stories out there. What happened to *Harper's*, the *New Yorker*? There are stories I want to pull up like a blanket. I need a real story, Pete, and I do not think it's John Fasio."

The other regulars came back from lunch and there was subdued but happy surprise at seeing their old colleague. They made fun of her celebrity status in a gentle, teasing way and said that the Fasio boomlet must be real if Channel 9 was sending their weathergirl out to check on the political winds.

* * *

She saw Fasio arriving back at his office after lunch, looking wild and pursued, like a real candidate. He was trailed by his faithful scowling lapdog, Gerber, as he ran up the steps of Borough Hall. That one made her shiver. Bonnie did not like Murray Gerber. Never had. He was one of those eager types who try not to show it. She had never understood the ambition of men who operated on the sidelines. It seemed almost voyeuristic.

Fasio looked up, saw her watching him, started to wave at the bright flash of Bonnie's familiar smile, but pulled back his hand, smiled and moved on. Gerber scowled.

Maybe there was a story there, after all, she thought. Something wrong with those two. She wondered what kind of mayor Fasio'd be. Open, probably. Or, at least, he'd put on a show of being open. The good-old-boy, northern style, kind of mayor. He left behind a feeling of being chummy. It was that big bear hug of false intimacy. It made you think you were being embraced, allowed inside some secret place. She had an idea that it was a fabrication to throw people off the scent. There was something . . . almost a repressed misery in his eyes. She did not think him capable of intimacy. But that was a guess.

The Queens borough president's cabinet meeting was brief and to the point. The borough president wanted action on a number of fronts and he wanted—in Churchill's famous words—action this day. Twelve deputies and assistants sat around a twenty-five-foot table in the conference room listening to his instructions while Fasio stood. The borough president always stood. He was too antsy to sit down, and, besides, standing gave him a psychological advantage. He loomed over his subordinates.

He wanted his executive assistants to produce quick reports on budget needs, projected weak spots in the forthcoming fiscal year; he wanted status reports on capital projects and suggestions for issues. He was running against a ticking clock, and he needed results fast. Already other candidates were beginning to show their heads as word of Mayor Billy Cohen's imminent departure filtered through the political network. And, Fasio suspected, more than one head was being shoved into the ring by Patsy Scotto. The borough president knew that he would leave behind a mess if he became mayor. Scotto's newspaper friends would make certain to jump on that. They'd chew him up.

The deputies and assistants sat on the edge of their chairs while John Fasio ticked off the list of demands, which were coming off the top of his smoking head. They reached, one by one, for the glasses of stale water to try to stave off the heat of Fasio's firestorm. Parks, roads, social services, building inspections, licensing, public safety, environmental—Fasio wanted everyone turning the files inside out looking for land mines and fresh ideas. He wanted the borough of Queens to shine.

"Any questions?"

George O'Brien, the head of the borough sanitation committee, held up his hand. He was a young civil servant fresh out of Yale with a degree in civil engineering. "You know, as to the Bayside incinerator . . ."

He never got to finish his question. "That's done. That's out of our hands," said Fasio, shuffling some papers in the folder in front of him. "That thing is approved as far as our site and environmental studies are concerned. Anything else?"

"Yes, but the homeowners association . . ."

"They're going to have to bite the bullet," Fasio said. "We can't exclude any community from service to the whole."

O'Brien looked startled. Fasio nodded. A signal to move on. Sam Morris was dead, and the incinerator was alive. No one had ever seen him move so resolutely, with such ruthless authority. Well, Fasio thought, they better get used to it. He wasn't going to be running a little village come May; he was going to be operating a city. The city. This was the face of the new mayor of New York, he thought. This is what I'll be like: no excuses, no pity, no shame. Only results. It was high-octane stuff and guys like O'Brien would either measure up or move out.

There were some tentative proposals—a parks deputy commissioner wanted to organize a spring festival—but Fasio wanted them in writing. "Clean, thought-out, and on my desk by Monday."

They all nodded. "Otherwise," he said with a frosty smile, "I am going to come upside your department and inside you out."

He turned and marched back into his own office. Murray Gerber took charge of the end of the meeting. He assigned the man from parks to sweat out the report over the weekend, had the budget people pumped and ready to pull all-nighters. No hand would be idle in the near future.

"The borough president is under a lot of pressure," said Gerber to the assembled cabinet. "As you know, there are going to be some big changes coming down . . ."

"When, Murray?"

It was Imo Manca, the deputy borough superintendent of public affairs. Imo was one of the old-timers. In office for five borough presidents. Had to be seventy and fighting off mandatory retirement. Before he came into government Imo was a newspaperman, which gave him some purchase in the press room when he was trying to sell the good side of a bad story.

Gerber shook his head. "Soon," he said. "Not tomorrow. But soon."

He looked around the room. They were starting to calm down after the riot of Fasio's battle commands. Gerber doubted that they could handle the pressure. After seeing Fasio's impatience and speed, he didn't think that any of them would be coming along when they moved to Gracie Mansion.

The cigar was lit. He was puffing smoke and whipping his hand across the pages of ordinances and regulations and proclamations. He didn't even look up when Murray Gerber came back into his office.

"You think they got it?" he asked.

Gerber shook his head. Fasio didn't have to see it—he felt it.

"Neither do I," Fasio said.

The orders signed, the directives issued, the proclamations discharged, John Fasio sat back in his chair and nodded at the side cabinet. "Scotch," he said.

Gerber poured the drinks. It was that moment between afternoon and evening when Fasio caught a second wind. A moment of calm in the roiling white water of his urgent goal.

"Irma called," said Gerber.

Fasio closed his eyes.

"She says that she won't be able to make the party," Gerber continued.

"Send a car for her," said Fasio.

Gerber cleared his throat. "She didn't sound . . . well."

Fasio's chair banged against the desk as he lunged forward. Some of the scotch spilled onto one of the proclamations. He hit the intercom. "Jane, get me Irma!"

He got out of the chair, started to pace. Gerber was silent. The intercom buzzed. He picked up the phone as if he were grabbing his wife's throat.

"I'm sending a car," he said. "You have between now and eight o'clock to get yourself in shape."

He slammed the receiver into the cradle.

"What's doing with the, uh, financing?" he asked Gerber.

His assistant fumbled through his folder, although the folder contained nothing related to the recent large influx of cash into the "Fasio-For-Mayor" committee. He was trying to assemble his thoughts.

"Actually, we're in pretty good shape," said Gerber.

"How's that?"

"Well, you know, we're picking up lots of support."

"Really?"

"Lots. There are some big contributors."

"You mean, like special-interest money?"

Murray stammered. He didn't know how far Fasio wanted to take this. "There's always some of that," Gerber said. "It's perfectly legal."

Fasio nodded, jammed the cigar in his mouth. "How much?"

"How much what?"

"What've we got in the war chest? I mean, right now. Today. What size check could I write this afternoon?"

"A million," Gerber replied, feeling the pinch of Fasio's direction.

"And how much of that came from the Bayside group, you know, the homeowners? Sam's people."

"Not much."

"How much?" It could have been steam instead of smoke coming out of Fasio's mouth.

"A fifth."

"Two hundred thousand," Fasio said wistfully. "And for all their money, they're gonna get that incinerator shoved down their throats."

"They got their money's worth," Gerber said with a touch of steel in his voice.

"Did they? Did they really? Did Sam?"

"Sam was a schmuck."

Fasio glared at Gerber, as if looks alone could smash the barrier between them. "You don't know what happened to Sam, do you, Murray? Because if you do, you better tell me now."

He half rose, menacingly, in his chair, and Gerber was certain that he would lunge over the desk and strangle him if he delivered the wrong answer. He could get out his gun and put two rounds into Fasio's heart, but that wouldn't stop him. He was convinced of that.

"John, I swear that I have no idea what happened to Sam." The silence hung between them—a thread of uncertainty between Fasio and murder.

"Don't lie to me, Murray. No more fucking lies."

"I swear, John. You know what kind of city this is. The man was murdered by a maniac. You think I'm a maniac?"

"I think you're a crook," said Fasio. Then he turned away. "But no more crooked than me."

15

AT JOHN FASIO's insistence, the band was playing a choppy rendition of "Happy Days Are Here Again," defying all the neo-Democrats who wanted to appeal to a broader, softer political coalition by changing tunes in midstream. But not John Fasio. He could never separate that snappy song from the great patriotic and family-blood emotions of his youth. He pictured his father standing in the back of some steamy VFW hall, shaking hands with the men of affairs, grinning from ear to ear, cutting deals for working-class people to get civil service appointments. Doing good.

The son would hover nearby and listen to his father speak passionately of the precinct engines and the election districts; Big Jim was a master political mechanic and could tell which ones were running smoothly and which were off in the timing department and required a tune-up. Fasio could hear him still, twenty years later, mentioning the benefactors and holding up the spread of checks like a fan, and laughing triumphantly. Big Jim called them benefactors—the money-men who gave lavishly to the chosen candidate.

And now his son was the chosen candidate. John wondered how his father would do in the fund-raising department compared to, say, Murray Gerber. But more important, he wondered what his father would think of his son as a big-shot candidate. How he would measure up. Big Jim had died before John showed himself. He wondered if Big Jim would find his son's success his own vindication. He didn't think so.

Fasio held Irma in his arms and danced under the twinkling lights of the turning globe in the center of the Sky Ballroom in a section of the borough called Astoria. It was a densely ethnic part of Queens. In the ballroom, on other nights, Greek women pledged fidelity to men with old-world expectations, and ancient Balkan feuds came under a temporary truce. This night, patrons of the art of politics came to pay homage and make their semisecret money pledges.

Dancing to the old FDR anthem, Fasio felt the massed attention of hundreds of eyes watching him and his wife move across the floor. He felt something else: a confused glow of old memories and shifting faith.

"Better?!" he barked into his wife's ear.

She looked at him with a tragic smile. She was dancing. She was trying her best. But nothing was better. He could barely hold her in his arms. It was like dancing with a dead weight. And so he looked away.

The ballroom glittered with $500-a-plate guests, 250 of them, he estimated. Another $125,000 in the war chest. And more. Someone was always throwing in an extra zero. Donations poured in now that the power seemed to be moving his way. After the word had been leaked that he would be the new mayor, the money had come in like melting snow—at first a trickle, then a flood. It was unsettling how easy it was to begin the flow. He didn't even have to say yes. Murray did it for him. Murray did it all. Fasio remained protected on some higher plane, smiling grimly. He would not ask Murray how he did it when the fresh reports of cash came in, because he already knew without asking that only a fraction of the giant war chest came in like this, legally and above board. The rest arrived in sealed envelopes, with covert understandings of just exactly what was expected in return. If Murray said that something was a priority matter, Fasio knew better than to ask why. For instance, the matter of the cable franchise had become a priority affair, and the only thing that Fasio asked was to be kept in ignorance. It was enough to have his mother's bills paid and his campaign chest fat and to be left unaware of just how much of his soul he had sold. He would make it all up when he got elected; that was the bargain he made with himself. Sheltering the homeless, feeding the hungry—that's what he bought with his retailed virtue.

He wondered, Is this how it happens? Is this what happened to my own father? He pushed that thought out of his mind, as he danced with the weight in his arms and drove out his persistent disquieting suspicion about the murders of Sam Morris and his wife. No, he wouldn't believe the worst. He couldn't. Murray bent some rules, violated the technical codes, like some lovable rogue, but he was essentially a decent man. He was not a killer.

Fasio saw the local politicians watching him with naked appetite. They were the ones who came out night after night to one dinner or fund-raiser after another because that was the way it worked—you support me and I'll support you. Miss one political mixer and you better have a good excuse. And you better send in the check anyway. The crush of followers was familiar. They were interchangeable with the political crowds who came to Gracie Mansion, except that on the outerborough side of the Queensboro Bridge they were ten pounds heavier and two or three years out of fashion. Still, it was the same cut of hungry lawyers, underemployed municipal technicians, sleek pollsters, and hopeful businessmen. The market in the opening days of a campaign was always salivating with handlers, consultants, managers, and corporate middlemen.

And there were the stiff, silver-haired judges surrounded by flocks of lawyers planting seeds of ingratiating flattery. The judges stood aloof, holding out their arms delicately, as if they were offering rings to be kissed instead of hands to be shaken. They smiled from the sanitary distance of caution at a ribald joke.

Fasio noticed a commotion. It was the mayor arriving, and he took Irma's hand and led her off the dance floor. The crowd cleared a path, like rolling out a red carpet between the approaching politicians. Fasio knew that Billy Cohen didn't like to come out for these affairs; he preferred, now that his mayoral career was in its gracious, crowning twilight, to stay at home and watch old movies on cable. But he had no choice; he had to come out for this. Fasio was his boy. But at his side was Pasquale Scotto.

These guys! thought Fasio with disgust, seeing them arrive together. They played mind-twisting, hardball politics, and then, at the end, embraced, as if nothing happened. Scotto was there—even in his decline—to show some muscle and, more important, to display his unbroken nerve. And to confuse the gossip that he was Fasio's adversary. His presence was enough to demonstrate that he stood at Billy Cohen's elbow. Scotto looked around the room, took in the crowd like someone counting the house at a theater opening.

The arrival of the mayor and Scotto had a noticeable effect on the room. It heightened the gaeity. A torch of false fellowship lit up the hall, as men who saw each other every day acted like it was a big reunion, pushed expensive cigars on each other and chased the waiters with the drinks as the laughter grew louder and tales grew more reckless.

The mayor greeted Fasio with a hug for the benefit of the scorekeepers. Scotto shook his hand and held his arm—a show slightly less enthusiastic than Billy Cohen's. There was a chill in the greeting that made Fasio shiver.

In the car on the way out, the mayor had tried to smooth things over. "John's doing well," he had said.

"Oh, yeah?"

Scotto had sat back in the plush leather seat, his legs spread out. He had gazed out of the window of the mayor's bulletproof limousine, watching the traffic move out of the way for the official car.

Billy Cohen had heard the skeptical push in Scotto's tone. "He's getting organized; he's coming up with some cash. I happen to think that he has a future, Patsy. People like him. He's got a touch. I believe that it would serve the party well to promote candidates like John."

Scotto had coughed. Then he had said, "Listen, Billy, I think you should be careful with this kid."

"You know something?" Cohen had asked.

"Is there something to know?"

Cohen had smiled. He wasn't going to quarrel with Scotto. "He's popular," he had said. "Lights up a room. I've seen it. A gift. He attracts attention. He's got a lot of people coming on board."

"Still got Gerber, on board, I notice."

"What the hell have you got against Murray Gerber?"

"I'm making an inventory." Scotto had erupted with a short, sharp laugh that had turned into a moist cough. "You got something to drink in this bus?"

Cohen had poured him a glass of Evian water from the small refrigerator in the back under the jump seat.

When he had recovered, Scotto spoke softly. "The reason you gotta be careful, my friend, is that there is something very strange about a guy who is financially shaky one day and the next socks away more than a million dollars in a political slush fund."

The mayor had looked shocked. "Where would he get such money? And how the hell do you know?"

Scotto had waved a hand. "I got friends," he had said airily. "People tell me things."

"Is this for real?"

Scotto had leaned closer. "I happen to know that this guy

Gerber—who is still a crook in my book—made some very large deposits in a Citibank account that is used by Fasio."

"You got friends in Citibank?" Billy Cohen had asked with amusement.

Scotto had shrugged.

"Where's the money from?"

"I'm working on it," Scotto had said.

"It could be perfectly legal contributions."

"I don't know."

"You better work on it quick," Cohen had said with a sigh. "I intend to resign on the third Monday in May."

Scotto had seen a worried look plant itself on the mayor's face.

Harvey Levy was standing by the window of the Channel 9 executive dining suite, whispering into Thatch Conway's ear. The British owner of the television station had a dread of being late and was scheduled to host a formal dinner at 8:30 on his yacht, the *Lady Nelda*. He kept looking at his watch. He was also gazing at the silent monitor above the bar. It was a few moments before the eight o'clock newscast.

Important social lions, some investors, a few celebrities, and one or two gossip columnists had been invited for the affair aboard the *Lady Nelda*. Conway was eager to impress his growing circle of friends. The fact that his name was favorably mentioned in a gossip column mattered to him.

"I'm a little nervous," said Levy, looking around to see if they were being watched.

Thatch laughed and took Levy by the arm. "My dear fellow," he said cheerfully. "This thing is business!"

"Yes," said Levy, torn by the allure of sudden and intoxicating power and money and the dread of venturing out into deep water, "but it is not entirely legal, is it?"

Thatch shook his head. "Nonsense," he said dismissively. Then he, too, lowered his voice in spite of the fact that they were alone at the window overlooking the river. "Do you think that big business—any big business—is conducted in a completely straightforward manner? One has to outwit one's opponents, don't you think?"

Harvey Levy looked at him curiously, as if he had missed some crucial portion of the conversation. Thatch Conway nodded and led his American protégé to a couch.

"Look, my friend, someone is going to get that cable franchise," said Conway, as if dealing with an idiot child. Levy let him lead him along with this baby step, as if his dim appreciation of the deed protected him from culpability. "Now, your American rules are rather strict, compared to British, and even global standards for conducting business. Very strict. Too many regulations. That's what Bush and Quayle were always saying. We are overregulated. That's why they set up that 'Competitiveness Council.' Cut down on the red tape."

He held up a hand against an expected protest from Levy. "I'm sure that there are very good reasons for a lot of the regulations. Reasons that have to do with protecting the public against conflicts of interest and out-and-out scoundrels. But you see, I'm not a scoundrel, and, besides, this cable business in New York state is not regulated by the FCC. It is one of the few two-tiered systems in the country. Some states are regulated by the FCC, but New York is not. And the state bows to the city. The net result is that there is such a profusion and confusion of overlapping authority that no one even knows the regulations or who is responsible for what. That's what's taking them so long to settle the thing. It needs a czar. Or maybe a borough president. There really is no problem, as long as we don't broadcast treason or lose money. I believe that is the only real cardinal sin in America—going broke."

He smiled broadly. It was a disarming smile, and he seemed pleased by his argument, as if it answered Levy's reservations.

Still, Levy felt uneasy.

"I am meeting with his man again tonight," he said.

"Good," said Thatch glancing at his watch. "I am trusting you. I've already laid the groundwork with a great deal of money, as you well know."

Levy nodded. He wasn't certain why he was doing what he was doing. Except that the opportunity had presented itself. Maybe that's what crime boiled down to: an opportunity presented. Out of nowhere, he was given a message to pass along to Thatch Conway from Fasio, via Murray Gerber. It was shadowy and oblique, but Harvey Levy understood the meaning clearly: plainly stated, Thatch could buy a cable franchise in Queens. It would take enough money to drive John Fasio's campaign for the mayoralty—that is, it would take millions. But, in the end, it would be worth it. Thatch Conway would become the cable operator for the borough of Queens, and there were two million people living in Queens, and by the arithmetic of the hour, they would each spend several dollars every month for the blessings of cable television.

The operating costs were small. Even the ten million payment to wedge Conway to the front of the line was inconsequential. He would make it back with ten times the interest in the first year. A cable franchise with all of its basic subscription income and pay-per-view side benefits would make the profits from the Channel 9 license look like a mom-and-pop compared to a supermarket. The only question Thatch Conway had was, could Fasio deliver? Levy thought that he could. The local planning boards and study committees and special commissions could be influenced in Conway's favor. Fasio had the power.

Levy had already arranged the first payment of a million dollars. It had been surprisingly easy. He'd merely informed the financial officers of companies owned or controlled by Conway to write out contributions to Fasio's campaign committee. There were enough companies and enough individuals for the amounts to remain within legal limits. It had the stench of crime, but Levy was blinded by Conway's calm approval. And a growing ember of greed.

* * *

She was tapping the pointer at the weather map in the Channel 9 studio. "I'm afraid that there's no way to avoid heavy outerwear tomorrow," said Bonnie Hudson. "It'll get up to the low thirties, but it'll feel colder because of the wind. The five-day forecast doesn't give much relief. Thirties, and possibly plunging down to the twenties by Monday. But the good news is that there's no precipitation, or at least not much according to the National Weather Bureau's betting line. My own opinion is that they're only guessing. But that's a guess."

"You know, Bonnie, you haven't given us a good weekend for a while," said anchorman Jerry Kantor jovially, making his happy-talk contribution to the broadcast. Lately, Bonnie had been almost dulcet in her reading of the forecasts. That was a very misleading indicator. It was almost a cover story. Giving her a press pass and a license to go out and report had sweetened her disposition to the point where it deceived the majority of the staff into thinking that she had merely undergone a rough transition and was now one of the safe Stepford newsreaders. "I was hoping for some mild weather for a change," said Kantor naively.

"Why is that, Jerry? Are you thinking of walking to your limousine?"

Suddenly, his mouth was flapping. He was blinking. You never knew with her, he thought. One minute she was almost sugary, and the next a hidden blade had cut his throat.

"I don't have a limousine," he said lamely. Turning to the camera, thinking that he should make it clear to his audience that he was not one of those pampered network anchormen, he continued, "She was joking. We have a car service, but it's not a limousine. They only use Lincoln Town Cars."

The director was rolling his hand, indicating that the anchorman should proceed to the next story, which was a late-breaking item about an abandoned baby found in an alley in Brooklyn. The umbilical cord was still attached.

"This . . . just in," he said in a quivering voice. Then he looked up again, and over at Bonnie, who was always amazed at what came out of her own mouth. "You know, Bonnie, I happen to drive a small, compact car. That's my personal car."

At that point, they cut to a commercial for Cadillac and Jerry Kantor started to babble incoherently. They managed to finish the broadcast, but anchorman Kantor was lost in some fog of guilt and worry. "Bonnie, do you have a limo?" he asked, chasing her as she fled the studio.

"Yes," she shouted over her shoulder, "it was in my new contract. That, and the larger wardrobe allowance." Then she stopped, turned around, and threw, "Oh, yeah, and the guest appearance bonuses!"

"I don't have a limousine," he said, stopping, staring after her as she took off again and ran for the elevator.

Harvey Levy was on the elevator; she saw him just as the door closed. She ran down the stairs and caught him just as he was about to enter the double-parked car.

"I gotta talk to you," she said, pulling him away.

He looked at his watch. It was 8:35. "I'm late." He looked over at the car. Inside Bonnie saw him again: Murray Gerber. She turned to Levy. "Harv, you going to work for Fasio?"

"Talk to me in the morning."

"It's Friday."

"Call me."

She watched them drive away, feeling a premonition of something—a story.

16

JACK LINGERED AT the fund-raiser, sobering gradually. He saw Bonnie standing in the corner of the Sky Ballroom, deep in conversation with a tall, attractive man in an expensive pin-striped suit. Lawyer, thought Jack Mann, feeling all the aches of jealousy and envy that he thought had been contained under the scar tissue of his unhealed emotional wound. Five years younger, he guessed. Jack's face burned as he spun around and walked away at a quick clip, heading for his appointment with Tommy Holman in the ballroom's bar.

"You look like shit," said Holman as Jack rolled onto a stool and ordered a double scotch on the rocks.

"This is the bright side," said Jack. "You'd hate to see how I really feel."

He emptied the glass of scotch, held the bartender's sleeve, and told him to refill the glass.

"You driving?" asked Tommy.

"Well, I'm certainly in no condition to walk."

He was no longer accustomed to quick liquor, and as the blood rushed to his temples he found himself in the fuzzy territory of a mild, tipsy no-man's-land. He was moving a step or two behind the rest of the world, and a strange smile landed on his face like a bird and stayed there.

"Okay, okay," began Jack, the famous teller of bad jokes. It was a method of regaining control. "So, this guy and his wife get killed in a car accident—speaking of drinking when you drive, or driving when you drink."

Holman rolled his eyes. He would have poked someone in the ribs, except there was no one there to poke.

"They go to heaven, this miserable couple, and St. Peter takes them around and shows them the golf course and the condo and the swimming pools," continued Jack. "The wife is thrilled with all this splendor and she turns to the husband, who has this terrible glowering look on his face, and she says, 'Don't you like it?' And he says, 'If it wasn't for all that oat bran and high fiber crap, we could've been here ten years ago.' "

The bartender, who Holman had thought was out of range, laughed. Holman didn't. He was always afraid that he missed the punch line. He only laughed when people fell down. He laughed at the sound of cracking bones, not cracking jokes.

He waited until the bartender walked away and then asked Jack about Gerber. "You stay with him?"

"He could not shake us," said Jack. "We were as glue to his skinny ass. That is, until we had to come here and meet you. We lost track of him somewhere between the Long Island Expressway and San Francisco. An honest mistake. But we know where he is. We knew where he would wind up. We are on him again. We have our methods."

"Yes," said Holman. "I can see that. He's right outside now—this very minute—sucking up to the governor and the mayor. Which is probably something that will be in your report. Did you know that he was here?"

"That is as it may be," replied Jack, who was acting more drunk than he really was, "he remains at the end of a very long tether. As I said, we are on him like a bad debt."

"You are? I would guess, judging from your condition, that the only thing you're on is cloud nine. Or Channel 9."

Jack indicated his partner sitting at the far end of the bar, nursing a beer. Jerry Bandolino was keeping an eye on Gerber and would signal Jack if they had to get moving again.

"We've been on him, Tommy, like ducks on a pond, like Bandolino on a hamburger," said Jack. "And you know that you can't get any closer than that."

Holman smiled, reassured. "Right. Okay. What's his day like? Tell me what you discovered."

"His day? Busy, I would say. Busy, and yet completely predictable. He awakes, he breakfasts on sour grapes and twigs, and then he goes—as usual—to his girl's house to exercise his loins," said Jack, consulting his notebook. "He stays his hour. No more, no less. They must have an hour-long Jane Fonda tape that they do it to, no doubt."

"Go on, for Christ's sake."

"Then, alone, he goes up and does some shopping. Killing time. Gets a shirt at Bloomingdale's. Crappy thing—checks, white and black, Polo. Overpriced. Way overpriced. Cost $125. The man is a fashion dysfunctional."

Someone came up to the bar and ordered a screwdriver. Jack and Tommy paused and spoke of politics while the drink was fixed and taken away.

"He does not make you?"

Jack shrugged. "He's a cop. Always looking around. Always suspicious. Watches chairs and plants to see if they move. He's also a guilty cop . . ."

"How so?"

Jack put his arm on Holman. "For one thing, he's a crook," he said matter-of-factly. "He didn't actually purchase that horrible flannel shirt. That is, he never paid for it. He stole it. Isn't that amazing? The man's a crook! I've seen the type before. Doesn't need the shirt. He could afford to pay for it. He just likes the thrill of stealing, the zip he gets from flirting with being caught. Outwitting security."

"Really?"

"No shit. Got the merchandise-control tag off and put it

under his coat. Neat. Very neat." Jack held his hand up for another drink, which the bartender brought quickly.

"He stole it?"

"And a hat."

"No shit?!"

"Yep," said Jack with some happy overlay of satisfaction on his mood of tipsy gloom. "The man's a thief. Funny thing about people like that, they get the bug. You can't be a little thief, or a sometimes thief. You're just a born thief. Flat out."

"C'mon, it was a fuckin' shirt!"

"Wrong. You know, Tommy, you're wrong. That's what makes me a cop and you wrong. It's not a loaf of bread the guy stuck under his coat, and I'm not Javert."

"Who?"

"See, if a man has an urge to steal something—say he sees some shiny object and he has to take it—it is an irresistible thing. And he can't just own it. He can't actually go over and pay for it. That would spoil the fun. He has to take it. Possess it. Because that way, he's won it in battle, that way it gives him some extra, secret kick. He feels in his scrawny little heart that he is entitled to take it. He won it, fair and square."

Jack shrugged, then continued. "That's a sickness. And it's progressive. It doesn't stop there. You steal a comic book as a kid, and the next thing you know, you're stealing dollar bills out of the cash register as a teenager. Before you know it, you're Richard Nixon stealing a whole fucking country."

"You're making a pretty big thing out of a shirt . . ."

"And a hat."

"You don't think maybe you're exaggerating? Maybe you had a little too much vino?"

"No," he said. "In vino there is veritas."

"What the fuck does that mean?"

"In wine there is truth. Question is, now that we know he's a thief, what's he stealing? Pennies out of dead men's eyes? Shirts and hats? Shaking down construction crews? When he was on the job, he had a reputation. But I thought that it was just, you know, his style, maybe. Some guys come on like pirates. It pleases them to be thought of as vaguely criminal or dangerous. Boosts their standing with people impressed by that sort of macho thing. They like to swagger. It's not always greed. But this guy! . . . This is something else."

"You gotta slow down. Forget the psychological shit. I wanna know where this fuck went and what he did. I got a client."

Jack nodded and sipped at the drink, stuffed some peanuts in his mouth, staving off unconsciousness. "Then," he said with dramatic flair, like a counselor around a campfire telling a ghost story, "after stealing a designer shirt that I would not wear to my own funeral, he goes to the meet."

"The meet?"

"The meet!"

Forgetting his need for caution, Jack took a triumphant swig of the whiskey.

"What meet?"

Jack leaned over and almost staggered Holman with his breath. "He meets . . . Ta, da! . . . Harvey Levy."

"Who the fuck is Harvey Levy?"

"Who the fuck is Harvey Levy?! God, if you'd been having an affair with a certain weather person, you'd know goddamn good and well who Harvey Levy is. He's the guy who has the hots for my old girlfriend. Always has. The son of a bitch! And he's the guy who had dinner with Murray Gerber tonight at a very discreet, very dark restaurant in Manhattan. I think it was Ethiopian."

"I don't get the connection," said Holman.

"Well, neither do I. But Harvey Levy is now a big shot at Channel 9."

"So?"

"So, Channel 9 is where Bonnie now works."

"Big fuckin' deal." Holman had lost interest. There was a

redhead across the room making a big point of her chest. She would turn and flash it at Holman, then turn away. The bar was dark, but Jack could see that she was ten years past youth. Like a lot of rebounding women in Queens who jazz up their act, she was the type who provoked a double-take in a dark bar and regret in a bright light.

"I think it may be a big deal."

"Write a report."

Holman slipped away to tell his client, Patsy Scotto, who was waiting in the men's room for the latest bulletin on Murray Gerber. Added to the report from Scotto's man at Citibank, Holman's update was giving shape to Jack's design.

The mayor was feeling a little queasy after eating a plate of pasta with a heavy cream sauce. Four doctors, including a gastroenterologist, were hovering over him as he lay groaning on the couch in the back office of the ballroom. The doctors were fretful, but doing absolutely nothing. There was not much they could do. He suffered from a lactose intolerance, could not eat cream, and the episode had to run its course. Soon the cramps would diminish. The doctors urged him to pass gas—it would relieve some pressure. The mayor was torn between the urge to help himself and the desire to preserve his official dignity.

Detectives Donald Fine, the driver, and Sam Jackson, the bodyguard, were pacing back and forth in the room. There was no clear security threat, yet the mayor's well-being was disturbed and each thought that they should be doing something more. Detective Jackson had phoned the command center, and an emergency team—including a surgeon and diagnostician— stood ready to chopper out to Queens. The nearest hospital in Jamaica was placed on high alert. "What do you make of it?" the deputy chief in charge of operations had asked Jackson on the cellular phone.

"A bellyache," Jackson replied, having spoken to one of the doctors. "The cream sauce."

"Do we have a Grade One emergency?" demanded the deputy chief, who was sweating under the weight of command. Jackson put one of the doctors on the phone, who explained to the mayor's doctor in a conference hookup what had happened.

"Lactose intolerance," said the mayor's doctor without hesitation. "Should never have eaten the cream sauce, but he's weak when it comes to cream sauces."

They agreed that nothing further was necessary unless it persisted or shifted. If Cohen developed a fever or if the pain spread, the emergency procedures would be put into operation. As things stood, they would wait.

Having seen that the mayor was in no immediate danger, Fasio wandered out of the ballroom office and found that no one in the hall was aware of the mayor's distress. They assumed a backroom meeting where plots and deals were being hatched. Medical excuses were just cover stories for intrigue. He drifted out to the main hall, where he was grabbed under the arm by an old man with wisps of white hair floating across his troubled forehead.

"Do you remember me?" cried Danny Pearse, one of the old-timers, a crony of his father's. Pearse, who ran a car service in the downtrodden section of Jamaica, who had been there for fifty years, was a fixture at party functions. Association with the Democrats helped his business with liberal blacks, but his attachments went back to New-Deal ward politics when clubhouse custom meant Thanksgiving baskets of food for hungry constituents. The informal charities of the party forged iron bonds with men of Pearse's generation.

"Of course I remember you," replied Fasio.

Pearse nodded happily. He smiled painfully and pinched Fasio's arm. "I was a friend of your father. Great man." He spoke in a reverent rasp to show his feelings for the late Big Jim Fasio. "A great man! Took all the weight and troubles for himself when he didn't have to."

It was necessary to endure the repetition of his father's myth, a political liturgy muttered like a Hail Mary among the keepers of the flame in the small borough clubs. Big Jim Fasio was a famous champion to a certain breed of Democrat who saw his downfall as a great secular passion play. Over the years he had become an example of heroic sacrifice.

"He stood up in a great wind when all the little twigs bent and broke under the pressure," Pearse went on, nodding rapidly for emphasis.

Pearse was a bent old man by now, but he maintained old habits; he still wore a bouquet of linen in his breast pocket, still rubbed his hands in respect for the son of the martyred, unofficial saint.

"Did you know that I spoke to him, not a month after they made those terrible accusations?" The way he said "accusations" left no doubt as to his opinion of the charges. "He was down at the club. They let him out on bail and he came around to the clubs to assure us that he had done nothing wrong. As if he needed to reassure us! He spoke of you."

Fasio looked up. It must have been an old tale, told a thousand times, but still he wanted to hear.

"He said that it was nothing," said Pearse. "A bunch of shit. He wasn't afraid. He'd fight it hard because of you. He didn't want you to live with that stain. He never thought that they'd convict him."

"No," said Fasio.

"Never thought that they'd give him up."

Pearse said "they," and by that he meant a murky group of powerful and wicked party leaders who pulled strings, made decisions, and allowed scapegoats to fall for the sake of the stated high-minded goals, but, more probably, intended to protect their own security and comfort. "They" continued to live in splendor and serenity while men like Big Jim Fasio paid the high price of misplaced loyalty.

Pearse shook his head. There were tears in his eyes. "You know, Big Jim used to come down personally to the district to make sure that we all got out to vote. And we were a safe district. Nobody but a Democrat was going to take Jamaica. No, sir. But Big Jim said it was important to roll up a big vote. Show the bastards that we had teeth. Show the bastards! That's why they had to get him, y'see. He wouldn't play it safe."

Fasio didn't quite see the connection, but it was an explanation that old-timers like Pearse used to justify their beliefs.

The old man coughed, one of those wet belly-coughs that signified an entrenched, enduring illness. He held a cigarette in his hand.

"I remember you coming to the house one Christmas," said Fasio.

The old man's face lit up. "That's right. I was there. You were just a kid. I didn't think you'd remember me. It was a Christmas we were a little short. Some of the districts weren't getting their food baskets. I had to come to your house and get enough cash to cover the district."

"Did my father give you the money?"

"Of course! Did he ever turn away someone in need? Not that I can recall. He was a real man. A man's man!"

Whenever he thought about his father, Fasio was sad. Not shattered, but almost melancholy, as if the whole thing was something distant and indistinct. He could remember the details, but the emotional wallop had turned over the years into something blurry and illegible. But this man, Pearse, this stranger, felt something more intense.

"Big Jim," he said, shaking his head. "The bastards!"

"You know, my father forgave them," said Fasio, lying. "In the end, he didn't hold a grudge. Wouldn't have done any good. He thought it better to get it behind him."

"But he was the best!"

He looked. The old man's face was composed. His brow was furrowed, but he was not crying. Not exactly. His eyes were wet and tears fell in a straight line down the corrugated surface of his face. Two ropes. It seemed almost as if his eyes were bleeding tears.

Fasio was stunned. He had never seen such thoughtful and considerate grief, and this in a man who had been only marginally connected to his father. He was ashamed that his own emotions were so well managed.

"My father was a good man," said Fasio slowly, his voice unbroken.

"I can't say."

His name was David Michaels and he was a federal attorney employed by the justice department. He was in New York on an assignment. That's as much as he would tell Bonnie Hudson. She was not put off by the mystery.

"You're an attorney?"

"Yes."

"You went to law school?"

"Of course."

She could see that his suit was custom-made, a cut above the usual government attorney uniform. His eyes were sheltered inside deep sockets on his sculpted face. The broad brow and the stubborn beard of his Irish ancestry gave him a masculine appeal that Bonnie found beguiling. He spoke with a sarcastic undertone, denying the importance, or possibly warning against accepting the complete accuracy, of what he was saying.

"Harvard?"

"Yale," he said forcefully.

"Yale," she said, nodding. "I hate Yale."

"Why is that?"

She was conscious of the fact that she was being uncharacteristically coquettish. It did not please her, but she found it impossible to talk to this attractive man without some coy technique.

"Bush," she said. "Yalie, male bullshit bonding."

He nodded, looked around, checking out the room. She

wondered if she had lost him. "Yeah, I know what you mean. We call it Bushshit."

They stood for a moment, silent, pawing the ground, sipping their wine in the plastic glasses. It was painfully awkward.

"You're that weathergirl," he said.

She laughed. "That's my usual ID."

He smiled. "I like that, 'Hey, it's only weather!' "

At least he got it right.

"I usually hate the news," he said. "Can't watch it. Those people! But I think you're terrific."

"Really?!"

"Well, all those other people, they seem so eager to please, begging you to stay tuned for the latest ax murder. My God! It's so grim and they're so . . . cheerful!"

"You mean stupid."

He shook his head. Laughed. "I didn't want to say it."

"It's okay. We are stupid. It makes us a lot more lovable. Smart people are a pain in the ass."

"You're not."

She nodded. "I'm just one of the family," she said.

"No, you're not. You're not like a newscaster."

"Ohhhhh, that's a mistake," she said. "We're not newscasters. None of us."

"You're not?"

"Oh, sure. Technically, we're professionals. But you have to think of us as members of a wacky family. That's the secret. Every station, every network, puts together a news program as if they are assembling a family. There's crazy Aunt Alice almost busting to tell you about the breakup of the royals. There's dusty old Uncle Dan Rather telling us in his most reflective and earnest way that the European Common Market is something that we should think about. It's essential! Good old brittle Uncle Dan. Every once in a while he tries to crack a joke, but he has no gift for it and it snaps off like an icicle."

Federal lawyer David Michaels was laughing and saying, "It's true! It's true!"

"Of course it's true," said Bonnie. "Think of us as a family. That's how we're cast. It's like a movie. We want to find a family that you'll let into your living room and tell you, in our friendly, folksy manner, about the stuff going on down on Main Street. You know, the guy eating his neighbors, the drive-by murders, the crack houses, the racial tensions, not to mention the juicy sex scandal with the conscientious, trustworthy judge and the married socialite. And then you have the funny weather person, who's usually a little overweight—for comic effect—and just a tad unreliable because he or she keeps making awful puns so we'll know that it's not really serious business."

"I'm going to have a whole new look at this news stuff," he said.

"Just don't take it too seriously. Look at it like Thanksgiving dinner talk."

She had loosened him up. "By any chance, you're not working on the Sam Morris murder?" she asked.

He was jolted back to paying attention. It had been a flirtation; now it was something else. Some family clown, he thought. "No," he said, "I'm not working on that murder, and if I was, I wouldn't tell you." His voice was harsh, but not unforgiving.

"I just thought, you know, it might have federal implications, him being a councilman."

"How about another glass of wine?" he asked, seeing her empty cup.

"Sure," she said.

"I'll be a few moments—I have to call my wife."

Well, so what, she thought? I'm not interested in men right now. I'm a professional after a story! Then she shook her head and thought of the subtle smile he had shone upon her. You jerk! she thought.

When he went off, Bonnie saw Jack sitting at the bar. He was watching her in the mirror. It was a long distance, but she knew those eyes and just how far they could travel. She felt the turbulence of unresolved emotions.

17

IRMA WAS COOKING breakfast and the smell of bacon and pancakes wafted through the old Victorian house like a remembered perfume. John Fasio was in bed, enjoying for a moment the pungent change in the atmosphere. He could hear his wife singing in the kitchen. A blend of humming and words.

He leaped out of bed and flung himself into the shower, and under the hard spray of the water, he began to sing opera in his off-key, aggressive style. He ran through a medley from *Madame Butterfly* and *La Traviata*. It was hard to believe that this was a house in mourning.

It was just after nine in the morning and Irma had already been to early mass. It was an overdue sacrament. Yesterday, something happened. They had spent the Saturday after the fund-raiser alone. Doing nothing. In the evening, they sat together watching an old movie, a love story, with Gary Cooper and Audrey Hepburn. *Love in the Afternoon.* It was schmaltzy and sentimental, but it didn't matter. It was also a reminder of mislaid passion. For a moment, John Fasio was overwhelmed with tenderness. She was grateful for the softening. They undressed like strangers, full of surprise and delight, and made love for the first time in a year. She wailed and cried and he held her into the small hours. When she awoke, she was almost happy.

And so was he. For a change he would have a sumptuous breakfast, then go visit his mother, who seemed to be adjusting nicely to the retirement home in Staten Island. Things seemed to be working out fine. The world was sunny with promise as he belted out a tune from *The Student Prince*.

When he looked up, he saw her through the opaque glass of the shower stall. She was shouting something at him and he shut off the water, leaned out of the shower, and kissed his wife wetly on the lips. She laughed and it tinkled lightly like her old schoolgirl laugh.

"Phone," she shouted.

"I'll call them back."

He grabbed her around the waist, his intentions plain, but she pulled away, still laughing, and wiped at the spreading splotch of water. "It's that columnist," she said.

"Barney?"

He took the bath towel and put it modestly around his waist. Irma slipped out of the room and went back to her cooking, singing merrily. He stepped into the bedroom, where the light on the telephone console was blinking.

"Mr. Slade!" he chirped into the receiver.

"John," said the columnist for the *Daily News* in his official working press voice. "Sorry to bother you on a Sunday, but there's something . . . I'm working on a story."

"There's a switch," he said lightly. An uneasy feeling rose from his stomach. Not just the fact that Barney Slade called him at home on a Sunday—he'd broken the Sabbath rule often enough. But he detected in the newspaperman's voice some undertone of grave solemnity.

"I need a comment," said Slade in arid simplicity.

They'd never been formal. They were almost friends. They'd squandered more than one night bouncing around clubs until daylight; they'd confided superficially together, hinting at great truths and enjoying a wild taste of each other's company. But always they'd operated on an assumption of discretion and unstated immunity. Neither one would sell the other out. Neither one would betray the other. Neither one would cross that boundary of decorum into rude badgering. Not for a mere story. They liked each other too much.

"What's the story?" asked Fasio.

There was a hole in the conversation. A black, bottomless silence in which Fasio felt a shivery chill as he sensed doors being closed on their friendship.

"The story is a scandal in Queens."

"Really?"

"A scandal involving important politicians."

Fasio laughed. It sounded hollow even to himself. "You been out late, Barney?"

"Up early."

"What is this scandal?" Fasio had control of his voice by now. He had stiffened it. He could do that in a crisis.

"The story is that Jim Hayes has a special task force working in your backyard."

"Anything more?"

"Not a lot."

"You get this from Hayes?"

"I can't tell you that."

The legs had gone out from under Fasio. He sank onto the bed.

Jim Hayes. There was a bloodhound! He was the United States attorney for the southern district, which included all of New York City. It was his task to prosecute all alleged federal offenses within his jurisdiction. But, above all, Jim Hayes was known as a scrupulously incorruptible brick in the judicial system. He survived Democratic and Republican administrations, so pristine was his reputation. Hayes was a demon on hunting down corrupt politicians. And he was not cursed with prosaic ambition. Born rich, he was an American aristocrat. He was driven by old notions of public service.

But that was not what frightened John Fasio. It was the fact that he blamed Jim Hayes for pursuing Big Jim Fasio into his grave. It was one of the first cases Hayes had handled as a young prosecutor.

The tenor of the call from Slade had only one meaning. Hayes was sending out a big signal. He was trying to smoke someone out into the open. It was an old prosecutor's trick. A newspaper story would send the crooks scampering for cover. And Hayes would see who ran.

"I am going to write a story for Monday's newspaper," said Slade. "It's going to say that high Justice Department sources confirmed that a special task force was looking into allegations of corruption in Queens involving high political leaders. Secret bank records have been impounded, witnesses brought covertly into federal offices to give evidence and information about to be presented to a grand jury . . ."

"You can't do that, Barney."

"Why not?"

He couldn't say. He said, instead, that he would feed Slade something better if he would wait a day or two so that he could check it out.

"This is a hot story," said Slade.

"Barney, I'm telling you, this is news to me," Fasio said innocently. "Just give me a chance to check it out. It could be something, it could be nothing. Maybe Hayes is trying to find out if anyone has the clap in the new administration. C'mon, Barney, he knows I'm gonna be the next mayor."

Slade hesitated. "I have this pretty good," he said. "It's a big fucking story."

"Not yet. So far you got smoke," said Fasio. "Let me find out. I'm telling you, you'll be the first."

"Okay," agreed Slade reluctantly. "I'll wait a day and give you a shot at finding out what's going on. But you call me early tomorrow," said Slade, hanging up.

Fasio dialed the mayor's private number. He got a dead fish

on the line. Billy Cohen knew something. He wondered how much.

They had an awkward conversation about the fund-raiser. Nobody raised the topic of Hayes or an investigation. But suddenly, everything was on hold. There would be no talk of an announcement and a transition—not until this was settled. Each man assumed that one or the other telephone line was tapped. Jim Hayes didn't announce his presence without first establishing that there was something out there to occupy his time, without listening to the ground. Fasio felt a rising fear.

"Listen, you take care of that tummy," said Fasio.

"I will," said Billy Cohen. "No more cream sauce."

Fasio dressed, then got Murray Gerber out of bed. "Pick me up as soon as you can," he barked; all the melody had gone out of his voice. Irma heard the difference and stopped singing. When he marched to the dining room, she placed the food in front of him on a large plate.

Gerber cleared the sleep out of his voice. "What's up? I thought we were going at eleven."

"Don't ask," said Fasio, hanging up the phone. He dug into the pancakes and bacon. But he didn't taste anything except the bitterness of that last call.

They couldn't meet on Saturday, not that either of them had anything better to do. She had the weather, and he had some reports to write. But a Saturday rendezvous would have been too thick with futile implications. Business, Bonnie had said at the Sky Ballroom on the Friday when she asked for a meeting. Business, Jack had agreed with his heart floating up around his thorax. He would have agreed to surgery, just to be with her.

They met on neutral territory—a place with none of their personal history or romantic fingerprints to confuse the agenda. Strictly business, they had agreed. They would meet on Sunday—a day of aftermath and conservative matters. Not rekindling old flames. They settled on a garden off Hudson Street in

Greenwich Village. As if there was a place anywhere which would not graze a tender memory.

It was noon and the church bells were pealing like distant, dusky hope. Almost spring, he thought, inhaling the crisp air and circling the block for the fifth time. He was early.

He was always early. It was an old habit. Because he was the youngest, his mother would insist that his four brothers take him along when they went out. That was the condition. Okay, they agreed, but we won't wait for him. And they never did. They didn't have to wait. Jack Mann made certain of that. His clock was set half an hour early for the rest of his life. Not that he minded. He found that it gave him an advantage. He got to scout the area, learned where things were, who lived where, what kind of place he was circling. Moods, tone, and temperament were revealed to him in his early wanderings. It also gave him a taste for solitary walks and watchful ways and deep thoughts. And one other thing: he seldom had to rush, except to get there early.

He saw her hurrying down Hudson Street in her plunging, single-minded way, wearing the blue coat, the one whose texture and depth he remembered from the days when she had granted him rights, when he could take her in his arms and she would come willingly, as if they were two parts of the same thing. He blinked, seeing her in that familiar and now off-limits coat. He tried not to expect much, but it was no use. The sight of her invariably aroused yearnings and expectations beyond his ability to control.

"You're early," she said, smiling. She always said that.

"You're late," he said, looking at his watch, which showed that she was for once on time.

They sat on cement benches and tried not to look at each other.

"I'm trying to investigate a story," she said to open the conversation on the agreed-upon business rules.

"Really?" He had always known that she wanted to break

out of the weather portion of the news. She wanted substance. Or whatever passed for substance on the evening news.

She nodded. "They even gave me a press card." She smiled. "A token of my important new status."

He patted her hand—a mistake, electric, even through the gloves.

"I'm looking into the Sam Morris case," she said.

"That's a good story," he said, then shook his head. He could never get used to the moral inversion of working journalists. It was a mental twist; it took something bad to make a good story.

They had long since had the head-on ethical collision over that flip-flop. She had explained that journalists did not commit the crimes. They only published the sorry record.

Of course, Jack did not completely buy her explanation. He still thought that there was something cruel and heartless and maybe even a little voyeuristic about spending a lifetime entombed in the human catalogue of weakness and transgression.

"Did you know him?" she asked.

"Sam? Oh, everybody in Queens knew Sam Morris. You couldn't hang around the courts without bumping into him. And there was a time when I worked plainclothes near City Hall. You meet all the councilmen when you pull a downtown assignment. He liked cops."

She was studying her gloves. "What did you make of him?"

He blew out some air and looked up at the sky. "Not a bad guy. A little annoying. You know, always pushing some Bayside thing. But he had a decent record, as I recall."

"You ever meet his wife?"

"Gerry? Oh, sure. She was a schoolteacher and used to hang around with Sam. Really awful what happened to her. I mean, even when I was on the job, I could never understand someone killing a helpless person. Someone who could not do them any harm. You know, I hate it when they use the term 'senseless killing.' But in her case, it really doesn't make any sense."

"That's what interests me," she said.

"What?"

"That it makes no sense. Unless someone had to kill her."

"It was a burglary," said Jack.

"I don't think so," she said. "I was out in the One-Eleven and talked to the detective who was catching. He said that the house was burglarized—things were taken, drawers were emptied, money and jewelry was stolen—but it didn't look like a maniac. Which is what you'd have to be, am I right? To kill that poor woman like that?"

He nodded.

"You think anyone could walk away from that scene and not be noticed?"

"It's pretty deserted down there."

"Not that deserted," she said. "There are eyes on that street and those streets are patrolled."

"Could happen."

"Maybe. Could we check it out?"

He looked at his watch. "I gotta make a couple of calls first."

Fasio walked deep into Cunningham Park. Gerber followed twenty feet behind, checking to make certain that they were not being followed. There were cars—sedans—that could have been tailing them as they drove from the house, but they peeled away one by one.

The men on the bocci court didn't even look up when the borough president passed by. They rolled the balls and commented in Italian on the lie and sat on the benches wearing old gray felt hats and Sunday coats. They looked up into the sun, as if they could inhale whatever warmth was present in an early spring.

Finally, in a remote section of the park where they could see anyone approaching and were certain of not being overheard, they leaned against a tree.

"What do you hear?" asked Fasio, looking over Gerber's shoulder to see if anyone was watching.

"Nothing," said Gerber, who thought that he detected a weakness in Fasio.

But the borough president looked at him straight in the eye. "Don't give me that shit," said Fasio.

Gerber shrugged. "There was a guy, Friday, at the thing."

"What guy?"

"An assistant federal prosecutor. Nobody knows what he's doing here. Just a guy. David Michaels. That's his name."

"Check him out."

Fasio turned and made another sweep of the area. Now it was confirmed. There was something going on. And Gerber was holding back.

"How come you didn't tell me?"

Gerber rolled his eyes. "I figured if you wanted to know, you'd ask."

That was undeniable. Fasio had left a lot unsaid between them. He didn't ask because he didn't want to know. But he knew. That cascade of new money didn't just spill in out of thin air.

Fasio started to speak, then stopped himself.

Gerber was watching him. Waiting.

There were men like Gerber who only understood action.

"I'll check him out," Gerber said.

"Did you . . . Are you . . . ?" Fasio couldn't meet Gerber's squinting eyes.

"John, I only did what I thought was right. I didn't do anything that I can't live with."

Fasio knew that he hadn't gotten an answer. But he also knew that he didn't want an answer. In any case, it was too late.

Gerber was not concerned. He had, after all, dodged bullets. He had disarmed men with knives. He had plundered whole sections of the city, and it gave him a certain sense of immunity. There would always be people like Hayes coming after him. But what did the prosecutor have? Sam Morris was dead. The Bay-side Homeowners Association had only third-hand knowledge of the payoffs. The people who could bring Gerber down would also bring themselves down.

He wondered about Harvey Levy. He was a man who had the conceit of scruples. Gerber played along, allowed him to think that they were engaged in no great sin. They were conducting business as usual—an inference encouraged by Thatch Conway.

In the end, he knew, Harvey Levy was aware that he was descending into darkness. He was too smart to miss the signs. He knew what he would do if it came down to it. He had no compunctions about murdering Harvey Levy, or anyone else. His only interest was in getting away with it.

And if he didn't, that didn't trouble him much, either. Murray Gerber had long ago decided that life was not as precious as living as he wanted. It was an old cop option. When things got too hot, when pressures got too bad, there was always a gun to eat. That wasn't the worst way to go out.

"Murray, let's go see my mother," said Fasio.

"Fine," said Gerber, who had no one close that he had to see.

18

THE MAYOR WAS shaving, going over the same spot on his face again and again, lost in blunt, nasty thoughts. The only sound was the buzzing of the little motor of the electric razor and the boats passing Gracie Mansion on the East River. Billy Cohen stared into the mirror and saw a fresh wrinkle on his cheek. He attacked it with the razor, as if he could shave it off.

He was no stranger to trouble. It went with the territory. Politicians are like firemen, he liked to say in his backroom talks to the volunteers. We rush out at the first sign of smoke and pour water on the threatened forest. Still, this thing with Fasio had his nostrils aquiver. He didn't know what to make of it, nor what it was—not exactly—but it came on with the gasping hush of a major crisis.

He didn't think that it involved Fasio directly. Not possible, he surmised. The sin of the man's late father weighed too heavily on the son for that. No, it was probably some lesser pilfering and extortion among the aides. The question was, how far down? If it was distant, out of the borough president's reasonable line of sight, then it was survivable. Fasio would condemn it, the mayor would condemn it, and the mayor would go ahead with his plan to resign, Fasio his nominee to replace him. Of course, there was a chance that the scandal was close—maybe even a deputy. It was conceivably as close as Gerber. That meant significant trouble. No one could separate the interests of Murray Gerber from the interests of John Fasio. They were fastened together in the minds of insiders and the public. Partners. Maybe Fasio was innocent, maybe he didn't know about corruption, but it didn't matter if it involved Gerber. The reasonable indictment would be that in such a close relationship, if there was something wrong, he should have known. Gerber's involvement would be enough to doom John Fasio's career.

But Billy Cohen told himself that he was being premature. All he had to go on was an enigmatic call from the assistant United States attorney informing him that an investigation of corrupt officials in Queens was underway and that he should not tell anyone. He was told that and no more. It was not enough to derail his plan to quit and run for governor. Not enough to condemn John Fasio as his successor. If it was a small transgression and if it was remote, Fasio would ride it out and Billy Cohen would be there with him. Cohen might even profit, looking brave and loyal to his beleaguered colleague.

But there was that unmistakable and disturbing stench of smoke . . .

He heard a knock on his bedroom door and before he could answer, his assistant, Nat Berry, came in, brandishing an agenda. Berry was in his winter wardrobe, a three-piece woolen suit and a splash of color in his necktie. The cocky show of turquoise was his only concession to the fact that it was a weekend. Berry devoted a lot of time and thought to his appearance. It was, he believed, an essential part of the job for a member of the mayor's praetorian guard: a smart and well-tailored uniform.

Billy Cohen depended upon his excessive efficiency.

Berry read from his copy of the agenda to remind the mayor that he had scheduled meetings with commissioners to discuss the transition, had an informal luncheon planned with an Israeli diplomat passing through New York, and was penciled in as a speaker at a seminar of Afro-American educators. His evening was free.

Sundays were quiet, but a mayor of New York City was never really idle. Sunday was just one more day in the life of the government, only with less traffic.

"I have to see Scotto," Cohen said deep in thought. Nat Berry marked it down on a clipboard pad that never left his hands when he was in the presence of the mayor.

"When?" he asked.

"Now. As soon as possible."

There was no discussion about shifting appointments or making excuses, or even about the rank or urgency of the engagement. Like the efficient aide that he was, Berry recognized the sound of the fire bell when he heard it.

"Phone?"

Billy Cohen shook his head and gave Berry a look of pained disappointment.

"Yes," said the assistant quickly. "I'll postpone the commissioners and handle the rest."

Berry thought that the mayor should have asked his opinion about Fasio. After all, he had insights. He knew that there was a crisis simmering just by listening to the whispers in the mayor's side of telephone conversations. Berry had become a clandestine cryptologist, just by being a bystander and decoding meaning from every third word. The mayor should value his analysis, he thought, although he knew from the signs and sighs he read in plain body English that the mayor did not want his opinion.

"God, I hate going out to Brooklyn," said the mayor, wistfully.

"I'll arrange it."

They walked back and forth along the windy shore of Little Neck Bay, attracting a choreographed sweep of curtains as they went. Bayside had grown skittish since the murder of Councilman Sam Morris. Twice, patrol cars from the local precinct had cruised past, slowing down while the uniformed officers inside studied Jack and Bonnie with deterrent intensity.

"Must be getting calls from every house in the neighborhood," said Jack, who knew the routine from his days on the force. "By now they've checked out my car and, of course, they know you."

"I didn't dress warmly enough," said Bonnie, shivering, pulling her spring coat close to her throat.

"Should have checked the weather forecast," he said, and she gave him a dirty look.

"According to the guys in the One-Eleven, he was killed first," said Jack, looking at the house intensely. "Then whoever did it went upstairs and killed her."

"How do they know that?" asked Bonnie.

Jack shrugged. "If he killed the wife first, the husband would have put up a struggle. There was no sign of a struggle. So the likeliest reconstruction is that the perp did his killing, then took his time stealing the stuff, then made his getaway. Maybe somebody saw something, but if so, the guys didn't pick it up when they made the canvass of the neighborhood. Five times they went back and forth, checking houses."

"Let's check out that house there," she said, pointing to a gabled old wooden confusion of styles nearly hidden behind a thicket of maples and elms two blocks away from the Morris house.

"You can't even see the street from that house," argued Jack. "We even missed it."

Bonnie nodded. "Maybe someone hid in those trees," she said. "Besides, people who value their privacy like that tend to notice what's going on and who's in the neighborhood. You know—paranoid maniacs."

She had a point, he thought. He was always surprised at her coplike common sense.

As they walked up the overgrown driveway, they heard a dog

barking. It sounded like a large dog. "You have your gun?" asked Bonnie, getting her can of mace spray ready.

"It's only a dog," replied Jack, who could never convince Bonnie that nature and animals were not necessarily her enemies.

"Cujo was only a dog," she replied, pushing aside a branch.

It was a neglected house, with paint peeling and loose boards and a broken porch. The grass was overgrown into under-growth, as if the house was vanishing among the weeds. There was a pile of buckets in the front yard, along with a profusion of debris, from mangled bicycle tires, broken crockery, chunks of furniture, to a World War II soldier's helmet, the remnants of a compass, some mousetraps, and some pieces of metal and wood that had been out in the weather so long that they had lost their identity and were escaping back into their natural state.

"Who's there?" shouted a voice from the second-floor win-dow.

They stepped back and saw the vague outlines of a face in the window.

"What do you want?" It was an old voice, but it crackled with menace.

"Police," said Jack, holding up his retired shield.

The face at the window hesitated. Jack thought he saw metal—the barrel of a gun, perhaps. He moved Bonnie subtly toward a bush so that he could fling her out of the line of fire if the thing turned out to be a gun bearing down on them.

"Nobody sent for the police," said the voice, a little uncer-tain, now that it was faced with an official presence.

And suddenly Jack realized that the voice belonged to a woman. An old goat of a woman, living like a hermit in a great metropolitan hub, he thought.

"There've been some prowlers," said Jack by way of expla-nation.

"There are always prowlers," said the woman. "You're prowlers."

Bonnie laughed. It broke the tension.

"Could we speak to you?" asked Bonnie.

The woman hesitated again. The metal went away from the window. "You're not a police officer," she said to Bonnie. It was no longer the barbed-wire sound of an obstacle. It was, not soft, but educated and uncompromising. The voice of a school-teacher.

"No," replied Bonnie. "I'm not. But he is."

"You're that weathergirl."

It sounded like an accusation.

The old woman took her time coming downstairs. She was very small and very old. It was not a gun, after all. She carried a broom handle. She invited them in. The house, inside, was surprisingly tidy. They sat on a flowered couch while the woman made tea. Now that she had granted them entry into her home, she was a considerate and fussy hostess. She placed delicate lace napkins on their laps, poured brewed tea into cups of English china, and served fresh seedcake.

Bonnie guessed that she was close to ninety, judging by the skin tone and bent posture and the aspect of her face. Her name, she said, was Sophie Lyons, and she had lived alone for the past thirty years, since her husband died. Her sister had come to live with her for a while, she said, but they didn't get along—bick-ered—and so her sister had gone home to Long Island. Now she lived in happy seclusion.

"I like things done in my own particular way," she said, watching that the tea and cake balanced on the knees of her guests did not spill or crumble. "The police have been here several times, you know. I've told you, I didn't see anything that day. It may have happened when I was napping. I nap a great deal."

Jack couldn't help but glance toward the door, and Sophie Lyons took his meaning: The clutter in the yard. "I cannot do a thing about the yard," she said. "It's just too much work. I can clean the inside. I have some help—a woman comes twice a week. She shops and cleans and keeps her mouth shut about me. But I wouldn't trust anyone else."

The old woman smiled. "It's not very inviting, is it?" she said, and both Bonnie and Jack remembered their first feeling of aversion. The instinct was to bypass the place. "When I was still using the subway—some twenty years ago—I would always dress in a certain way. A hat. A great, big, eccentric hat. And a cheap bag with a hammer inside. I would always manage to look a little crazy. People don't bother crazy people."

Jack laughed at the cunning.

They sat and ate their cake and sipped their tea silently, and Bonnie thought for a moment that she and Jack had been bewitched, stumbled upon an enchanted cottage in a magic forest. The old woman had a smile that hinted at a great secret. Maybe it was the secret of survival, or just age.

The house was, in its own way, enchanted. This part of Bayside, said the old woman, was relatively undisturbed. No one believed that she possessed anything of value, so while burglars and malefactors might be tempted to attack the newer, more promising homes, hers was left alone. It held out no promise. The debris on the lawn served as a moat.

"Do you know any of your neighbors?" asked Jack.

She pondered that. So far she had spoken in general terms about things that didn't matter. But now Jack was closing in, and he could see that she was calculating whether or not to go further. It was not unlike her decision to allow them into her home.

"Yes," she said finally, "I know a great deal about my neighbors. I do know what you're getting at, Officer. Did I know Sam and Gerry Morris."

"Yes," said Jack, and yes, Bonnie nodded.

"Well, I did. They lived here for many years and I, as I have said, have lived here even longer. I saw him when they first moved in and I got to know his wife when she left teaching and stayed home. We became . . . friends."

It was then that Bonnie saw stacked in the corner all the newspapers. A great wobbly pile of tabloids and broadsheets, rising five feet off the ground, growing more and more wrinkled and yellow as her eye moved from top to bottom.

"She was quite an interesting woman," said Sophie Lyons of Gerry. "Very well educated. Not just because she was a schoolteacher. Anyone can get a degree, especially these days. No, I mean educated in a deeper sense. She read a great deal and we exchanged books and spent many afternoons here, in this room, talking. When she could still get around. Then I went to visit her."

She looked around, as if seeing Gerry for the first time, and Bonnie could see a buildup of grief in her eyes. But Sophie was tough and she bent and took another sip of tea and turned back to them with a fresh smile.

Bonnie understood. It happens to people who pass a certain age, she thought. They grow accustomed to life's calamities and inevitable deaths and adopt a fatalistic calm in the face of tragedies.

"Of course, I didn't always get along with him," she added, referring to Sam.

"You didn't?" pressed Jack.

"Well, he was always after me to help more in the homeowners association."

"You didn't belong to the association?" asked Bonnie.

"Oh, I belonged," she said, shaking her head. "I just didn't follow the party line. You'd think he'd know better than to try to bully me."

"About what?" asked Jack.

She smiled. "That damned incinerator. He kept asking for more and more money to fight against it. Dues and special assessments. A month ago, right before that awful thing happened . . . he came up to the door with his hand out, saying that this was the crucial moment, it was do or die about that thing. As if he was still fighting Hitler!"

Jack held out his cup for a refill. "You were in favor of the incinerator?" he asked.

"Yes!" she said emphatically, pouring the tea. "I was for it. Do not misunderstand: no one relishes the idea of a great factory belching carbon fumes in her backyard. But, dear lord, they have to put it someplace, don't they? This seems like an ideal place, if I was in the incinerator business." She shook her head. "Filthy things. But then, so is the garbage, isn't it? It's got to go someplace."

"And he was against it?" asked Bonnie, smiling pleasantly.

The old woman grew heated. "The whole homeowners association was against it. That's all they were against, as far as I could see. They stopped working on anything else. I couldn't even make Gerry see that maybe there was another side to the question, although in her heart I'm certain that she had other opinions. She'd just shake her head and point out the window and start to cry. That's all she had in the end, you see, was the window. I guess I can't blame Sam much for wanting to keep the incinerator out of Gerry's window."

They sipped and ate their cakes and gazed out of Sophie's window at the bay, with Westchester across the water and Connecticut far away in the distance of their imagination.

"Did that break up the friendship?" asked Jack.

She shook her head. "Something like that wouldn't break up a friendship. I had too much regard for Gerry. No, I even stayed in the homeowners association."

"Even with the added expense?" asked Bonnie.

"Well," said the old woman with a sigh, "the extra dues and assessments were enormous. I just have my annuity, you see. I was a businesswoman. My husband and I owned a small factory. We manufactured shirt studs. Those plastic stiffeners for the collars. We had some savings, and there was the money when we sold the business. But, you know, if you live too long, money becomes a problem."

She smiled again, with a tinge of criticism for the careless younger people who didn't appreciate all the pitfalls and snares of growing old.

"How expensive was it?" asked Jack.

She waved her hand. "The annual dues alone were five hundred dollars. But it was like Mister Blanding's Dream House. Every month, there was a new contribution.

"Some things made sense. A neighborhood patrol. I could have supported that. But then they wanted so much money for lawyers."

"Lawyers?" asked Jack.

"To fight the incinerator." The old woman sighed. She was tired. Jack gathered the plates and trays and took them into the kitchen. It was growing dark.

"They were planning on building it down there." She pointed to a spit of land near King's Point, where the bay ran into Long Island Sound. "They had to hire very expensive lawyers. There was a special fund set up just to fight the incinerator. Each homeowner had to give five hundred extra. Then another five hundred. Then another."

"That's an awful lot of money," said Jack.

"Yes. When you have two or three hundred active homeowners each putting up that kind of money, you have quite a war chest."

"And it went to lawyers?" asked Jack.

She nodded. "Not that it did any good. They're going to start building the incinerator this summer. At least that's what Gerry told me. The day before she was . . ." She paused and bit back her emotions. "All that money and they're putting it up anyway." She shook her head.

The governor called from Albany in a state of distress, demanding to know what the hell was going on. He'd gotten a courtesy call from Jim Hayes, informing him that a special task force was investigating corruption of certain high officials in Queens. Hayes could not in conscience tell the governor more, except to add that he should not inform anyone of the call and that he was not the target of investigation.

"Patsy, what the fuck is going on?" asked Toedtman.

"I have no idea, Mike," replied Scotto.

"Don't pull my chain. You know everything."

"I'm sick."

"Bullshit. What the hell's going on?"

Scotto said he didn't know, but that there were bad rumors about Fasio.

"What rumors?" Toedtman demanded.

"Mike, I'm telling you, I don't know," he said with all the sincerity he could muster.

"Christ, can't get shit out of Hayes," complained the governor.

"I know."

The governor softened. Whatever was breaking in the city, it was nothing vital to his own fate. "You think it's serious?" he asked mildly.

Scotto didn't say anything. The governor took the hint.

"Keep in touch," said the governor, hanging up.

Now the mayor sat in Scotto's dining room while his assistant and a driver waited outside in an official car sipping coffee from paper cups.

Patsy Scotto laid out two glasses of whiskey and sat down carefully opposite Billy Cohen.

"How are you feeling?" asked the mayor.

Scotto shrugged. "You know, the cold weather's bad."

Scotto never used foul language in front of the portrait of his dead wife, Rose, which hung over them.

"Yes," said Billy Cohen, who could not count himself young in his mid-sixties. "I feel it, too."

Outside, Scotto could see the frowning profile of Nat Berry in the car.

"You know why I had to see you?" said the mayor.

Scotto stared into the whiskey. "I thought you were concerned about my frail health."

"There's nothing wrong with your ears."

"No."

"So, what's going on?"

Scotto leaned back in the chair. He looked over at Billy Cohen, as if gauging whether or not he could be trusted with a hard truth.

"Patsy, you know I'm on the verge of stepping down and letting John take my place; I do not want to walk into a buzz saw," said Cohen.

"I can understand that."

"So?"

Patsy Scotto shrugged. "I know what you know."

"What's that?"

Patsy drank the whiskey. He was orchestrating this, thought Cohen. He had rehearsed the meeting, but that was to be expected. Patsy Scotto only approximated spontaneity. His was the theater of surprise. He would go as far as he intended and no further.

"Rumors. I know that there's a special prosecutor looking into some business in Queens," Scotto said. His voice had a knowing hard edge.

"Jim Hayes gives away ice in the winter. God! You'd think he'd warn us."

"Well, you have to look at it from his standpoint. We could be involved."

"In what?"

"Whatever he's investigating."

Billy Cohen pushed a little harder. "This business about the bank account Gerber set up for Fasio, does it have anything to do with that?"

Scotto shook his head and frowned gravely. "There's a couple of million dollars gone into that thing already."

"So it's dirty?" asked Billy Cohen, whispering.

Scotto shrugged. "Where would a couple of million come from?" He shook his head again. "It's suspicious, if nothing else. The man only earns a couple of hundred thousand a year. You have to be pretty frugal to save up two million in a month. Then there's his high living. I'm certain Hayes will be looking into that. It's just a guess, but a good one. And Gerber. My, my, my!"

Billy Cohen saw that Patsy Scotto had his bloodhounds loose on the trail of John Fasio. He didn't know whether Hayes was feeding Scotto or Scotto was feeding Hayes; it didn't matter. In the end, John Fasio was going to be turned inside out.

Before Cohen left, Nat Berry came in, excused himself, and asked to use the bathroom. Scotto showed him the way and when they were momentarily alone, Berry whispered, "He's starting to get very nervous."

Scotto nodded. He took gifts of intelligence whenever they were offered.

When Cohen and the others had gone, Scotto dialed the private unlisted number of Tommy Holman and pressed him to step up his investigation into Fasio and his henchman, Gerber. Scotto was determined to keep feeding fresh material to Assistant United States Attorney Jim Hayes.

19

I GOTTA GO," said Jack after he hung up the phone. Tommy Holman had beeped him to call; it turned out to be an emergency job.

"A policeman's work is never done," explained Bonnie to Sophie Lyons, who shook her head in gentle disagreement.

"I believe that the expression is, 'A man works from sun to sun but a woman's work is never done,' " she recited.

"Same thing," replied Bonnie. "We're liberated."

"Thing is, I gotta go," Jack said.

Tommy had told Jack to go tail Murray Gerber. It was something that just came up. Holman couldn't find Bandolino, so Jack would have to handle the assignment by himself.

"It's okay," said Bonnie easily. "I can handle things from here."

"I'll drop you at a cab stand," Jack offered.

Bonnie wasn't ready. "I'll be okay," she said.

Jack was reluctant, but she was emphatic. She would call for a car service or take a bus, or do something. No big deal. He could just leave. "Call me later," she said, as he headed reluctantly for the car.

Then Bonnie and Sophie settled back like two cats into the

plush cushions of the comfortable old couch in the surprisingly snug house near the bay. They brewed more tea and gossiped about Sam and Gerry Morris and the Bayside Homeowners Association.

Then Sophie asked bluntly, "Do you like what you do?"

Bonnie was surprised. Most people thought that she was enjoying herself being a television celebrity, a gossip-column item, a public personality—that her on-air quips and sarcasm represented high spirits and a kind of gushing glee over her being paid to do such simple and desirable work.

"What do you think?" she asked Sophie. "Do I like it?"

The old woman shook her head. "I think you don't."

"Really? How come?"

The old woman was silent for a moment, thinking. "Because almost everyone on television seems so foolish," she said finally. "They make such a fuss about nothing. And then they skip over things of real importance."

Bonnie laughed and nodded. Then she said, "But I'm different?"

Sophie smiled. "Yes, you know you're different. So is that man you're with." She nodded at the door from which Jack had exited.

"He's different, all right," agreed Bonnie.

She thought a moment about what Sophie had said about her job. Mostly, she answered such profound questions routinely—without thinking about them. But there were moments when a question—even a familiar question—jolted an unsuspected twist to old assumptions. Maybe it's the way it was asked or who was asking, but the result was a different order of answer. "Television is hard," she said to Sophie. "I don't mean that it's hard like heavy lifting. I mean that it's hard like smiling too much. It hurts to smile when you don't mean it."

"I can see that. We call it a pained smile."

Bonnie nodded. "People think it's easy because we pop up at dinnertime like something out of a microwave—all those blow-dried snacks. They think we leave our brains in the blow-dryers! But it takes an effort to be on television. You have to work at it, I can tell you."

"You don't. Work at it, that is."

"Yes, well, but I don't have any ambition. That's the secret of my great success."

"You certainly picked a strange occupation."

"I didn't. It picked me."

Suddenly, Sophie surprised Bonnie and changed the topic back to the murders.

"This business about the homeowners and the killings—you think maybe it's connected?"

Bonnie shrugged. "I don't know. It just seems funny that they were murdered in that particularly horrible way and that the homeowners association isn't doing anything."

"Like what? What could the homeowners do?"

"I don't know; maybe picketing and lobbying everybody for more cops."

"That's funny. I hadn't thought of that. Yes, it is strange, now that you mention it. But maybe people are just frightened."

"And it's all wrong for a burglary."

"Why is that? What do you mean?"

"Everything about it. Too messy and not messy enough. The whole feel of it. It's too . . . I don't know. Look, why kill Gerry? One killing can make some sense, in a perverted, sick way. You kill Sam in some kind of panic or rage because he interrupts your work, that happens. But burglars flee after a killing. They don't go around and pick out cheap jewelry. They run for their lives. Why go upstairs and murder some helpless old woman who couldn't have been a witness anyway? Christ, the woman couldn't even get out of bed."

"Maybe Gerry was killed first," suggested the old woman.

Bonnie shook her head. "The pattern was the other way around. That's what the cops say. If he killed her first, Sam would have put up a struggle. First Sam, then Gerry. Methodical."

Sophie shuddered. "You should talk to Harold," she said. "He might know something. At the least he can tell you about the homeowners association."

"Who's Harold?"

"The head of the homeowners association," said Sophie.

His full name was Harold Browder. A silver-tongued real estate man with one of those woodsy offices in a low-level commercial property off Bell Boulevard, the main thoroughfare in Bayside. He was a blustery charmer who boasted of his contacts and inside knowledge and promised the members of the association that he would stop the incinerator from being built.

"You think Sam had real inside contacts—that he could really have stopped the incinerator?" asked Bonnie, accepting her third cup of tea and noticing that it was growing fully dark outside.

Sophie nodded. "Slowed it down a lot, I can tell you. It's been on the drawing boards for a while. The first proposal was two years ago. They lobbied—I have no idea how people lobby, but I guess they twisted some arms, used muscle, begged. I know that they didn't collect all that money for nothing," she said.

Bonnie said that she thought Sophie was right. She would go see Harold Browder.

"He lives right nearby," said Sophie. "Two blocks west, and one block south. It's a lovely house—all new pine. But knowing Harold, it would be on the market tomorrow if the price was right. He is first and foremost a businessman."

Bonnie took the address and some careful instructions about how to get there and set out to find Harold Browder, picking her way through the broken branches and vanishing driveway of Sophie Lyons' property.

"I think we better not make any more deposits to that Citibank account," said John Fasio.

He was driving Murray Gerber home before going to visit his mother, for Gerber had been struck by one of his blinding migraines. He was too sick to chauffeur Fasio to the Victory Home in Staten Island.

Gerber spoke, eyelids closed. "I deposited some money Friday. It was a chunk from some donors connected to some business interests. Strictly campaign money and aboveboard."

"How much?"

"A million, five," said Gerber.

Fasio grunted. "Shit! Shit!" he growled.

"No problem," said Gerber. "It's clean."

Fasio grunted again. He didn't understand Gerber. He was so calm in the face of an impending disaster. Jim Hayes was coming after them both, he was almost certain, and Gerber behaved as if there was nothing to fear. Maybe it's a cop thing, thought Fasio. Maybe these guys face down people with loaded guns and not much else bothers them. It was incomprehensible to John Fasio. He was too afraid to even press his assistant about the danger. He should, he told himself. But he couldn't.

Fasio left Gerber outside of his development in Fresh Meadows, then headed west toward Staten Island. It was late in the afternoon, and he felt alone and vulnerable. He wondered if his father had had the same lost feeling.

At the Victory Home, the manager came out of the office when he heard that John Fasio was in the building. The "guests" had just finished their dinners, and the aides were moving the tall carts slowly down the hallways picking up the trays. The home smelled of baby food and talcum powder.

"Your mother is doing great things," said the manager, rubbing his hands together.

"Is she?"

"Oh, yes. She's organized some of our guests into a political discussion group. Even gotten some registration forms to vote. I guess politics is in the blood in your family."

He was grinning as if he'd just made a huge joke. Fasio

smiled back thinly. "Yes," he said, "Mother has always been active in politics. She might even be after your job, you know. Is it elective?"

Carl Smith laughed too loud; there was a nervous undertone in his reaction, as if he worried about every threat to his position.

They were walking along the orange and blue corridor. The guests quickly made a lane for the manager and Fasio. The sight of old people scurrying out of his path left Fasio uneasy. A fascist state, he thought. But then, he was in a state of controlled terror anyway. He couldn't bear to think about the next few days.

"I'll leave you two," said the manager, at the door to his mother's room. "Thank you for the check," he whispered tactfully.

Fasio shuddered. Murray sent the quarterly check for $13,000, he thought. Drawn, as usual, on the Citibank account. One more nail in his career. But, he had decided when the practice began, he had no choice. The decent homes were $200 a day. And that was just for residential care. The nursing care for those who were sick as well as elderly ran two and three times that much. And you had to spend yourself below the poverty line before Medicare kicked in. Fasio would not allow his mother to become a charity case. He couldn't. Not and stay in politics.

His mother was sitting in front of a television set, her dinner tray on the folding arm. It was Sunday, so the menu was extravagant. She had been unable to finish the thick cut of roast beef and the healthy portion of mashed potatoes and the fresh carrots. A plastic cup of Jell-O lay untouched. Saving it, thought Fasio. That's what happens in institutions—the "guests" squirrel away bits of food for later.

"Mother," he said, and she looked up quickly and smiled. He was relieved. There was always the chance that she would be gone. Not dead, but intellectually and emotionally departed, leaving behind only the husk of her shriveling body to be fed and cleaned by the nursing home minions. That's what he would find one day when he walked into her room: the empty envelope.

"There you are," she said brightly. "I thought you weren't going to come today."

He walked over and bent down to kiss her and she took him in her wrinkled arms, folded them around his head, and kissed him all over his face. He was momentarily gladdened, but it went on just a little too long. Like the high spirits of a manic depressive, it was not a reliable mood.

She stopped, feeling his reluctance, the tension as he pulled imperceptibly away—a pressure so slight that it was almost a breeze. But Celia felt it and understood it, and he was grateful for that much.

Soon, he thought, she would not be able to control herself and would be unable to let go.

"How's Irma?" she asked.

"Not feeling great," Fasio lied. "She wanted to come. She says that she'll make it next time."

Celia turned to the window, to the lights of the Verrazano Bridge in the distance. He could see something in her eyes— more than sadness or regret. The certainty that she would never cross that bridge again.

"How's little Jimmy?" she asked, and his heart turned over in his chest. She turned to look at him and he saw that other part of the family genetic code: a cruel and complicated retaliation. She knew that her grandson was dead, or, at least, that she would be saying something vicious, and had done nothing to stop that particular bullet from shooting out of her mouth.

She turned away again.

He let it pass. He could even understand it. She was fighting against extinction, like someone drowning, gasping for air.

There was something on the screen. It was a baseball game. From a spring training camp.

"Since when do you like baseball?" he asked.

She looked at him and smiled. "I thought it was football," she said.

He perched on the bed, and she sat in the chair, and they

pretended to watch the baseball game. "So, the manager, Mr. Smith, tells me that you're causing trouble. Organizing rebel outposts, leading a guerrilla band. Is that right?"

She shrugged. "It's boring here."

He laughed. "So, what does your group think of supporting me for mayor?" he asked lightly.

She turned away from the set. "Is that what you're going to do?"

"It looks that way."

She turned back to the set. "It's a nasty job," she said.

He shrugged. "Someone has to be in charge, Ma. And you know me."

"I know you."

"Someone has to get into office and really help people, you know? They all talk, but no one feeds the hungry, houses the homeless. You know that's what I always wanted to do."

For a moment her eyes softened a little. "I know you always wanted to help," she said. "As a little boy . . ." She stopped.

"I'd be a good mayor," he said.

"We'll see."

"You think Papa would be proud of me?" He sounded wistful.

She didn't flinch. Her voice was hard now. "He would have made sure you had enough money in the campaign chest."

He almost laughed. "I'd like to start with a clean slate," he said.

"I don't think that's such a good idea," she said.

He didn't say anything. She sounded as if she knew everything.

She shrugged. "I'm tired, Johnny."

Harvey Levy was in a cold panic. He couldn't find Thatch Conway; his personal secretary said Conway was en route, between places, unreachable. Might be gone for a week. Might be gone for much longer. All the instructions for Levy would come in from Conway's London headquarters.

Harvey had called the secretary because he had heard from the starched company attorney that he was going to be served with a subpoena to appear before a federal grand jury investigating official misconduct in Queens.

The Channel 9 attorney had received instructions from London, and had said that he would meet with Levy on Tuesday to go over the possible areas of grand jury interest. Unless matters became more pressing, and then they would meet earlier. He also said that it might be a good idea for Harvey Levy to hire his own attorney. The interests of the company might not coincide with the interests of Levy. Levy detected in the voice of the company attorney the sound of a departing boat whistle.

Levy felt isolated, vulnerable, furious. Not that he had done anything wrong. Or, not that he was aware of doing anything wrong. He was merely a conduit. That's what he kept telling himself. It was a business matter he handled for Conway. But when he thought about it, he could see that Thatch Conway had left himself several avenues of escape. For one thing, Conway was not himself familiar with American business habits. He could say that he left such things to his deputy. As far as the money was concerned, Conway had no firsthand connection to the transfers. They were all conducted by intermediaries—on the explicit instructions of Harvey Levy.

While Levy was in this fretful state, Murray Gerber called from an outdoor phone and gave Levy a cryptic message. They were to meet at an old location at an hour past their last meeting time. He took that to mean they should meet at nine o'clock at the Ethiopian restaurant on West Eighty-ninth Street.

The assignment was to stick to Murray Gerber, but Jack didn't expect Gerber to leave his apartment. He watched him go inside with his head bent low, as if he had one of his migraines. He called Tommy Holman, who told him to stay there anyway. Just in case. Jack got back in time to see Gerber making his way to his car.

Jack stayed with him through the Queens-Midtown Tunnel, but on the way uptown Gerber's car slowed, then charged the lights, as if eluding a tail. Jack tried to pick up the trail again, circling, but Gerber was gone.

Holman was understanding when Jack called. After all, Murray Gerber was a professional. He could shake the best surveillance if he had to.

Harvey Levy arrived at the restaurant five minutes late and found Murray Gerber waiting outside. Gerber said that it might be a bad idea for them to be seen eating together in public so they had better walk. Besides, someone wanted to meet him. Gerber was dressed for the weather, with a knit hat and his black peacoat. They headed east to Central Park.

"I am going to be subpoenaed," said Levy miserably.

Gerber nodded. "Everybody gets subpoenaed, sooner or later," he said. "You have nothing to worry about."

It was not soothing. Something had changed. And it was not for the better. They were walking near the park and it was dark, and figures in the shadows were pushing shopping carts heavily laden with black plastic bags of empty cans and worthless possessions bulging out of the sides and tops like tumors. They hurried into the park.

"John wants to talk to you," said Gerber.

Levy brightened. Finally. John Fasio, himself, was getting involved. Surely he would show the way out of this dilemma. They headed down a path sheltered by trees and flanked by large hedges. The moon flickering through the branches played off of Gerber's face.

"Lemme ask you, you're not worried?" asked Harvey Levy.

Gerber shrugged. "There's not too much you can do about it, either way. But, no, I'm not worried. I've had bigger headaches."

"Really?"

"Really. When I was a young cop I got shot. Bullet stayed in my chest. Floating. It could still come unstuck any time, puncture an artery and kill me. Disability doctors said that I could go out on a 50 percent pension. But I figured, what the hell . . ." He shrugged and kept walking, tugging Harvey Levy along with his story.

"Where is he?" asked Levy.

"Ahead." He nodded to the front. "Didn't want to take the car into the park."

"He's not worried, either?"

"Are you serious? C'mon!"

They reached a spot just before the road that ran north and south. There were whispers in the underbrush. Rats, thought Harvey Levy.

"I'm telling you, when I first heard 'subpoena'—!"

"There he is!" said Murray Gerber.

"Where?" Harvey Levy turned to see where Gerber was pointing. The first thing he felt was the blunt edge of Gerber's knee in his back. At almost the same instant, the iron arm wrapped around his neck. The knee propelled him forward, and the arm pulled him back. His spine snapped like a dry twig. As he died there on the rim of Central Park's Great Meadow, in a section known as "The Ramble," he had a strange, comforting thought: Murray Gerber was right, after all; he no longer had anything to worry about.

20

THE MURDER OF Harvey Levy was incomprehensible.
Bonnie Hudson was at home having her first cup of coffee
when she got the news. It was just after seven when anchorman
Jerry Kantor called; he had been summoned to the station early
to put a gentle, friendly spin on the Channel 9 family tragedy.
When he telephoned Bonnie, he sounded grim and ardently
candid—the way he did when he went on the air with an urgent
bulletin—and Bonnie's first impulse was to make fun of him. But
then she heard what it was that he was saying.

"They found his body in The Ramble."

"What?" The death of Harvey Levy was a complete shock.

"His body, they found it in The Ramble."

The components of terrible events are usually scattered and
impossible to grasp. Most people blink and look at one part and
then another, dazed by the confusion and magnitude of havoc.
They are unable to absorb it all at once.

"The Ramble," Kantor repeated.

Certain things registered. The Ramble registered. It was a
notoriously deserted part of Central Park where ambiguous sexual assignations took place and deadly traps were laid. Kantor
paused, allowing the sordid implications to marinate.

"His spine was broken," he said finally, as if each detail had its own corrupt significance and had to be broadcast singly.

Bonnie had been standing, but she sank onto a chair.

"The police assume it was a mugging."

She looked around for a cigarette, then realized that she had quit smoking years ago. She bit her lip.

"Harvey?" she asked dumbly, like all of the spectators and survivors she had interviewed over the years who could not comprehend the simplest facts of life and death. Maybe, they seemed to be beseeching, the story would change. Maybe it had been misheard or misspoken or misunderstood. Maybe it was somebody's idea of a joke.

"I know that you two were close," he said.

He sounded almost pleased by that.

Then his voice quickened. He was past the consoling part. "They just identified the body. We're putting together a package for the six o'clock broadcast and thought you might want to come in early . . ."

She didn't want to hear any more and hung up. She turned on the television, and it was there, all over the morning news: television executive found dead in Central Park. Police have no clue as to why Harvey Levy was in such a region of the park after dark. But of course the context and the unspoken implications were clear.

And then came the cloying, gushing, insincere tributes from the remote colleagues. They went on and on about traits that had nothing to do with Harvey Levy. He was depicted—against all genuine truth—as a kind and gentle man who always demanded the best from his staff. He was said to be—by those who had never worked with him—an editor's editor who knew how to run a television station. There were interviews with bug-eyed staffers who grew tongue-tied at finding themselves on the other end of the microphone, mouthing, finally, ignorant platitudes. Always ending with the overheated lie: "He'll be missed."

She called Jack, and he said that he was watching a program on it now. She hung on while he watched.

"This is bad," he said.

"Yeah, even Harvey would agree with that, Jack."

"It's not just that . . ." He hesitated. The telephone, she realized, had a strangling effect on him. Cops spoke like spies on the telephone, she had discovered. They assumed that there were things to hide even in the most innocent conversations. It was the habit of keeping civilians behind the barricades.

He said that he had things to tell her, and she said that she had things to tell him. They agreed to meet and try to assemble the scattered bits of information.

Fasio wanted to appear calm, undisturbed, and the master of events, in spite of the manifest breakdown of his universe. But everyone around him was running for cover and, in spite of his resolve, he was frantic. The onset was so sudden. Yesterday he awoke singing, and then came the crack in the sky: news of the investigation into corruption among high officials in Queens County.

A heartbeat skipped, but when he thought about it, there was no reason for panic. There were no flagrant crimes to hand to a grand jury—none that couldn't be scornfully dismissed. He was a high public official running for an even higher office. Naturally, he delegated tasks to underlings. Sometimes, these same trusted agents mishandled their duties. It happened. Misfeasance was always possible, especially when dealing with great stakes and a flood of money. But nothing venal could be laid at his door. He was above that. They could trace no stolen money to his campaign account. They could accuse him of no exchange of favors. Politics, after all, was conducted on a money basis. That's how people ran for office—on large wads of donations. Perfectly legal. No, the charges and rumors were a hot-air balloon floated by his enemies. Of no importance. That slander he could survive.

But now this. A murder. This was not just some hanky-panky with shifting and uncertain bank accounts that could be explained; this was the death of a witness. The circumstances looked bad. The murder of a witness could be construed as a wicked attempt to silence the rumors of scandal. Ironically, death did not bring silence, but rather a kind of hushed proof.

Monday dawned under a typhoon of wild speculation. As soon as the body of Harvey Levy was identified, the office of the United States attorney was in an uproar. Everyone mobilized, as if war had been declared. According to their view of events, their principal witness in whatever it was they were constructing had been killed to put them out of business. It only made them more determined. Investigators and attorneys had all reported for work, pawing the ground to go after Fasio.

Fasio found himself besieged. Suddenly, the governor was unavailable for the borough president's calls. Toedtman's secretaries and aides made large, elaborate lies about all-day meetings and nonstop conferences, and Fasio could hear in the stammering evasions the sound of a brush-off.

Fasio was in a panic. But he had his racing suspicions. Scotto hated him. He felt it. Maybe, he thought, if he called, he could discover the reason for Scotto's attitude. Maybe Scotto could even get Hayes to call off the dogs. He was blind with hysteria.

Scotto took Fasio's call, but spoke to him in crisp monosyllables, making it clear that he was declaring himself an onlooker. "You know, the lawyers and judges are gonna be checkin' every canceled check and alibi," Scotto said ominously. "I'm sure you don't have a thing to worry about. Am I right? Listen, I gotta go."

Irma had taken to a sickbed now that she detected the imminent meltdown of her last stronghold—John Fasio's well-being.

Fasio wanted to believe that he could survive the furor. He told himself that corruption was unprovable. Especially in the midst of a frantic campaign.

Now this random murder of some television executive was

being elevated for political reasons into a diabolic conspiracy! He could appeal for fairness, claiming that in the absence of proof on the corruption matter, a tragic but unconnected murder was being thrown up like sand to blind the public to his presumptive innocence.

Of course he expected some to run for cover; that's what had happened to his father. The summer supporters were finding ways to put distance between themselves and the borough president on the shaky grounds that the apple doesn't fall far from the tree. The irony was that it was not too long ago that they had staunchly proclaimed his father's innocence.

Still, even he had to admit that Levy's death smelled bad. But it was very unfair. What did that murder have to do with him? By the time he arrived at his office at nine in the morning, he was already sick of the hints that there was a connection between the murder and the rumors of a scandal. He didn't know who the hell this Harvey Levy was.

"I can't believe you had that headache last night," he said to Murray Gerber. He was pacing his office waiting for the phone to ring. He was nervous because he had put in a call to the mayor and it was slow in coming back.

"Well, there's a very simple way around that," said Murray Gerber.

"What's that?" said Fasio, who had a growing feeling of dread about the enemies mounting against him.

"Well, we could point out that I was with you when you went to visit your mother last night," said Gerber simply. "That was roughly the time when this guy Levy was murdered."

Fasio was stunned.

"We'll just say that I drove you out to Staten Island. I stayed in the car while you went in and visited your mother. And then I drove you home. Isn't that what happened?"

It was at that moment that the bottom fell from Fasio's stomach. Gerber was so quick to lie. It was glib. But Fasio also thought that there might be some advantage in providing an alibi for his aide. It was, of course, convincing. There was no one to challenge it. He didn't think that Murray was guilty of killing Levy. No, he refused to believe that! But there was something terrible about uttering a lie. Such a clear-cut lie.

Why should he need to provide an alibi? He thought of saying that to Gerber. Let's just tell the truth. But he could see in Gerber's face that it was not an option.

The lie would put an end to the speculation. Thinking back, Fasio recalled that indeed he had parked in a dark end of the lot at the Victory Home when he went to see his mother. No one was there to see him. No one could dispute his story. It might have happened just as Gerber said it had happened. He began to think that maybe that was just the way it did happen.

"Call me Harry," said the man with the silver toupee and the ear-to-ear grin.

Jack and Bonnie were escorted by a woman with a brittle smile back to Harold Browder's inner office—a little triangle made out of cheap stained shingle and glass. The office's side walls were speckled with outcroppings of shelves on which stood small stuffed animals and one or two indecent backroom jokes mounted on plaques—IF YOU DON'T SEE WHAT YOU WANT, HARRY'S STILL GOT HIS PANTS ON!

There was, behind his desk, a map of this section of Bayside. It dominated the wall, the streets and parks and plots of land marked off in faint little rectangles. There was a large orange arrow pointing to Bell Boulevard and under it the inscription YOU ARE HERE! Red flags indicated houses on the market, and blue flags, those that were sold. Red was winning.

The desk was cluttered with contracts and Polaroid pictures of sad, lonely homes. They were cramped houses on tiny plots of overtrimmed ground. Yellow signs driven into the soil declaring the homes for sale. The pictures reminded Jack of the blurred photos that hopeless men and women sent in to dating magazines. The lawns looked like bad haircuts.

"The weathergirl," said Harry with his oversized marriage broker grin. "I watch you all the time."

She had tried to see him on Sunday, when she left Sophie Lyons' house, but he had been away. At a dinner, he said now. They were always having dinners, he explained. Had to keep out in the market, passing the cards around. You never know when someone's going to be buying or selling, and he wanted his business card right there on the top.

Jack noticed that Browder's suit was a little old, but expensive. The wristwatch was a Piaget, at least $6,000. The shoes were well shined, well cared-for. Also expensive. In spite of the fact that the housing market in Queens had suffered a decline along with the rest of the country, Harry Browder was doing better than most, he decided.

"You are head of the Bayside Homeowners Association," said Bonnie, smiling disarmingly.

"Yes, that's me. Homeowners Association, Civic Association, Chamber of Commerce, Citizen's Patrol . . . you name it." He announced his titles as if he were handing out business cards.

"So, you knew Sam Morris," asked Jack. The remark was a little more blunt than Bonnie's style, but it had a sobering effect.

Harry Browder shook his head vigorously. He was a man who had no enemies. He was a friend to policemen, ex-policemen, weathergirls, and city councilmen.

"A terrible shame," he said changing directions, shaking his head in mourning for poor Sam. "Gerry. Especially Gerry."

He reached behind him and took a bottle of Cutty Sark out of a cabinet. He produced three glasses. Now Bonnie recognized the smell: his breath was heavily minted. Harry drank too much. His hand trembled when he poured. They let him pour three drinks but left theirs untouched.

"These days," he said, allowing the rest of that sentiment to fall into the abyss of social disintegration.

"You think it was a burglary?" asked Bonnie.

His eyes looked haunted when he faced her. He swallowed

his liquor neat. Then he laughed. "It was definitely not a suicide," he said with heavy sarcasm. "I knew Sam well enough for that."

"He had a lot of reasons. If someone was looking for reasons. More than most, just on the surface."

"What reasons?" There was a flash of temper from Harry Browder. "He had no reasons! This man was a war hero, a fighter, not someone who'd . . . Besides, how could it have been a suicide? The man was stabbed! Nobody kills himself with a knife."

"Still, he was depressed over Gerry."

Harry shook his head, nodded in agreement, then struggled for words. This was a glib charmer who was never at a loss for something to say, yet he was tongue-tied. Jack thought he had been brooding over the killings for a while.

"You didn't know Sam, did you?" Harry was looking at Jack. His hands were folded on the little mountain of contracts and pictures on his desk. He was leaning forward. "No, you didn't know Sam. See, I knew Sam, and he was always looking on the bright side."

"How do you mean?" asked Bonnie gently.

Harry Browder poured some more whiskey into his glass. "I keep the doors locked now," he said. "No one works at night alone. I have to keep someone here to watch the ladies." He nodded toward the women working the phones in the bay of the real estate office. "You can't show homes only during the day. People work. At least, if we sell a home we want the people to work." He laughed at what was an old joke.

"What about the incinerator?" asked Bonnie suddenly.

"What about it?" shot back Browder.

"Well, he lost that fight, didn't he?" she said.

Browder looked from one to the other. He didn't understand this. He prided himself on being a judge of people; he knew a buyer from someone wasting his time the moment he walked through the door. But these two were mystifying.

"I don't know what you're talking about. Sam told me that

it was a misunderstanding. That he was going right to the top and get this straightened out. That incinerator was not going to be built in Gerry's face, I can tell you."

"When did he tell you this?" asked Jack.

"That day! That same day he was killed. He called me on the phone. At home. He said that he had been dealing with a middleman but that from now on he was going straight to the top. His words. 'Straight to the top.' "

"Who do you think he meant?" asked Bonnie.

"John Fasio! Who else?"

"And the borough president would have stopped the incinerator?" asked Jack.

"He was in charge of the site study commission. He knew the impact studies. He had the power to recommend or not recommend to the mayor and the Environmental Control Agency. Our arguments were pretty good. I know that."

"Why would John Fasio do that?" asked Bonnie. "I mean, turn around and change his mind? Why would he risk making a fool of himself?"

"Are you kidding? Listen, my friend, I don't know if you understand politics, but let me educate you." He had become a little expansive. His eyes almost twinkled. "You know how you get elected to public office?" He didn't wait for an answer. He rubbed the fingers of his right hand together. Money, he was telling them in sign language.

Both nodded. The homeowners had paid to get the attention of John Fasio, and Browder was saying that they had a right to a fair hearing. Nothing illegal or even unethical about that, if the contributions were aboveboard and duly noted.

They were getting up to go, shaking hands, old friends, when Bonnie turned and asked Browder one more question. "Who was the middle guy? The one Sam dealt with personally?"

"Gerber," he said quickly. "Murray Gerber. His administrative assistant. Right-hand man. That's how I knew Sam was serious when he said he was going to the top."

21

QUIT LOOKING AT me," she said emphatically.

Jack was staring straight ahead. "What are you talking about? I'm driving, for Christ's sake!" he protested. "I'm watching the damn road!"

Bonnie was in the passenger seat of the wheezy old Buick, also gazing straight ahead. They had both been rattled by the mention of Gerber's name. A connection—a direct connection—to John Fasio! It was a chilling breakthrough. The implications were huge, beyond their immediate ability to grasp. In spite of the fact that Jack had been a cop, and had seen murder before, the killings had always been sloppy, hot-blooded crimes of passion. To do something like this—take a life with such calculated ferocity—required an element of madness. Bonnie was equally rattled. She was a hard-nosed reporter who had seen her share of mutilated corpses, but she was thunderstruck by taking part in the chase of a savage killer. Someone had murdered Harvey Levy! The questions buzzed in her head—why Levy? Why was Sam Morris killed? And what was Gerber's role? She shuddered. That man was capable of anything. He could murder Sam and his crippled wife. She began to see some reason for that. The potential for scandal. But a kung-fu assault on poor

Harvey? What the hell was going on? She was after a good story, but this was too much. This was insane.

They were on their way to Jack's apartment, where he had the copies of reports he'd stolen from the Holman agency on the Fasio surveillance. He had never trusted Tommy Holman's motives, and was trying to see for himself where the investigation led. Bonnie had made a fiery argument that the important case was the murder of Sam and Gerry Morris. Now the killing of Harvey Levy left them both upset. The evidence accumulated over the past weeks did not give them a clear-cut picture, and they needed something more to get it right. That's why he suggested that they go together to his apartment to study the files.

"I'm not looking at you!" he flared again.

"Don't give me that crap," she shot back. "I could always feel you looking at me."

She was, of course, right. He had her on his peripheral scope, and he had her perfume swimming in his head and the silk sound of her movements in his brain. Of all the melodies played on that old unfinished tape of their aborted relationship, that was the tune that haunted them both: the fact that they knew each other so well. Dancers moving to remembered rhythms and moods.

"Jack, I don't know if I can do this." She spoke softly, but she seemed to be accusing him of something.

He was moving through traffic on Northern Boulevard, heading west to his apartment at 147th Street. He pulled roughly to the curb, still staring straight ahead. His hands were white, gripping the wheel.

"Listen," he said angrily, "I didn't do anything. I didn't push myself back into your life, I didn't arrange this job so that I could be close to you, I didn't invite you out to Queens to reinvent the wheel. I didn't even look at you. You said that we're done. Okay. Fine. I'll drop you at the subway, at a cab stand, or leave you right here. So get off my back because this is not a frolic for me."

She was silent for a moment. She gazed down at her gloves. "Frolic?" she said, amused, smiling.

"Rollick, frolic, lark." He shrugged. "I am not having a great time."

The wave of temper began to fade. "I didn't want to cause you pain," she almost whispered.

"I know that. Don't you think I know that? That, even that causes me pain. You always caused me pain," he said sadly. "Even when I was happy, even when I was delirious with joy, even when I was singing in the damn shower—there was always an ache."

"Oh, God, Jack!" she said, still unable to look at him.

"Not that it isn't worse when you're physically present to plunge the dagger into my heart personally."

"You prefer that I don't do my own dirty work?"

She didn't have to look to see him smile and nod.

They both stared ardently out of the front windshield. Women crossed in front of them wheeling strollers. Kids with backpacks ran home from school. Men with squinty eyes looked through the windshield, trying to figure out exactly what drama was taking place between the two grim people planted like cement in the front of the car idling at the curb on Northern Boulevard.

"Let's go study the files," she said finally.

He put the car in drive and lurched out into a thick stream of traffic, igniting horns and yells and a soft giggle from Bonnie Hudson.

The mayor was running late, and the other VIP guests at the luncheon honoring large donors to a shelter for the homeless were spread throughout the lavish private rooms of Manhattan's exclusive, oak-panelled Century Club, waiting for the ceremonies to begin.

Pasquale Scotto was in a tall holding room off the main dining room, expecting to take his place at the head table when the mayor entered the building. He was resting in a large leather chair, holding a brandy snifter and a cigar—a picture of triumph and contentment. John Fasio was ushered into the room, and the door was closed behind him. They were alone.

"You look great," said Scotto sarcastically after studying Fasio for a moment. He had a lizard smile on his face.

Fasio shook his head, went over to the sideboard, and poured himself a large glass of whiskey. Outside, he could hear the guests for the charity luncheon. The voices were high-pitched, excited.

The old man was right, thought Fasio. His suit was growing limp from nervous sweat.

"Sit down, Johnny," said Scotto gently. One of the rare moments when Scotto was mild.

Fasio obeyed, after filling up the whiskey glass.

"Some bozo from the press is gonna notice that," said Scotto, nodding at the liquor glass.

Fasio shrugged. He was almost past caring.

Scotto took a sip of his brandy and inhaled a breath of the cigar. He knocked an ash onto the carpet. "They can afford a new rug," he said conspiratorially.

"Patsy, you know, you are really starting to get on my nerves," said Fasio. He looked at one of the immense windows.

"That happens," said Scotto. "Funny thing, people piss people off more than anything else. Some schmuck comes along and fucks up a nicely running city—bang! You wanna kill the rat bastard! Happens all the time." He shrugged.

"What the hell are you talking about?"

Scotto smiled. "Lemme ask you something. You're a bright guy; somebody killed that asshole, Levy, am I right?" he said. "Couldn'a been an accident, am I right? Couldn'a been like they say, a fag caught in a meat market?"

"How would I know?"

"Well, I thought you knew him. I heard it. Someplace. Who told me that? Somebody."

"I only heard the news reports. He was killed in the park. What the hell would I know about it?"

Scotto had a knowing patience. Like someone waiting to spring a trap. "Well, if he was a campaign contributor, you'd know, am I right? Especially if he was a big giver. A very big giver." He waved a hand in the air. "Not his own money; he didn't have any money. That's what I hear. I mean, this guy works for that Englishman, Conway, right? And we all know that Conway wants a piece of that cable deal in Queens." He shook his head. "I heard that. Somebody told me. This Conway hands out some piles of cash, using Harvey Levy, because he's too busy for that stuff and this Levy is one of his bagmen. Business. Strictly borderline legal. But now he's a player."

Fasio's stomach performed a somersault. The cable was number one priority, Murray Gerber had said. They had never exchanged explicit terms of the deal, but Fasio had known what he was doing when he moved Thatch Conway's application ahead of the others at the last meeting of the cable advisory board. He didn't ask, and Murray didn't offer, and when Harvey Levy was found murdered—on top of Sam and Gerry Morris's killing—the suspicions in Fasio's gut had turned sour. "Lots of things could happen," he said to Scotto.

Scotto took another sip of brandy and a whiff of his cigar.

Fasio emptied the whiskey. He was starting to feel the effects. His head was unsteady. He did not resist the woozy aftermath of the liquor. He smiled, looking at Scotto. The old man was sitting there like a hundred-year-old turtle, with thick skin and slow, deliberate moves—like some durable and impervious force of nature. An old turtle.

"You know, I don't even think he was a fag," said Scotto. From the tone and the smile, Fasio saw that Scotto was toying with him, pushing him around with his paw.

"So maybe he was doing a late aerobics," said Fasio with a bitter laugh.

"Maybe. Maybe. I happen to think it was a hit, myself. All

the earmarks. You see a lot of that in Brooklyn—usually guys bent over a steering wheel with one hole in the back of their head." He shrugged. "Maybe I'm jaded."

"Patsy, did you happen to know Mr. Levy? 'Cause I sure never met him."

"Now that you mention it, I could have known him. I meet so many people. You, too, I bet. I bet you could have met him and not even know it. I heard—and I wish I could remember where—that he was a big fan of yours."

"Maybe you should report this."

Scotto shook his head. "Nothin' to report. Yet. Besides, I'd have to talk to a lawyer and you know what that means. Hate those fuckin' lawyers. Nah, I thought, you know, reasonable men could put their heads together and maybe settle this shit. It's getting a little ugly."

It was an offer. Fasio was being tempted. Signals were being sent, but he didn't know how he felt about them. He didn't know how deeply he was involved. It all depended upon Gerber, and his trust in his lieutenant was sinking fast.

"I didn't even know the man," he said of Harvey Levy. "I wouldn't know him if he walked into this room . . ."

"Oh, if he walked into this room now, you'd know him," said Scotto with a moist laugh.

Fasio shook his head, then lost his temper. "Why are you crowding me on this?" Scotto was coming at him. He felt the push of the old man's strength.

Scotto shrugged. "Don't mind me. This guy Levy, he was pumping Conway money into somebody's pocket," said Scotto, quietly. "At least a million, from what I hear." Then he stopped, put down his glass.

"Oh, yeah?"

Scotto perked up. "Listen to me." Scotto was leaning forward, his face red with excitement. "There are records. I happen to have people who work in Citibank who have told me—confidentially—that you are receiving large contributions. These

large contributions can be traced. You are gonna hafta explain,
Johnny. Not to me. To a grand jury. They won't give you the
benefit of the doubt. It's the other way around." He leaned even
closer. "If you drop out, maybe I can help you. Depends." He
looked around. "I don't think you iced anyone. But I think that
prick who rides with you could have arranged it. Just drop out,
Johnny, and I'll be a friend."

Stung, Fasio finally caught up with his voice: "Why? Why do
you want me out so bad? What've you got against me?"

"You're a thief," said Scotto simply.

Jack and Bonnie were on the ratty couch of his basement apartment, reading reports. They had spent the last of the morning
and part of the afternoon going through the dossiers. The files
and papers were scattered on an eight-foot table in the center of
the room. There were copies of bank accounts left by another
investigator. There were copies of old police reports Jack had
gotten from an old friend in the records division of police headquarters. Some went back twenty years, to the arrest of Big Jim
Fasio. There were summaries and charts and ledger sheets on
the assets and balances for the Fasio campaign. At Holman's
office, Jack had slipped the folders under his coat when no one
was looking.

"It seems pretty sordid," said Jack, flipping through a folder
marked FINANCE.

The folder had account balances on "The Committee To
Re-Elect John Fasio," "The Better Government Committee of
Greater New York," "The Queens Council For Civic Improvement," and a laundry list of other campaign organizations.
Many were recent charters and all had had a sudden influx of
cash from a variety of good-government sources. The good-
government committee assets came from a range of business
interests connected to Thatch Conway.

Jack calculated the total in the accounts at more than two
million dollars.

Bonnie was studying the accounts of the Bayside Homeowners Association. She paused. "Look at this," she said, pulling Jack closer to her side of the couch.

"What?" he asked.

She pointed to a line under debit. It was for $15,000. A notation said: "Hundred dollar bills."

"Wait a second," said Jack, and he turned to a pile of bank statements. He was breathing heavily and rummaging through them. Then, he pulled one out of the pack. "Look at this."

It was a deposit slip for $15,000 in hundred dollar bills to the account of James Morse. She stared at it. The dates were the same: February 17th.

Jack slapped his head and went into another pile of records. There was a list of donors to "The Queens Council For Civic Improvement." One of the chief donors was James Morse, who was also listed as a major contributor to the campaign to reelect John Fasio. James Morse was collecting funds from a variety of donors, and he was also skimming off some cash. The transfer and deposits were quick and confusing.

"What do you think?" asked Jack.

"I think we should find James Morse," said Bonnie.

She bent over and studied the files. The names were cross-checked by social security numbers. There were eight accounts in eight banks under the name of James Morse. He was a recipient of money from the Bayside Homeowners Association and from the committees to support John Fasio. His holdings had shot up from a few thousand dollars in January to more than a million.

"Put your arm around me," said Bonnie, shivering.

"Yeah, I know, it's frightening," said Jack, wrapping Bonnie in his arms.

"It's not that," she said. "Don't they have heat here?"

"Not in the daytime," he said.

They turned to look at each other, feeling for the first time in a long while the flame of their old emotions. "Maybe we can generate some body heat," he said, taking off her scarf.

"I can't believe you said that." She grinned, helping him with his shirt.

By now John Fasio had come to believe that his only hope lay in a rescue by Billy Cohen. It was a wild and irrational grasp at a straw. But he was desperate and slightly deranged after his private meeting with Scotto.

He was seated on a dais of the Century Club. There were two seats between him and the mayor. The celebrities formed a constant, distracting flow to the head table, paying their respects, chattering inanely, making certain that they were in the frame of the pictures.

The mayor was cutting off a piece of chicken; he was a veteran of slipping food into his mouth between handshakes. At the first break in the line, Fasio came up behind him.

"Billy, I need your help," he said. He couldn't keep the fear out of his voice.

The mayor swallowed, turned halfway around, and put a consoling hand on John Fasio's arm. "You know that anything I can do for you, I'll do," he said.

"I know, I know. Listen, maybe we could push the timetable a little." He sounded like a junkie asking for credit. He could feel the mayor's body temperature begin to fall.

Billy Cohen laughed. "Well, you know, there are some things you can't rush."

Fasio tried to get control of himself, but the whiskey and Scotto's threats had taken a toll. "It's only a month, Billy. What's a month? You don't have to do anything more than announce that you intend to resign and name me as your candidate for the office."

Photographers were snapping away, sensing that the conversation at the head table was more than routine. Security guards kept them back far enough so that they couldn't hear, but the urgent tone was clear.

"See, that's the thing, John. Once I do that, it's a fait accompli."

The mayor's voice sounded like a fist. Fasio knew that he was fighting a lost cause. He couldn't help himself. He kept pushing.

"What's wrong with a fait accompli? You were all set last week. What's wrong with pushing it ahead a little?"

The photographers were now blazing away. The television crew, which was awaiting the speeches, switched on their lights and began rolling. The reporters had come alive, like deer in a forest who sense the presence of danger. And at the far end of the table, Patsy Scotto lit another cigar.

"Can't we talk about this later?" said the mayor softly, trying to lower Fasio's voice.

"Why? What the fuck has changed?"

Fasio looked up. He was staring into a firing squad of television cameras. The newspaper and magazine snipers were in jittery motion, jockeying for the ultimate picture of his demise.

He rushed out of the club.

22

P ASQUALE SCOTTO FELT the wind blow through his coat; there wasn't much inside to stop it. His lungs felt like thin glass. When he coughed, he thought that he might shatter. Only this last great goal kept him going."Why do you come here?" asked Tommy Holman, seeing the old man's unusual frailty, wracked by the wind and the cough.

They were standing on the wharf near Sheepshead Bay where the charter fishing boats were tied down and still under canvas. The air off the ocean smelled of brine and a whiff of far-off anchorages.

"I used to come here a lot," said Scotto softly, trying not to explode again in coughs. "When Rose was alive. She'd sometimes kick me outta the house." He held out a hand, to show the way that Rose banished him. Then he turned. "I like it. It's private." He had a way of crowding meaning into small chops of words. "Not too many private hideouts anymore."

They found a wooden bench and sat. There were some Sunday sailors working on the hulls of the fleet, scraping and painting away the winter. The old man kept brushing away something that wasn't there in his eyes.

"So, what've we got?" asked Scotto, taking out a cigar, looking at it, smelling it, and rolling it around in his hand.

"We've got a problem," replied Holman. It was strange, thought Scotto, but this ex-cop was frightened of him. It was Scotto who had rescued Holman when he offended a mob hitter. It was Scotto who'd thrown him work after Holman was bounced off the police department. That was Scotto's tactic: he planted people in his debt in critical jobs.

Scotto inhaled, smelling something. "What's the problem?" he said. He didn't sound worried. After all, he had heard the worst possible news from the doctors. He wasn't going to be upset by some local political difficulty.

Holman tried to weigh his words, but he was never very good at dainty excuses. "I think someone made copies of the files," he said quickly.

Scotto didn't blink. His voice was low. "What files?"

Holman looked grief-stricken. This was bad. This was serious. "I think the whole Fasio-Gerber file."

"Everything?"

Holman nodded. "I think so," he said hesitantly. "I'm pretty sure."

Scotto shook his head. Finally, he asked, "Who?"

Holman shook his head. "Well, the only guy who had the opportunity—who was alone in the office—was the new guy, Jack Mann," said Holman. "The guy we put on Murray Gerber's ass."

"Who's he making copies for?" asked Scotto.

Holman hated to speculate, but he had to give the old man an answer. "Well, I'm not positive, but he used to go with this weathergirl, you know the one on Channel 9."

Scotto thought. Then he remembered. "Yeah, yeah, yeah. What's that thing she says? Oh, yeah, 'Hey, it's only weather.'"

"I like her," said Holman brightly.

Scotto gave him a gloomy look. "You like her?!"

Holman was embarrassed. "As a weathergirl. On television. She's pretty."

It was a great burden, thought Scotto; he was stuck with an

addled, simpleminded oaf as a lieutenant! Where were the streetsmart mercenaries who had once filled the ranks of the party? Where were the rough-hewn precinct philosophers who knew every quirk of every group and ethnic tribe in their voting district? Where were the urban mechanics—uncertified PhD's in human behavior—who made up the marching soldiers of the local Democratic party?

They were the reason he went into politics in the first place. Not just his father's prodding to take that road, to grab legitimate power. Politics, behind the scenes, that was the road to power, his father had said. That was where you could do good.

But that wasn't Scotto's only reason. He wanted to be near the grown-ups, which is how he thought of the political warriors. To hear them calculate the voting patterns for this block and that block. To listen to the leathery wisdom. He loved the game, playing against political chessmasters, pitting his moves against the brilliant counterplay of scheming experts. It was a challenge and a high instruction in real life.

He had sat in rooms with sidewalk scholars who read Chaucer while awaiting election results; he had known men who, on a night of a long-shot victory, would quote *Henry V.* Of course, he'd come into it at a time of hope and expectations; a time that was highlighted and ennobled by the great crusade of the Second World War. It was a time when the women were trained to service and silence. And it was never dull, and it was never too mean.

But now he was weighed down by the sodden yoke of the Holmans. Maybe it was good that he was dying, he thought. His time was up when he had such puny collaborators. They no longer knew what it was that they were fighting for. In the old days, the passions were always flying high like battle flags. They followed a bright torch of populist folk wisdom.

There were other resources in the good old days. They knew the meaning of sacrifice then; they gave themselves up for the good of the party. Now Patsy Scotto couldn't get one lousy borough politician to curb his fuckin' appetite.

Somewhere along the way, politics had gone sour and rotten. It had become a quick-buck industry, instead of the devout church he had entered like an acolyte.

"Well, a weathergirl! What the hell," said Scotto sympathetically.

"It's not that simple. She's a reporter for Channel 9," said Holman. "That's the same station that Harvey Levy worked for."

"So?"

Holman sighed. It was miserable, dragging this out himself. "So, she's not just a weathergirl. She's a police reporter."

"No! Don't hand me that shit."

"She worked for a newspaper and she's been investigating."

"What? What the fuck has she been investigating?"

"Sam Morris. The homeowners association. She's bound to look into Harvey Levy's death."

"Fuck!" said Scotto, getting up.

Then he turned and glared down at Holman.

"I think you better handle this," he said to Holman.

"How?"

Scotto thought for a moment. He remembered the early report Jack had made and submitted to Holman. "Isn't this guy Mann the same one who followed Gerber Sunday night?"

"Right."

"So, he can place him in the city; Gerber is running around telling everyone that he was with Fasio out on Staten Island the night of the murder and we know that he was in Manhattan. Probably heading for a meeting with Levy. Am I right?"

"Definitely."

"So, what if someone called Gerber and tipped him about this cog in the Fasio bandwagon?"

It took a moment, but then Holman grasped it. Scotto wanted to smoke out Gerber. "Right," he said.

*   *   *

The new station manager's name was Ian Shea. He was taking over the news division, as well as the rest of the station's programming. One of his first demands upon assuming power was to see Bonnie.

She was flustered. Shea was a man in his forties—one of the English public-school types, with perfect tailoring, a perfect haircut, chiseled features, and a scornful manner. He was smoking a cigarette, reading a report, and sitting behind Harvey Levy's old desk. The sight of him there gave her a jolt.

He had an unpleasant expression on his face and a glass of whiskey on his desk. He didn't offer Bonnie a drink. She held that against him, as well.

"You were absent from work yesterday, Miss Hudson," he said crisply.

"Yes, well, I was very upset," she said. He removed his glasses, stopped reading the report, and stubbed out the cigarette. "I did call in," she added.

He got up, and she was struck by his height. "You are a professional," he said.

Well, she was not British. She was an American. We won that war. "I regard my appearance today as an act of professional heroism," she replied.

He laughed without much mirth. He lit another cigarette. He said that he had been fully briefed by Mr. Thatch Conway about her useful influence on the ratings, that she had a license to test the envelope, as it were, of the weather segment.

But she was not to go too far. He had watched some of her tapes, and while he, himself, did not always grasp American idiom or humor, he appreciated the fact that she had a distinctive and appealing style that suggested someone who was, by nature, droll.

"I love Monty Python," she said flippantly.

He looked at her with an expression of complete puzzlement.

"I can assume that you will be doing the weather tonight?" he asked mockingly.

"You bet," she said. "But there's another thing. I guess nobody got around to mentioning it."

He was settling down to his papers, putting on his glasses, dismissing her.

"I'm working on a story," she said, not budging. He removed the glasses again. "A big story," she added.

"Something to do with the weather, I presume?" he asked. "A new hurricane?"

"No," she said. "This is a political story. Something breaking in Queens with the borough president."

He put on the glasses and began reading the papers on his desk while addressing her. "Mr. Conway spoke to me about that. He asked me to convey his strong desire that in the future you confine your gifts to the weather. Thank you."

She got up. "I'd like to speak to Mr. Conway about that," she said.

"Fine," he said evenly. "Make an appointment with his secretary," he said dismissively. "Meanwhile, remember, please, only the weather." He looked up and smiled. "With the exception of those little sallies into comedy at which you excel."

She slammed the door on her way out.

Soundman Max Gross was waiting by the elevator. She had a call waiting. It was from Jack.

Jack had been able to copy only a fragment of the records before. Enough to point the compass, whet his appetite, clear his head. Now he was back, poring through the rest for the answer to the questions set off by the first round. The banking records were too cumbersome to spread out. At least in the overheated atmosphere of Holman's office. So Jack Mann had to leaf through them, one by one, surreptitiously. They were kept in categories: Committees, Donors, Misc. The neon blonde secretary was looking at him with suspicion, but Jack Mann was still employed by the agency. She comprehended enough from her eavesdropping to know that he was not in good favor and that it might be prudent to ban him from reading the files. But that decision was beyond her authority. Tommy Holman would have to rule on that.

Bandolino asked if he could help, and Jack thanked him but said this was something he had to handle himself. The old detective withdrew to a couch where he bit his fingernails.

Jack found the name of James Morse under "Donors." The large checks donated by Morse went to "The Committee to Re-Elect John Fasio," along with several other committees. Jack snuck copies of the canceled checks into his pocket. Thousands of dollars. Hundreds of thousands.

He kept digging into the files, searching for some clue to the true identity of James Morse.

"You sure I can't do nothin'?" asked Bandolino. He was sorry that he had let Jack down on the surveillance and still looked for any excuse to make it up.

"Hey, Bando, no problem! I can handle this. But, listen, you really wanna help me out? I could really go for a coffee and bear claw."

"Great."

He had his coat on in a second. The secretary waved Bandolino away when he asked if she wanted anything. She was on the phone with Holman, and trying to concentrate. The door slammed as Bandolino almost ran out. "Yes, well, that item you mentioned is here now, Mr. Holman," said the secretary. ". . . No, the other item, ya know? Just went down for coffee."

Jack almost laughed. But he still had time, even if Tommy Holman was now aware that he was plundering the files. He started going through the LARGE DONOR file.

"Mr. Holman would like to talk to you," she said archly, holding out the telephone.

"Thanks, Sherry," he said, loping over to her desk, pinching her cheek, trying to act nonchalant.

"It's Cherry," said the secretary.

"Never would have guessed." Then he picked up the receiver and sat on her desk. "Hey, Tommy! Where the hell are you? Gonna hafta report you to the boss."

"I'm in the car."

He could hear tension in the voice on the other end of the phone. Tommy Holman could not disguise his moods.

"Yeah, well," Jack said. "I'm just cleaning up some reports, you know? I gotta type out that surveillance on M the other night. And I still got some expense reports . . ."

"Listen! Listen! I don't want you to touch the files. You hear me?"

"Too late, Tom Tom. I got my hands all over them."

He hung up and under Cherry's malignant gaze went straight back to the LARGE DONOR file. The phone rang again.

"Thomas Holman Associates," began the ever cheery Cherry. Then her voice dropped. Jack could hear the whispered words as she turned away. "Yes, he's still here . . . What? He's going through the records . . . No. Mr. Bandolino is still out now. But I don't think he'll be gone long . . . Okay. Tell him what? . . . Okay, Mr. Holman. When will you be back? . . . Yes, I know, Brooklyn-Queens Expressway traffic. Ya don't hafta tell me about that. I'll try to handle it."

There was a secret portion of the file cabinet. It had a lock. Jack used his pocketknife and broke it open. Inside he found the records of Pasquale Scotto's instructions. Figured. Jack always suspected that Patsy Scotto was the guiding hand behind the surveillance.

At the back, he spotted a red folder with bank records of large donors. Inside were the canceled checks. There was a copy of a $250,000 check from James Morse to the committee and a copy of a check from TC Ltd. for $250,000 to James Morse, both drawn on the same date. He began copying the names and the dates. There were company names listed, giving large amounts to John Fasio's campaign. The companies had one thing in common, according to the IDs on the checks. They were all subsidiaries of Conway Enterprises.

He knew now the links between the killings and the campaign slush funds. He knew where James Morse came in, and, more important, who he was. There were a few mysteries remaining, but nothing crucial.

"Uh, Mr. Mann, Mr. Holman asked me to ask you to please leave the files until he returns," pleaded the secretary, who remained behind her desk. She looked a little frightened.

"Hey, Sherry, I'll only be a minute."

"He was very specific, Mr. Mann."

"Do me a favor, just shut up," he said. He was stuffing the copies of the checks into his coat pocket. Just then, Bandolino returned, half out of breath, with the coffee and bear claw.

"Mr. Bandolino," yelled the secretary, "Mr. Holman just called, and he had very specific instructions—"

"C'mon," said Jack, grabbing Bandolino under the arm. He scooped up his own coat. "We got a job."

"What about the coffee?" asked Bandolino.

"Bring it," said Jack.

"Mr. Bandolino!" called the secretary as they headed out the door. Jack was gone before her words could catch up.

"What's goin' on?" asked Bandolino as they hit the cold air.

"The shit has hit the fan," said Jack. "Take your car and meet me at Montauk Point."

"Way the hell out on Long Island?"

Jack shrugged. "That's what he said. He's the boss."

"What's happening there?"

It was the first place Jack could think of that would put Jerry Bandolino out of the picture for at least four hours.

"I don't know, yet. Tommy told us to get there, use separate cars, and not to call him until ten o'clock tonight." It was 4:30.

"Can we stop to eat?"

"You stop. Just don't call in until ten."

23

D ID I COMPLETELY wear you out?" Bonnie asked kittenishly when she picked up the receiver.

"What?" boomed back the voice on the other end of the phone.

Bonnie started to say something but stopped. It wasn't Jack on the telephone. She looked at the receiver, as if it had duped her. She blushed. "Who is this?" she asked under a dome of embarrassed indignation.

There was a slight hesitation on the other end of the line. Then, recovering, more assured, the voice said, "I'm calling for Jack. I was looking for him." The voice sounded frosty, but nevertheless familiar. "You are a friend of his?"

She was disturbed by the formality of the caller's style, as if this was something scripted and rehearsed.

"Yes, I'm Jack's good and true friend," she said. "Who the hell are you?"

There was that stammering pause again. She had that effect on men. Her head-on approach made most of them blink.

"I'm, uh, trying to reach him."

Who was this, she wondered. Cryptic and sinister, she thought. Still, she was more curious than alarmed.

She put a business suit on her own voice. "I am expecting to hear from him."

There was a beat or two of hesitation, as if the caller was making adjustments in plans. "Yes, well, would you tell him that if he is seeking some fresh information about certain matters that he has been investigating, he can come to Borough Hall at 6:30."

"Which borough hall? Where?"

All she heard was the click of the other receiver.

She gathered her coat and her purse and turned to Max Gross. "Listen, if Jack calls, tell him to meet me at Fasio's office," she said breathlessly. "And don't tell anyone else where I've gone."

"What about the six o'clock broadcast?"

She looked at her watch. It was 5:00. She had promised Shea that she would do the evening weather forecast. He did not seem like a man who took the breach of such assurances lightly. "Tell them that I was bleeding and had to be rushed to the doctor," she said.

"Bleeding? With what?" cried Max as she ran off.

"A miscarriage."

It was all over. He was certain. John Fasio tried to grasp the fact that his career as a public servant was finished. He stared at his desk. It was clean and uncluttered. He listened to the late-day bustle as the building emptied. Scotto had called him a thief. Well, he was a thief. It had begun with the free coffee and the free vacations. Then letting Murray fiddle with the accounts so that his mother's nursing home bill was paid. Finally, when the campaign chest was dry, he didn't ask how it got filled up. He obeyed Murray's priority calls. The money came from business interests, and those same business interests were connected to the business interests of the borough. He knew that.

He had rehearsed a defense. He had to deal with business-men, because they were the people who bid on the contracts. But he had given no special favors to anyone. No one could prove that he had. Everyone knew that fund-raising was a free-fire zone.

But he couldn't sustain the lie. He knew better. Scotto was right—he was a thief. He just prayed that he wasn't a co-conspirator to murder. Murray Gerber had recently become a completely unknown quantity.

"Is there anything I can do for you before I leave?" asked his secretary, poking her head in the door.

"No, thank you, no." He heard a wistful, wandering quiver in his voice.

"Good night, Mr. Fasio."

"Good night, Jane."

It sounded like good-bye.

No, there was nothing brazen that they could charge him with—if the special prosecutors were in fact after him. He could mount a reasonable defense. But he had no heart left to defend himself.

Funny. Billy Cohen had recognized long before he did that something had gone wrong. The old fart still had a reliable cunning.

There was a knock on the door, and Murray Gerber walked in. He looked grim, but undefeated. Fasio wondered if he knew what defeat was. Gerber was a technician, a plumber. If he had moral and ethical qualms about the way he did his work, John Fasio had yet to detect them.

In spite of everything, Fasio could not believe that Gerber was a killer. No, Sam had been murdered by an intruder. And Levy was a victim of urban peril. Still, why did Murray ask for an alibi? Probably because he didn't have one and he knew that he might fall under suspicion. That didn't make him guilty. But he wouldn't give him a false alibi anymore. That was asking too much.

* * *

Jerry Bandolino was halfway to his car when he remembered that he had left his cellular phone in the office.

As he headed back to the office, Bandolino saw Jack's old Buick turn toward the expressway, headed, he thought, out to their late rendezvous on the tip of Long Island.

The secretary was on her feet, holding the phone, when he walked in. "Oh, thank God," she said, handing him the receiver. She looked ashen. She had just explained to Holman that Jack had come back to the office and taken more files. She hadn't known how to keep him out.

"Listen to me," Holman told Bandolino. He was on the car phone. He had the command tone in his voice.

"Jack told me," Bandolino said crisply.

"He told you what?"

"About the meeting on Long Island. I was heading out to Montauk now. I just came back for my cellular phone."

Holman spoke quietly so that Bandolino would bend in and pay attention. "Listen to me. Jack's gone rogue."

"You're jerking me off!"

"Listen to me!" Holman's transmission was breaking up as he passed a power station.

"I can't hear you!?"

"Hang on! Don't hang up!"

Now he was yelling. The voice came in clearer.

"I can hear you now."

"He stole some files."

"Who? Jack?"

Holman couldn't afford to lose his patience. "Yes, Jack. He stole some important files."

"Jack?"

None of it was beyond reason. Bandolino believed every form of treachery, from cops stealing cocaine to support their own habits, to mothers selling their babies. He believed his wife running off with another cop. But Jack had seemed so . . . upright.

"Yeah, okay," he said, getting the gist of Holman's message. "He stole some files."

"Whatever he told you, it's a lie."

"Right." He picked up a pen and broke it in half.

"I want you to get over to Borough Hall." It was where the special prosecutor had set up shop. But Holman guessed Gerber. That was where Jack went.

"Right," Bandolino said.

"I want you to stop him from giving those files to anyone."

"Right."

"Start with John Fasio's office. And stop Jack. I don't care how you do it."

"Right."

Bandolino's voice was flat—a straight line. Like a bullet. He grabbed his own cellular phone and went out after Jack.

It was a windfall. Eight officers of the Conway Communications Company, CCC, had donated a total of $32,000 to the good-government committee, whose chairman was James Morse, whose social security number was identical to that of Murray Gerber. The good-government committee funneled $22,000 into the Fasio campaign fund. All the ensnaring checks and all the matching files and all the significant clues, one linking the next to another in an inexorable chain of proof, were in his possession. Jack drove in circles for two blocks just in celebration, then decided that he would head for home, marshal all of his meaningful facts, then turn them over to the special prosecutor in one incriminating package.

Through Holman, Scotto had the ammunition to destroy Fasio. But Jack was not certain that he intended to use it. It was all there in Holman's files, but Scotto was keeping the information away from the special prosecutor. Why?

The late-afternoon traffic was building. Jack stayed at the same speed as the flow. It helped him think. He used the cellular phone to dial Bonnie at her office. They had agreed to meet, but they would have to be a little more careful. There was still time before Holman could react to Jack's moves, but they couldn't loaf.

"She went to meet you," said Max Gross through the static.

"What do you mean?" asked Jack.

"She got a call from someone and then she said that she was going to Fasio's office and she would meet you there."

Jack looked around. He was driving west along Northern Boulevard, heading for his apartment. The streetlights were coming on, as it still grew dark early.

"How long ago?" he asked.

"Half an hour, forty-five minutes," said Max.

He hung up, pressed down on the accelerator, and headed toward Borough Hall.

There was almost no one left inside Borough Hall, but the police guards had not yet sealed the building. Bonnie walked up the staircase and heard her footsteps echoing down the empty hall. The lights were out in all the offices, save the large suite with double doors at the end of the corridor. The headquarters of John Fasio.

Murray Gerber was waiting for her there. He took her under the arm, paralyzing her with the ferocious power of his grip, and pulled her into his own den off to the side of Fasio's office.

"What the fuck are you doing?" she said loudly.

"Keep your voice down," he said through clenched teeth, closing the door behind them.

"What's going on here?"

The room was windowless. He pushed her into a seat. He had his jacket open and she could see the pistol riding on his hip.

Then the connecting door opened, and John Fasio came in. He smiled at Bonnie. "The weathergirl," he said, surprised.

"Where's Jack?" she asked sharply. Better not to show weakness now, she thought.

"He's coming," said Murray.

"Who's Jack?" asked Fasio.

Murray shook his head. "He's still playing innocent," he said to Bonnie.

Murray sat on the lip of his desk, one leg on the floor, the other cocked for balance. Fasio stood back, as if he sensed that this room was dangerous.

"Jack is that guy, the ex-cop, who's been hounding us," he said. "Following me. Working for Scotto. Gathering evidence. Jack Mann. Her boyfriend."

"What evidence?"

Gerber threw up his arms in disgust. "Man, don't you know what's going on yet? They are on our ass over the campaign donations. They're trying to knock you out of the damn race."

"Murray, I think you better . . ."

Gerber looked at Fasio with something close to hatred. "Stop it!" he screamed. "Quit playing innocent!"

"Murray," he began softly, "I am innocent. We are innocent."

"Oh, Christ! Where the fuck did you think we were getting the money to pay for your mother's nursing care? Why did you think I kept putting off the damn incinerator? Because I liked that schmuck, Sam Morris?" He waved Fasio away. "Stop being a baby. You are with me in this, John."

Bonnie felt a lump of terror rising in her throat. Murray Gerber spoke like a man burning bridges. "Hey, pal, I'm only a television weathergirl," she said.

"That's right," said Fasio. "Didn't you use to work for *Newsday*?" He sounded to her like someone trying to smooth the waters. She saw that he, too, was frightened by this sudden outburst of Gerber's.

"Yes, I did work for *Newsday*."

"Now she works with Jack Mann," said Murray. "The guy who's trying to murder us."

He was perched like an attack dog, ready to lunge if she made a move.

"Murray, what's going on here?" asked Fasio.

"We're waiting for Jack."

There was a knock on the door. Murray moved around Bonnie and let Jerry Bandolino in.

"Stand over there, Jerry," said Gerber. "Don't let her out. Jack will be along."

Bandolino obeyed.

"Murray, this is not a smart thing," pressed Fasio.

Gerber shook his head. "Listen, I'll tell you everything, if you promise to pay attention." He went behind his desk, reached down and opened the second drawer, pulled out a pistol with a silencer, looked up, aimed and shot Jerry Bandolino once in the middle of his forehead. Bandolino watched hypnotically, not making a move, uncertain of his role, right up until the moment his head split open. Then, with blood spilling out of his mouth and an eye rolling down his cheek, he collapsed in a heap.

Bonnie screamed, which was the effect Murray wanted. He heard Jack's footsteps running down the hall.

Jack stumbled into the mess, his old service revolver at his side. Murray Gerber easily took it away after tripping Jack in the doorway. Jack was grateful to see that Bonnie was still alive. But Bandolino lay on the floor, his stomach twitching and blood still pumping out of his dead, empty eye socket.

Jack had a strange thought: What was Bandolino doing here?

Fasio was cringing in a corner, horrified by what he had just witnessed. Bonnie was rooted to her chair, frightened, but, Jack saw with pride, amazingly composed.

Gerber had the gun pointed at Jack's heart. Jack toyed with the idea of lunging for Gerber's weapon, but thought he stood a better chance if he waited for an opening. There would come a moment, a lapse in attention. Better to wait.

"You're late," said Gerber. He sounded like a psychopath, gone over some psychological edge. Jack was almost clinically calm. He had seen such things before. Somebody starts killing and doesn't stop. When he was a rookie cop, he had come into a house where a man had killed his unfaithful wife, then murdered her mother, her sister, and even a stranger who happened to board there. When Jack asked why, the murderer answered simply, "Because they were there." Murder was a fever that had to run its course.

"I got held up in traffic," replied Jack. "Sorry."

"Doesn't matter," replied Gerber, putting Jack's gun in his holster. "You got here in plenty of time to kill poor old Jerry, there."

He saw the plan. Gerber would blame Jack for killing Bandolino. The rest was still murky.

"What about the borough president?" asked Bonnie. "He's a witness."

Gerber looked around at him. "Oh, he'll back me up. He's already given me an alibi for Sunday night."

Fasio looked confused, stricken. "But, I thought . . ."

"What?" asked Gerber contemptuously. "You thought that I was innocent?" He was plainly disgusted. "You're such an asshole! You even thought that you were innocent. Christ, you even thought that your father was innocent!"

"My father?! He was innocent!" cried Fasio, taking a step forward. "My father was innocent!"

Gerber laughed.

"My father was innocent, goddamit!"

There had always lurked a doubt in the back of Fasio's mind. His father's innocence had rested on the flimsiest of all platforms: windy silence. Big Jim would not discuss the case, except to say that he was the victim of injustice. His mother was even more enigmatic. She said, when asked, that she had as much to do with the missing money as his father. John always took that to mean she was delivering a careful verdict. A faithful wife's solidarity!

"Well, technically, yes. He wasn't guilty. He didn't actually steal the campaign money, if that's what you mean."

Fasio still looked troubled. There was that whole swirling period when the family finances plummeted and his father was in charge of a tempting political treasure.

There were always tempting infusions of cash, in any campaign, and the donors didn't ask for an accounting. In the old days, no one had asked for a strict accounting. At night, Big Jim would come home late from a round of fund-raisers and dump his briefcase full of cash and checks on the kitchen table. Fasio's mother and John would count while his father showered before coming down to dinner. John and Celia Fasio—so crimped and squeezed by budget pressures—were intoxicated by the crisp hundred dollar bills that had to be torn apart by wet fingers and thumbs.

It was, he remembered, a great effort to remind himself that it wasn't his money, an effort not to pocket a handful of bills. No one would have missed them, he told himself. Only he would know.

He remembered the college crisis, the feel of the envelope when his father handed him the money to pay for his tuition. He hadn't asked then and he didn't ask now where the money had come from. He didn't want to know.

But Gerber wasn't finished. "No, your father didn't steal the money to keep you in college."

Fasio looked relieved.

"Your mother took the money." Fasio stared at him. Gerber had something to add: "Your father only covered it up."

"You little bastard!"

He knew that it was true. He knew because he could still remember the look in his mother's eyes when they made tall piles of cash. She had the look of a beggar at a banquet.

After the scandal, he had heard her evasive explanations about the income that arrived in the nick of time to keep the family from economic collapse. She was involved. He knew. Probably always had known.

Gerber waved the gun at him, restraining him.

Fasio's head swirled.

Gerber spoke with contempt. "Your mother needed the money to send you to college. Your father knew she took the money. The only thing he ever took was the blame.

"Scotto wants to get you. He thinks you're in it, just like your mother was in it. The old man is using Holman to drop hints to the special prosecutor about the way we got campaign money. He's digging up all the shit with Conway and the homeowners association. I don't think he ever wanted to scare you off. I think he wanted revenge for what your father did to the party. He hates a crook."

A feeling of overwhelming despair threw John Fasio against the wall. The whole world was contaminated. His father, his mother—himself! His own fraudulent aspirations to do good. That's what his mother told him to do when he was a little boy wondering how he should spend his life. Do good, she said. Whatever else you do, she said in that high-minded voice of plain virtue, do good. Add to the overall stock of goodness in the world. No matter what else you do, do that much.

So said his mother, the thief.

Well, he thought, exhausted by the weight of all his new intelligence, maybe she was right, after all. He could still do good. There was still time.

John Fasio looked down and saw a knife in the second drawer. It was one of the long dirks favored by Gerber for silent killing. When Gerber's back was turned, Fasio reached down into the drawer and took it out.

Gerber turned his head in time to see the pointed end coming down like a curtain on his back. He jumped, but Fasio was too strong and too determined. Gerber was spurting blood and dying while Jack and Bonnie fled to the far corners of the room.

They watched helplessly as Fasio withdrew the dirk and

turned it around. "No!" cried Jack. He was too slow. The borough president plunged the dirk into his own belly and with enormous strength pulled it up to his heart, tearing and ripping through his organs in one last act of contrition.

The floor was awash in blood.

Epilogue

In the tumultuous aftermath of what came to be known as "The Carnage in Queens," John Fasio came to be regarded by the public as a tragic villain. He was denounced as a swindler and greedy exploiter of high office, but there was an underlying note of pity and regret from those who blamed fate or his father's tragic fall for all that followed.

Murray Gerber lived for ten days in a coma.

Celia Fasio died in her sleep before she could be told of her son's disgrace and death.

Irma became a recluse.

Mayor Billy Cohen changed his mind and decided to stay in office and run for reelection, which he lost to a reformer.

Bonnie went on the air some nights later to give her weather report. She burst into tears during the description of a hurricane moving up the coastline from Florida. She was granted a leave of absence, then quit to take a job as a police reporter for the *Daily News*.

Thatch Conway was indicted by a federal rackets grand jury and, after a plea bargain, was fined $100,000 for his attempt to manipulate the American system. Later that year, he bought outright a cable company that turned profits of $100,000 every single day.

But the real resolution to the story came for Jack Mann one day in June when he drove out to the lip of Brooklyn in his wheezy old Buick. It was a warm day, but he found the man in the attached house in Bensonhurst wrapped in a blanket, propped up in a chair. Pasquale Scotto had only wrinkled parchment left on his bones, a matter of days left in his body.

"I knew he was a thief," said Scotto in a voice that seemed to come from the grave. Jack had asked why he'd turned so ruthlessly against Fasio. "I couldn't let a thief get into City Hall."

Scotto shook his head.